The
Last Galley

Impressions and Tales

CONAN DOYLE

Serenity
Publishers, LLC
ROCKVILLE, MARYLAND
2011

ISBN: 978-1-60450-913-7

Published by Serenity Publishers
An Arc Manor Company
P. O. Box 10339
Rockville, MD 20849-0339
www.SerenityPublishers.com

Printed in the United States of America/United Kingdom

Contents

Preface

I HAVE WRITTEN "Impressions and Tales" upon the title-page of this volume, because I have included within the same cover two styles of work which present an essential difference.

The second half of the collection consists of eight stories, which explain themselves.

The first half is made up of a series of pictures of the past which maybe regarded as trial flights towards a larger ideal which I have long had in my mind. It has seemed to me that there is a region between actual story and actual history which has never been adequately exploited. I could imagine, for example, a work dealing with some great historical epoch, and finding its interest not in the happenings to particular individuals, their adventures and their loves, but in the fascination of the actual facts of history themselves. These facts might be coloured with the glamour which the writer of fiction can give, and fictitious characters and conversations might illustrate them; but none the less the actual drama of history and not the drama of invention should claim the attention of the reader. I have been tempted sometimes to try the effect upon a larger scale; but meanwhile these short sketches, portraying various crises in the story of the human race, are to be judged as experiments in that direction.

ARTHUR CONAN DOYLE.
WINDLESHAM,
CROWBOROUGH,
April, 1911.

Part One

The Last Galley

"MUTATO NOMINE, de te, Britannia, fabula narratur."

It was a spring morning, one hundred and forty-six years before the coming of Christ. The North African Coast, with its broad hem of golden sand, its green belt of feathery palm trees, and its background of barren, red-scarped hills, shimmered like a dream country in the opal light. Save for a narrow edge of snow-white surf, the Mediterranean lay blue and serene as far as the eye could reach. In all its vast expanse there was no break but for a single galley, which was slowly making its way from the direction of Sicily and heading for the distant harbour of Carthage.

Seen from afar it was a stately and beautiful vessel, deep red in colour, double-banked with scarlet oars, its broad, flapping sail stained with Tyrian purple, its bulwarks gleaming with brass work. A brazen, three-pronged ram projected in front, and a high golden figure of Baal, the God of the Phoenicians, children of Canaan, shone upon the after deck. From the single high mast above the huge sail streamed the tiger-striped flag of Carthage. So, like some stately scarlet bird, with golden beak and wings of purple, she swam upon the face of the waters—a thing of might and of beauty as seen from the distant shore.

But approach and look at her now! What are these dark streaks which foul her white decks and dapple her brazen shields? Why do the long red oars move out of time, irregular, convulsive? Why are some missing from the staring portholes, some snapped with jagged, yellow edges, some trailing inert against the side? Why are two prongs of the brazen ram twisted and broken? See, even the high image of Baal is battered and disfigured! By every sign this ship has passed through some grievous trial, some day of terror, which has left its heavy marks upon her.

And now stand upon the deck itself, and see more closely the men who man her! There are two decks forward and aft, while in the open waist are the double banks of seats, above and below, where the rowers, two to an oar, tug and bend at their endless task. Down the centre is a narrow platform, along which pace a line of warders, lash in hand, who cut cruelly at the slave who pauses, be it only for an instant, to sweep the sweat from his dripping brow. But these slaves—look at them! Some are captured Romans, some Sicilians, many black Libyans, but all are in the last exhaustion, their weary eyelids drooped over their eyes, their lips thick with black crusts, and pink with bloody froth, their arms and backs moving mechanically to the hoarse chant of the overseer. Their bodies of all tints from ivory to jet, are stripped to the waist, and every glistening back shows the angry stripes of the warders. But it is not from these that the blood comes which reddens the seats and tints the salt water washing beneath their manacled feet. Great gaping wounds, the marks of sword slash and spear stab, show crimson upon their naked chests and shoulders, while many lie huddled and senseless athwart the benches, careless for ever of the whips which still hiss above them. Now we can understand those empty portholes and those trailing oars.

Nor were the crew in better case than their slaves. The decks were littered with wounded and dying men. It was but a remnant who still remained upon their feet. The most lay exhausted upon the fore-deck, while a few of the more zealous were mending their shattered armour, restringing their bows, or cleaning the deck from the marks of combat. Upon a raised platform at the base of the mast stood the sailing-master who conned the ship, his eyes fixed upon the distant point of Megara which screened the eastern side of the Bay of Carthage. On the after-deck were gathered a number of officers, silent and brooding, glancing from time to time at two of their own class who stood apart deep in conversation. The one, tall, dark, and wiry, with pure, Semitic features, and the limbs of a giant, was Magro, the famous Carthaginian captain, whose name was still a terror on every shore, from Gaul to the Euxine. The other, a white-bearded, swarthy man, with indomitable courage and energy stamped upon every eager line of his keen, aquiline face, was Gisco the politician, a man of the highest Punic blood, a Suffete of the purple robe, and the leader of that party in the State which had watched and striven amid the selfishness and slothfulness of his fellow-countrymen to rouse the public spirit and waken the public conscience to the ever-increasing danger from Rome. As they talked, the two men glanced continually, with earnest anxious faces, towards the northern skyline.

"It is certain," said the older man, with gloom in his voice and bearing, "none have escaped save ourselves."

"I did not leave the press of the battle whilst I saw one ship which I could succour," Magro answered. "As it was, we came away, as you saw, like a wolf which has a hound hanging on to either haunch. The Roman dogs can show the wolf-bites which prove it. Had any other galley won clear, they would surely be with us by now, since they have no place of safety save Carthage."

The younger warrior glanced keenly ahead to the distant point which marked his native city. Already the low, leafy hill could be seen, dotted with the white villas of the wealthy Phoenician merchants. Above them, a gleaming dot against the pale blue morning sky, shone the brazen roof of the citadel of Byrsa, which capped the sloping town.

"Already they can see us from the watch-towers," he remarked. "Even from afar they may know the galley of Black Magro. But which of all of them will guess that we alone remain of all that goodly fleet which sailed out with blare of trumpet and roll of drum but one short month ago?"

The patrician smiled bitterly. "If it were not for our great ancestors and for our beloved country, the Queen of the Waters," said he, "I could find it in my heart to be glad at this destruction which has come upon this vain and feeble generation. You have spent your life upon the seas, Magro. You do not know of know how it has been with us on the land. But I have seen this canker grow upon us which now leads us to our death. I and others have gone down into the market-place to plead with the people, and been pelted with mud for our pains. Many a time have I pointed to Rome, and said, 'Behold these people, who bear arms themselves, each man for his own duty and pride. How can you who hide behind mercenaries hope to stand against them?'—a hundred times I have said it."

"And had they no answer?" asked the Rover.

"Rome was far off and they could not see it, so to them it was nothing," the old man answered. "Some thought of trade, and some of votes, and some of profits from the State, but none would see that the State itself, the mother of all things, was sinking to her end. So might the bees debate who should have wax or honey when the torch was blazing which would bring to ashes the hive and all therein. 'Are we not rulers of the sea?' 'Was not Hannibal a great man?' Such were their cries, living ever in the past and blind to the future. Before that sun sets there will be tearing of hair and rending of garments; what will that now avail us?"

"It is some sad comfort," said Magro, "to know that what Rome holds she cannot keep."

"Why say you that? When we go down, she is supreme in all the world."

"For a time, and only for a time," Magro answered, gravely. "Yet you will smile, perchance, when I tell you how it is that I know it. There was a wise woman who lived in that part of the Tin Islands which juts forth into the sea, and from her lips I have heard many things, but not one which has not come aright. Of the fall of our own country, and even of this battle, from which we now return, she told me clearly. There is much strange lore amongst these savage peoples in the west of the land of Tin."

"What said she of Rome?"

"That she also would fall, even as we, weakened by her riches and her factions."

Gisco rubbed his hands. "That at least makes our own fall less bitter," said he. "But since we have fallen, and Rome will fall, who in turn may hope to be Queen of the Waters?"

"That also I asked her," said Magro, "and gave her my Tyrian belt with the golden buckle as a guerdon for her answer. But, indeed, it was too high payment for the tale she told, which must be false if all else she said was true. She would have it that in coining days it was her own land, this fog-girt isle where painted savages can scarce row a wicker coracle from point to point, which shall at last take the trident which Carthage and Rome have dropped."

The smile which flickered upon the old patrician's keen features died away suddenly, and his fingers closed upon his companion's wrist. The other had set rigid, his head advanced, his hawk eyes upon the northern skyline. Its straight, blue horizon was broken by two low black dots.

"Galleys!" whispered Gisco.

The whole crew had seen them. They clustered along the starboard bulwarks, pointing and chattering. For a moment the gloom of defeat was lifted, and a buzz of joy ran from group to group at the thought that they were not alone—that some one had escaped the great carnage as well as themselves.

"By the spirit of Baal," said Black Magro, "I could not have believed that any could have fought clear from such a welter. Could it be young Hamilcar in the *Africa*, or is it Beneva in the blue Syrian ship? We three with others may form a squadron and make head against them yet. If we hold our course, they will join us ere we round the harbour mole."

Slowly the injured galley toiled on her way, and more swiftly the two newcomers swept down from the north. Only a few miles off lay the green point and the white houses which flanked the great African city. Already, upon the headland, could be seen a dark group of waiting townsmen. Gisco and Magro were still watching with puckered gaze the approaching galleys, when the brown Libyan boatswain, with flashing teeth and gleaming eyes, rushed upon the poop, his long thin arm stabbing to the north.

"Romans!" he cried. "Romans!"

A hush had fallen over the great vessel. Only the wash of the water and the measured rattle and beat of the oars broke in upon the silence.

"By the horns of God's altar, I believe the fellow is right!" cried old Gisco. "See how they swoop upon us like falcons. They are full-manned and full-oared."

"Plain wood, unpainted," said Magro. "See how it gleams yellow where the sun strikes it."

"And yonder thing beneath the mast. Is it not the cursed bridge they use for boarding?"

"So they grudge us even one," said Magro with a bitter laugh. "Not even one galley shall return to the old sea-mother. Well, for my part, I would as soon have it so. I am of a mind to stop the oars and await them."

"It is a man's thought," answered old Gisco; "but the city will need us in the days to come. What shall it profit us to make the Roman victory complete? Nay, Magro, let the slaves row as they never rowed before, not for our own safety, but for the profit of the State."

So the great red ship laboured and lurched onwards, like a weary panting stag which seeks shelter from his pursuers, while ever swifter and ever nearer sped the two lean fierce galleys from the north. Already the morning sun shone upon the lines of low Roman helmets above the bulwarks, and glistened on the silver wave where each sharp prow shot through the still blue water. Every moment the ships drew nearer, and the long thin scream of the Roman trumpets grew louder upon the ear.

Upon the high bluff of Megara there stood a great concourse of the people of Carthage who had hurried forth from the city upon the news that the galleys were in sight. They stood now, rich and poor, effete and plebeian, white Phoenician and dark Kabyle, gazing with breathless interest at the spectacle before them. Some hundreds of feet beneath them the Punic galley had drawn so close that with their naked eyes they could see those stains of battle which told their dismal tale. The Romans, too, were heading in such a way that it was before their very faces that their ship was about to be cut off; and yet of all this multitude not one could raise a hand in its defence. Some wept in impotent grief, some cursed with flashing eyes and knotted fists, some on their knees held up appealing hands to Baal; but neither prayer, tears, nor curses could undo the past nor mend the present. That broken, crawling galley meant that their fleet was gone. Those two fierce darting ships meant that the hands of Rome were already at their throat. Behind them would come others and others, the innumerable trained hosts of the great Republic, long mistress of the land, now dominant also upon the waters. In a month, two months, three at the most, their armies would be there, and what could all the untrained multitudes of Carthage do to stop them?

"Nay!" cried one, more hopeful than the rest, "at least we are brave men with arms in our hands."

"Fool!" said another, "is it not such talk which has brought us to our ruin? What is the brave man untrained to the brave man trained? When you stand before the sweep and rush of a Roman legion you may learn the difference."

"Then let us train!"

"Too late! A full year is needful to turn a man to a soldier. Where will you—where will your city be within the year? Nay, there is but one chance for us. If we give up our commerce and our colonies, if we strip ourselves of all that made us great, then perchance the Roman conqueror may hold his hand."

And already the last sea-fight of Carthage was coming swiftly to an end before them. Under their very eyes the two Roman galleys had shot in, one on either side of the vessel of Black Magro. They had grappled with him, and he, desperate in his despair, had cast the crooked flukes of his anchors over their gunwales, and bound them to him in an iron grip, whilst with hammer and crowbar he burst great holes in his own sheathing. The last Punic galley should never be rowed into Ostia, a sight for the holiday-makers of Rome. She would lie in her own waters. And the fierce, dark soul of her rover captain glowed as he thought that not alone should she sink into the depths of the mother sea.

Too late did the Romans understand the man with whom they had to deal. Their boarders who had flooded the Punic decks felt the planking sink and sway beneath them. They rushed to gain their own vessels; but they, too, were being drawn downwards, held in the dying grip of the great red galley. Over they went and ever over. Now the deck of Magro's ship is flush with the water, and the Romans, drawn towards it by the iron bonds which held them, are tilted downwards, one bulwark upon the waves, one reared high in the air. Madly they strain to cast off the death grip of the galley. She is under the surface now, and ever swifter, with the greater weight, the Roman ships heel after her. There is a rending crash. The wooden side is torn out of one, and mutilated, dismembered, she rights herself, and lies a helpless thing upon the water. But a last yellow gleam in the blue water shows where her consort has been dragged to her end in the iron death-grapple of her foemen. The tiger-striped flag of Carthage has sunk beneath the swirling surface, never more to be seen upon the face of the sea.

For in that year a great cloud hung for seventeen days over the African coast, a deep black cloud which was the dark shroud of the burning city. And when the seventeen days were over, Roman ploughs were driven from end to end of the charred ashes, and salt was scattered there as a sign that Carthage should be no more. And far off a huddle of naked, starving folk stood upon the distant mountains, and looked down upon the desolate plain which had once been the fairest and richest upon earth. And they understood too late that it is the law of heaven that the world is given to the hardy and to the self-denying, whilst he who would escape the duties of manhood will soon be stripped of the pride, the wealth, and the power, which are the prizes which manhood brings.

The Contest

IN THE YEAR OF OUR LORD 66, the Emperor Nero, being at that time in the twenty-ninth year of his life and the thirteenth of his reign, set sail for Greece with the strangest company and the most singular design that any monarch has ever entertained. With ten galleys he went forth from Puteoli, carrying with him great stores of painted scenery and theatrical properties, together with a number of knights and senators, whom he feared to leave behind him at Rome, and who were all marked for death in the course of his wanderings. In his train he took Natus, his singing coach; Cluvius, a man with a monstrous voice, who should bawl out his titles; and a thousand trained youths who had learned to applaud in unison whenever their master sang or played in public. So deftly had they been taught that each had his own role to play. Some did no more than give forth a low deep hum of speechless appreciation. Some clapped with enthusiasm. Some, rising from approbation into absolute frenzy, shrieked, stamped, and beat sticks upon the benches. Some—and they were the most effective—had learned from an Alexandrian a long droning musical note which they all uttered together, so that it boomed over the assembly. With the aid of these mercenary admirers, Nero had every hope, in spite of his indifferent voice and clumsy execution, to return to Rome, bearing with him the chaplets for song offered for free competition by the Greek cities. As his great gilded galley with two tiers of oars passed down the Mediterranean, the Emperor sat in his cabin all day, his teacher by his side, rehearsing from morning to night those compositions which he had selected, whilst every few hours a Nubian slave massaged the Imperial throat with oil and balsam, that it might be ready for the great ordeal which lay before it in the land of poetry and song. His food, his drink, and his exercise were prescribed for him as for an athlete who trains for a contest, and the twanging of his lyre, with the strident notes of his voice, resounded continually from the Imperial quarters.

Now it chanced that there lived in those days a Grecian goatherd named Policles, who tended and partly owned a great flock which grazed upon the long flanks of the hills near Heroea, which is five miles north of the river Alpheus, and no great distance from the famous Olympia. This person was noted all over the countryside as a man of strange gifts and singular character. He was a poet who had twice been crowned for his verses, and he was a musician to whom the use and sound of an instrument were so natural that one would more easily meet him without his staff than his harp. Even in his lonely vigils on the winter hills he would bear it always slung over his shoulder, and would pass the long hours by its aid, so that it had come to be part of his very self. He was beautiful also, swarthy and eager, with a head like Adonis, and in strength there was no one who could compete with him. But all was ruined by his disposition, which was so masterful that he would brook no opposition nor contradiction. For this reason he was continually at enmity with all his neighbours, and in his fits of temper he would spend months at a time in his stone hut among the mountains, hearing nothing from the world, and living only for his music and his goats.

One spring morning, in the year of 67, Policles, with the aid of his boy Dorus, had driven his goats over to a new pasturage which overlooked from afar the town of Olympia. Gazing down upon it from the mountain, the shepherd was surprised to see that a portion of the famous amphitheatre had been roofed in, as though some performance was being enacted. Living far from the world and from all news, Policles could not imagine what was afoot, for he was well aware that the Grecian games were not due for two years to come. Surely some poetic or musical contest must be proceeding of which he had heard nothing. If so, there would perhaps be some chance of his gaining the votes of the judges; and in any case he loved to hear the compositions and admire the execution of the great minstrels who assembled on such an occasion. Calling to Dorus, therefore, he left the goats to his charge, and strode swiftly away, his harp upon his back, to see what was going forward in the town.

When Policles came into the suburbs, he found them deserted; but he was still more surprised when he reached the main street to see no single human being in the place. He hastened his steps, therefore, and as he approached the theatre he was conscious of a low sustained hum which announced the concourse of a huge assembly. Never in all his dreams had he imagined any musical competition upon so vast a scale as this. There were some soldiers clustering outside the door; but Policles pushed his way swiftly through them, and found himself upon the outskirts of the multitude who filled the great space formed by roofing over a portion of the national stadium. Looking around him, Policles saw a great number of his neighbours, whom he knew by sight, tightly packed upon the benches, all with their eyes fixed upon the stage. He also observed that there were soldiers round the walls, and that a considerable part of the hall was filled by a body of youths of foreign aspect, with white gowns and long hair. All this he perceived; but what it meant he could not imagine. He bent over to a neighbour to ask him, but a soldier prodded him at once with the butt end of his spear, and commanded him fiercely to hold his peace. The man whom he had addressed, thinking that Policles had demanded a seat, pressed closer to his neighbour, and so the shepherd found himself sitting at the end of the bench which was nearest to the door. Thence he concentrated himself upon the stage, on which Metas, a well-known minstrel from Corinth and an old friend of Policles, was singing and playing without much encouragement from the audience. To Policles it seemed that Metas was having less than his due, so he applauded loudly, but he was surprised to observe that the soldiers frowned at him, and that all his neighbours regarded him with some surprise. Being a man of strong and obstinate character, he was the more inclined to persevere in his clapping when he perceived that the general sentiment was against him.

But what followed filled the shepherd poet with absolute amazement. When Metas of Corinth had made his bow and withdrawn to half-hearted and perfunctory applause, there appeared upon the stage, amid the wildest enthusiasm upon the part of the audience, a most extraordinary figure. He was a short fat man, neither old nor young, with a bull neck and a round, heavy face, which hung in creases in front like the dewlap of an ox. He was absurdly clad in a short blue tunic, braced at the waist with a golden belt. His neck and part of his chest were exposed, and his short, fat legs were bare from the buskins below to the middle of his thighs, which was as far as his tunic extended. In his hair were two golden wings, and the same upon his heels, after the fashion of the god Mercury. Behind him walked a negro bearing a harp, and beside him a richly dressed officer who bore rolls of music. This strange creature took the harp from the hands of the attendant, and advanced to the front of the stage, whence he bowed and smiled to the cheering audience. "This is some foppish singer from Athens," thought Policles to himself, but at the same time he understood that only a great master of song could receive such a reception from a Greek audience. This was evidently some wonderful performer whose reputation had preceded him. Policles settled down, therefore, and prepared to give his soul up to the music.

The blue-clad player struck several chords upon his lyre, and then burst suddenly out into the "Ode of Niobe." Policles sat straight up on his bench and gazed at the stage in amazement. The tune demanded a rapid transition from a low note to a high, and had been purposely chosen for this reason. The low note was a grunting, a rumble, the deep discordant growling of an ill-conditioned dog. Then suddenly the singer threw up his face, straightened his tubby figure, rose upon his tiptoes, and with wagging head and scarlet cheeks emitted such a howl as the same dog might have given had his growl been checked by a kick from his master. All the while the lyre twanged and thrummed, sometimes in front of and sometimes behind the voice of the singer. But what amazed Policles most of all was the effect of this performance upon the audience. Every Greek was a trained critic, and as unsparing in his hisses as he was lavish in his applause. Many a singer far better than this absurd fop had been driven amid execration and abuse from the platform. But now, as the man stopped and wiped the abundant sweat from his fat face, the whole assembly burst into a delirium of appreciation. The shepherd held his hands to his bursting head, and felt that his reason must be leaving him. It was surely a dreadful musical nightmare, and he would wake soon and laugh at the remembrance. But no; the figures were real, the faces were those of his neighbours, the cheers which resounded in his ears were indeed from an audience which filled the theatre of Olympia. The whole chorus was in full blast, the hummers humming, the shouters bellowing, the tappers hard at work upon the benches, while every now and then came a musical cyclone of "Incomparable! Divine!" from the trained phalanx who intoned their applause, their united voices sweeping over the tumult as the drone of the wind dominates the roar of the sea. It was madness—insufferable madness! If this were allowed to pass, there was an end of all musical justice in Greece. Policles' conscience would not permit him to be still. Standing upon his bench with waving hands and upraised voice, he protested with all the strength of his lungs against the mad judgment of the audience.

At first, amid the tumult, his action was hardly noticed. His voice was drowned in the universal roar which broke out afresh at each bow and smirk from the fatuous musician. But gradually the folk round Policles ceased clapping, and stared at him in astonishment. The silence grew in ever widening circles, until the whole great assembly sat mute, staring at this wild and magnificent creature who was storming at them from his perch near the door.

"Fools!" he cried. "What are you clapping at? What are you cheering? Is this what you call music? Is this cat-calling to earn an Olympian prize?

The fellow has not a note in his voice. You are either deaf or mad, and I for one cry shame upon you for your folly."

Soldiers ran to pull him down, and the whole audience was in confusion, some of the bolder cheering the sentiments of the shepherd, and others crying that he should be cast out of the building. Meanwhile the successful singer having handed his lyre to his negro attendant, was inquiring from those around him on the stage as to the cause of the uproar. Finally a herald with an enormously powerful voice stepped forward to the front and proclaimed that if the foolish person at the back of the hall, who appeared to differ from the opinion of the rest of the audience, would come forward upon the platform, he might, if he dared, exhibit his own powers, and see if he could outdo the admirable and wonderful exhibition which they had just had the privilege of hearing.

Policles sprang readily to his feet at the challenge, and the great company making way for him to pass, he found himself a minute later standing in his unkempt garb, with his frayed and weather-beaten harp in his hand, before the expectant crowd. He stood for a moment tightening a string here and slackening another there until his chords rang true. Then, amid a murmur of laughter and jeers from the Roman benches immediately before him, he began to sing.

He had prepared no composition, but he had trained himself to improvise, singing out of his heart for the joy of the music. He told of the land of Elis, beloved of Jupiter, in which they were gathered that day, of the great bare mountain slopes, of the swift shadows of the clouds, of the winding blue river, of the keen air of the uplands, of the chill of the evenings, and the beauties of earth and sky. It was all simple and childlike, but it went to the hearts of the Olympians, for it spoke of the land which they knew and loved. Yet when he at last dropped his hand, few of them dared to applaud, and their feeble voices were drowned by a storm of hisses and groans from his opponents. He shrank back in horror from so unusual a reception, and in an instant his blue-clad rival was in his place. If he had sung badly before, his performance now was inconceivable. His screams, his grunts, his discords, and harsh jarring cacophanies were an outrage to the very name of music. And yet every time that he paused for breath or to wipe his streaming forehead a fresh thunder of applause came rolling back from the audience. Policles sank his face in his hands and prayed that he might not be insane. Then, when the dreadful performance ceased, and the uproar of admiration showed that the crown was certainly awarded to this impostor, a horror of the audience, a hatred of this race of fools, and a craving for the peace and silence of the pastures mastered every feeling in his mind. He dashed through the mass of people waiting at the wings, and emerged in the open air. His old rival and friend Metas of Corinth was waiting there with an anxious face.

"Quick, Policles, quick!" he cried. "My pony is tethered behind yonder grove. A grey he is, with red trappings. Get you gone as hard as hoof will bear you, for if you are taken you will have no easy death."

"No easy death! What mean you, Metas? Who is the fellow?"

"Great Jupiter! did you not know? Where have you lived? It is Nero the Emperor! Never would he pardon what you have said about his voice. Quick, man, quick, or the guards will be at your heels!"

An hour later the shepherd was well on his way to his mountain home, and about the same time the Emperor, having received the Chaplet of Olympia for the incomparable excellence of his performance, was making inquiries with a frowning brow as to who the insolent person might be who had dared to utter such contemptuous criticisms.

"Bring him to me here this instant," said he, "and let Marcus with his knife and branding-iron be in attendance."

"If it please you, great Caesar," said Arsenius Platus, the officer of attendance, "the man cannot be found, and there are some very strange rumours flying about."

"Rumours!" cried the angry Nero. "What do you mean, Arsenius? I tell you that the fellow was an ignorant upstart, with the bearing of a boor and the voice of a peacock. I tell you also that there are a good many who are as guilty as he among the people, for I heard them with my own ears raise cheers for him when he had sung his ridiculous ode. I have half a mind to burn their town about their ears so that they may remember my visit."

"It is not to be wondered at if he won their votes, Caesar," said the soldier, "for from what I hear it would have been no disgrace had you, even you, been conquered in this conquest."

"I conquered! You are mad, Arsenius. What do you mean?"

"None know him, great Caesar! He came from the mountains, and he disappeared into the mountains. You marked the wildness and strange beauty of his face. It is whispered that for once the great god Pan has condescended to measure himself against a mortal."

The cloud cleared from Nero's brow. "Of course, Arsenius! You are right! No man would have dared to brave me so. What a story for Rome! Let the messenger leave this very night, Arsenius, to tell them how their Emperor has upheld their honour in Olympia this day."

Through the Veil

HE WAS A GREAT SHOCK-HEADED, freckle-faced Borderer, the lineal descendant of a cattle-thieving clan in Liddesdale. In spite of his ancestry he was as solid and sober a citizen as one would wish to see, a town councillor of Melrose, an elder of the Church, and the chairman of the local branch of the Young Men's Christian Association. Brown was his name—and you saw it printed up as "Brown and Handiside" over the great grocery stores in the High Street. His wife, Maggie Brown, was an Armstrong before her marriage, and came from an old farming stock in the wilds of Teviothead. She was small, swarthy, and dark-eyed, with a strangely nervous temperament for a Scotch woman. No greater contrast could be found than the big tawny man and the dark little woman; but both were of the soil as far back as any memory could extend.

One day—it was the first anniversary of their wedding—they had driven over together to see the excavations of the Roman Fort at Newstead. It was not a particularly picturesque spot. From the northern bank of the Tweed, just where the river forms a loop, there extends a gentle slope of arable land. Across it run the trenches of the excavators, with here and there an exposure of old stonework to show the foundations of the ancient walls. It had been a huge place, for the camp was fifty acres in extent, and the fort fifteen. However, it was all made easy for them since Mr. Brown knew the farmer to whom the land belonged. Under his guidance they spent a long summer evening inspecting the trenches, the pits, the ramparts, and all the strange variety of objects which were waiting to be transported to the Edinburgh Museum of Antiquities. The buckle of a woman's belt had been dug up that very day, and the farmer was discoursing upon it when his eyes fell upon Mrs. Brown's face.

"Your good leddy's tired," said he. "Maybe you'd best rest a wee before we gang further."

Brown looked at his wife. She was certainly very pale, and her dark eyes were bright and wild.

"What is it, Maggie? I've wearied you. I'm thinkin' it's time we went back."

"No, no, John, let us go on. It's wonderful! It's like a dreamland place. It all seems so close and so near to me. How long were the Romans here, Mr. Cunningham?"

"A fair time, mam. If you saw the kitchen midden-pits you would guess it took a long time to fill them."

"And why did they leave?"

"Well, mam, by all accounts they left because they had to. The folk round could thole them no longer, so they just up and burned the fort aboot their lugs. You can see the fire marks on the stanes."

The woman gave a quick little shudder. "A wild night—a fearsome night," said she. "The sky must have been red that night—and these grey stones, they may have been red also."

"Aye, I think they were red," said her husband. "It's a queer thing, Maggie, and it may be your words that have done it; but I seem to see that business aboot as clear as ever I saw anything in my life. The light shone on the water."

"Aye, the light shone on the water. And the smoke gripped you by the throat. And all the savages were yelling."

The old farmer began to laugh. "The leddy will be writin' a story aboot the old fort," said he. "I've shown many a one over it, but I never heard it put so clear afore. Some folk have the gift."

They had strolled along the edge of the foss, and a pit yawned upon the right of them.

"That pit was fourteen foot deep," said the farmer. "What d'ye think we dug oot from the bottom o't? Weel, it was just the skeleton of a man wi' a spear by his side. I'm thinkin' he was grippin' it when he died. Now, how cam' a man wi' a spear doon a hole fourteen foot deep? He wasna' buried there, for they aye burned their dead. What make ye o' that, mam?"

"He sprang doon to get clear of the savages," said the woman.

"Weel, it's likely enough, and a' the professors from Edinburgh couldna gie a better reason. I wish you were aye here, mam, to answer a' oor difficulties sae readily. Now, here's the altar that we foond last week. There's an inscreeption. They tell me it's Latin, and it means that the men o' this fort give thanks to God for their safety."

They examined the old worn stone. There was a large deeply-cut "VV" upon the top of it. "What does 'VV' stand for?" asked Brown.

"Naebody kens," the guide answered.

"*Valeria Victrix*," said the lady softly. Her face was paler than ever, her eyes far away, as one who peers down the dim aisles of overarching centuries.

"What's that?" asked her husband sharply.

She started as one who wakes from sleep. "What were we talking about?" she asked.

"About this 'VV' upon the stone."

"No doubt it was just the name of the Legion which put the altar up."

"Aye, but you gave some special name."

"Did I? How absurd! How should I ken what the name was?"

"You said something—'*Victrix*,' I think."

"I suppose I was guessing. It gives me the queerest feeling, this place, as if I were not myself, but someone else."

"Aye, it's an uncanny place," said her husband, looking round with an expression almost of fear in his bold grey eyes. "I feel it mysel'. I think we'll just be wishin' you good evenin', Mr. Cunningham, and get back to Melrose before the dark sets in."

Neither of them could shake off the strange impression which had been left upon them by their visit to the excavations. It was as if some miasma had risen from those damp trenches and passed into their blood. All the evening they were silent and thoughtful, but such remarks as they did make showed that the same subject was in the minds of each. Brown had a restless night, in which he dreamed a strange connected dream, so vivid that he woke sweating and shivering like a frightened horse. He tried to convey it all to his wife as they sat together at breakfast in the morning.

"It was the clearest thing, Maggie," said he. "Nothing that has ever come to me in my waking life has been more clear than that. I feel as if these hands were sticky with blood."

"Tell me of it—tell me slow," said she.

"When it began, I was oot on a braeside. I was laying flat on the ground. It was rough, and there were clumps of heather. All round me was just darkness, but I could hear the rustle and the breathin' of men. There seemed a great multitude on every side of me, but I could see no one. There was a low chink of steel sometimes, and then a number of voices would whisper 'Hush!' I had a ragged club in my hand, and it had spikes o' iron near the end of it. My heart was beatin' quickly, and I felt that a moment of great danger and excitement was at hand. Once I dropped my club, and again from all round me the voices in the darkness cried, 'Hush!' I put oot my hand, and it touched the foot of another man lying in front of me. There was some one at my very elbow on either side. But they said nothin'.

"Then we all began to move. The whole braeside seemed to be crawlin' downwards. There was a river at the bottom and a high-arched wooden bridge. Beyond the bridge were many lights—torches on a wall. The creepin' men all flowed towards the bridge. There had been no sound of any kind, just a velvet stillness. And then there was a cry in the darkness, the cry of a man who has been stabbed suddenly to the hairt. That one cry swelled out for a moment, and then the roar of a thoosand furious voices. I was runnin'. Every one was runnin'. A bright red light shone out, and the river was a scarlet streak. I could see my companions now. They were more like devils than men, wild figures clad in skins, with their hair and beards streamin'. They were all mad with rage, jumpin' as they ran, their mouths open, their arms wavin', the red light beatin' on their faces. I ran, too, and yelled out curses like the rest. Then I heard a great cracklin' of wood, and I knew that the palisades were doon. There was a loud whistlin' in my ears, and I was aware that arrows were flyin' past me. I got to the bottom of a dyke, and I saw a hand stretched doon from above. I took it, and was dragged to the top. We looked doon, and there were silver men beneath us holdin' up their spears. Some of our folk sprang on to the spears. Then we others followed, and we killed the soldiers before they could draw the spears oot again. They shouted loud in some foreign tongue, but no mercy was shown them. We went ower them like a wave, and trampled them doon into the mud, for they were few, and there was no end to our numbers.

"I found myself among buildings, and one of them was on fire. I saw the flames spoutin' through the roof. I ran on, and then I was alone among the buildings. Some one ran across in front o' me. It was a woman. I caught her by the arm, and I took her chin and turned her face so as to the light of the fire would strike it. Whom think you that it was, Maggie?"

His wife moistened her dry lips. "It was I," she said.

He looked at her in surprise. "That's a good guess," said he. "Yes, it was just you. Not merely like you, you understand. It was you—you yourself. I saw the same soul in your frightened eyes. You looked white and bonny and wonderful in the firelight. I had just one thought in my head—to get you awa' with me; to keep you all to mysel' in my own home somewhere beyond the hills. You clawed at my face with your nails. I heaved you over my shoulder, and I tried to find a way oot of the light of the burning hoose and back into the darkness.

"Then came the thing that I mind best of all. You're ill, Maggie. Shall I stop? My God! You nave the very look on your face that you had last night in my dream. You screamed. He came runnin' in the firelight. His head was bare; his hair was black and curled; he had a naked sword in his hand, short and broad, little more than a dagger. He stabbed at me, but he tripped and fell. I held you with one hand, and with the other—"

His wife had sprung to her feet with writhing features.

"Marcus!" she cried. "My beautiful Marcus! Oh, you brute! you brute! you brute!" There was a clatter of tea-cups as she fell forward senseless upon the table.

They never talk about that strange isolated incident in their married life. For an instant the curtain of the past had swung aside, and some strange glimpse of a forgotten life had come to them. But it closed down, never to open again. They live their narrow round—he in his shop, she in her household—and yet new and wider horizons have vaguely formed themselves around them since that summer evening by the crumbling Roman fort.

An Iconoclast

IT WAS DAYBREAK of a March morning in the year of Christ 92. Outside the long Semita Alta was already thronged with people, with buyers and sellers, callers and strollers, for the Romans were so early-rising a people that many a Patrician preferred to see his clients at six in the morning. Such was the good republican tradition, still upheld by the more conservative; but with more modern habits of luxury, a night of pleasure and banqueting was no uncommon thing. Thus one, who had learned the new and yet adhered to the old, might find his hours overlap, and without so much as a pretence of sleep come straight from his night of debauch into his day of business, turning with heavy wits and an aching head to that round of formal duties which consumed the life of a Roman gentleman.

So it was with Emilius Flaccus that March morning. He and his fellow senator, Caius Balbus, had passed the night in one of those gloomy drinking bouts to which the Emperor Domitian summoned his chosen friends at the high palace on the Palatine. Now, having reached the portals of the house of Flaccus, they stood together under the pomegranate-fringed portico which fronted the peristyle and, confident in each other's tried discretion, made up by the freedom of their criticism for their long self-suppression of that melancholy feast.

"If he would but feed his guests," said Balbus, a little red-faced, choleric nobleman with yellow-shot angry eyes. "What had we? Upon my life, I have forgotten. Plovers' eggs, a mess of fish, some bird or other, and then his eternal apples."

"Of which," said Flaccus, "he ate only the apples. Do him the justice to confess that he takes even less than he gives. At least they cannot say of him as of Vitellius, that his teeth beggared the empire."

27

"No, nor his thirst either, great as it is. That fiery Sabine wine of his could be had for a few sesterces the amphora. It is the common drink of the carters at every wine-house on the country roads. I longed for a glass of my own rich Falernian or the mellow Coan that was bottled in the year that Titus took Jerusalem. Is it even now too late? Could we not wash this rasping stuff from our palates?"

"Nay, better come in with me now and take a bitter draught ere you go upon your way. My Greek physician Stephanos has a rare prescription for a morning head. What! Your clients await you? Well, I will see you later at the Senate house."

The Patrician had entered his atrium, bright with rare flowers, and melodious with strange singing birds. At the jaws of the hall, true to his morning duties, stood Lebs, the little Nubian slave, with snow-white tunic and turban, a salver of glasses in one hand, whilst in the other he held a flask of a thin lemon-tinted liquid. The master of the house filled up a bitter aromatic bumper, and was about to drink it off, when his hand was arrested by a sudden perception that something was much amiss in his household. It was to be read all around him—in the frightened eyes of the black boy, in the agitated face of the keeper of the atrium, in the gloom and silence of the little knot of ordinarii, the procurator or major-domo at their head, who had assembled to greet their master. Stephanos the physician, Cleios the Alexandrine reader, Promus the steward each turned his head away to avoid his master's questioning gaze.

"What in the name of Pluto is the matter with you all?" cried the amazed senator, whose night of potations had left him in no mood for patience. "Why do you stand moping there? Stephanos, Vacculus—is anything amiss? Here, Promus, you are the head of my household. What is it, then? Why do you turn your eyes away from me?"

The burly steward, whose fat face was haggard and mottled with anxiety, laid his hand upon the sleeve of the domestic beside him.

"Sergius is responsible for the atrium, my lord. It is for him to tell you the terrible thing that has befallen in your absence."

"Nay, it was Datus who did it. Bring him in, and let him explain it himself," said Sergius in a sulky voice.

The patience of the Patrician was at an end. "Speak this instant, you rascal!" he shouted angrily. "Another minute, and I will have you dragged to the ergastulum, where, with your feet in the stocks and the gyves round your wrists, you may learn quicker obedience. Speak, I say, and without delay."

"It is the Venus," the man stammered; "the Greek Venus of Praxiteles."

The senator gave a cry of apprehension and rushed to the corner of the atrium, where a little shrine, curtained off by silken drapery, held the precious statue, the greatest art treasure of his collection—perhaps of the whole world. He tore the hangings aside and stood in speechless anger before the outraged goddess. The red perfumed lamp which always burned before her had been spilled and broken; her altar fire had been quenched, her chaplet had been dashed aside. But worst of all—insufferable sacrilege!—her own beautiful nude body of glistening Pantelic marble, as white and fair as when the inspired Greek had hewed it out five hundred years before, had been most brutally mishandled. Three fingers of the gracious outstretched hand had been struck off, and lay upon the pedestal beside her. Above her delicate breast a dark mark showed, where a blow had disfigured the marble. Emilius Flaccus, the most delicate and judicious connoisseur in Rome, stood gasping and croaking, his hand to his throat, as he gazed at his disfigured masterpiece. Then he turned upon his slaves, his fury in his convulsed face; but, to his amazement, they were not looking at him, but had all turned in attitudes of deep respect towards the opening of the peristyle. As he faced round and saw who had just entered his house, his own rage fell away from him in an instant, and his manner became as humble as that of his servants.

The newcomer was a man forty-three years of age, clean shaven, with a massive head, large engorged eyes, a small clear-cut nose, and the full bull neck which was the especial mark of his breed. He had entered through the peristyle with a swaggering, rolling gait, as one who walks upon his own ground, and now he stood, his hands upon his hips, looking round him at the bowing slaves, and finally at their master, with a half-humorous expression upon his flushed and brutal face.

"Why, Emilius," said he, "I had understood that your household was the best-ordered in Rome. What is amiss with you this morning?"

"Nothing could be amiss with us now that Caesar has deigned to come under my roof," said the courtier. "This is indeed a most glad surprise which you have prepared for me."

"It was an afterthought," said Domitian. "When you and the others had left me, I was in no mood for sleep, and so it came into my mind that I would have a breath of morning air by coming down to you, and seeing this Grecian Venus of yours, about which you discoursed so eloquently between the cups. But, indeed, by your appearance and that of your servants, I should judge that my visit was an ill-timed one."

"Nay, dear master; say not so. But, indeed, it is truth that I was in trouble at the moment of your welcome entrance, and this trouble was, as the Fates have willed it, brought forth by that very statue in which you have been graciously pleased to show your interest. There it stands, and you can see for yourself how rudely it has been mishandled."

"By Pluto and all the nether gods, if it were mine some of you should feed the lampreys," said the Emperor, looking round with his fierce eyes at the shrinking slaves. "You were always overmerciful, Emilius. It is the common talk that your catenoe are rusted for want of use. But surely this is beyond all bounds. Let me see how you handle the matter. Whom do you hold responsible?"

"The slave Sergius is responsible, since it is his place to tend the atrium," said Flaccus. "Stand forward, Sergius. What have you to say?"

The trembling slave advanced to his master. "If it please you, sir, the mischief has been done by Datus the Christian."

"Datus! Who is he?"

"The matulator, the scavenger, my lord. I did not know that he belonged to these horrible people, or I should not have admitted him. He came with his broom to brush out the litter of the birds. His eyes fell upon the Venus, and in an instant he had rushed upon her and struck her two blows with his wooden besom. Then we fell upon him and dragged him away. But alas! alas! it was too late, for already the wretch had dashed off the fingers of the goddess."

The Emperor smiled grimly, while the Patrician's thin face grew pale with anger.

"Where is the fellow?" he asked.

"In the ergastulum, your honour, with the furca on his neck."

"Bring him hither and summon the household."

A few minutes later the whole back of the atrium was thronged by the motley crowd who ministered to the household needs of a great Roman nobleman. There was the arcarius, or account keeper, with his stylum behind his ear; the sleek praegustator, who sampled all foods, so as to stand between his master and poison, and beside him his predecessor, now a half-witted idiot through the interception twenty years before of a datura draught from Canidia; the cellarman, summoned from amongst his amphorae; the cook, with his basting-ladle in his hand; the pompous nomenclator, who ushered the guests; the cubicularius, who saw to their accommodation; the silentiarius, who kept order in the house; the structor, who set forth the tables; the carptor, who carved the food; the cinerarius, who lit the fires—these and many more, half-curious, half-terrified, came to the judging of Datus. Behind them a chattering, giggling swarm of Lalages, Marias, Cerusas, and Amaryllides, from the laundries and the spinning-rooms, stood upon their tiptoes and extended their pretty wondering faces over the shoulders of the men. Through this crowd came two stout varlets leading the culprit between them. He was a small, dark, rough-headed man, with an unkempt beard and wild eyes which shone, brightly with strong inward emotion. His hands were bound behind him, and over his neck was the heavy wooden collar or furca which was placed upon refractory slaves. A smear of blood across his cheek showed that he had not come uninjured from the preceding scuffle.

"Are you Datus the scavenger?" asked the Patrician.

The man drew himself up proudly. "Yes," said he, "I am Datus."

"Did you do this injury to my statue?"

"Yes, I did."

There was an uncompromising boldness in the man's reply which compelled respect. The wrath of his master became tinged with interest.

"Why did you do this?" he asked.

"Because it was my duty."

"Why, then, was it your duty to destroy your master's property?"

"Because I am a Christian." His eyes blazed suddenly out of his dark face. "Because there is no God but the one eternal, and all else are sticks and stones. What has this naked harlot to do with Him to whom the great firmament is but a garment and the earth a footstool? It was in His service that I have broken your statue."

Domitian looked with a smile at the Patrician. "You will make nothing of him," said he. "They speak even so when they stand before the lions in the arena. As to argument, not all the philosophers of Rome can break them down. Before my very face they refuse to sacrifice in my honour. Never were such impossible people to deal with. I should take a short way with him if I were you."

"What would Caesar advise?"

"There are the games this afternoon. I am showing the new hunting-leopard which King Juba has sent from Numidia. This slave may give us some sport when he finds the hungry beast sniffing at his heels."

The Patrician considered for a moment. He had always been a father to his servants. It was hateful to him to think of any injury befalling them. Perhaps even now, if this strange fanatic would show his sorrow for what he had done, it might be possible to spare him. At least it was worth trying.

"Your offence deserves death," he said. "What reasons can you give why it should not befall you, since you have injured this statue, which is worth your own price a hundred times over?"

The slave looked steadfastly at his master. "I do not fear death," he said. "My sister Candida died in the arena, and I am ready to do the same. It is true that I have injured your statue, but I am able to find you something of far greater value in exchange. I will give you the truth and the gospel in exchange for your broken idol."

The Emperor laughed. "You will do nothing with him, Emilius," he said. "I know his breed of old. He is ready to die; he says so himself. Why save him, then?"

But the Patrician still hesitated. He would make a last effort.

"Throw off his bonds," he said to the guards. "Now take the furca off his neck. So! Now, Datus, I have released you to show you that I trust you. I have no wish to do you any hurt if you will but acknowledge your error, and so set a better example to my household here assembled."

"How, then, shall I acknowledge my error?" the slave asked.

"Bow your head before the goddess, and entreat her forgiveness for the violence you have done her. Then perhaps you may gain my pardon as well."

"Put me, then, before her," said the Christian.

Emilius Flaccus looked triumphantly at Domitian. By kindness and tact he was effecting that which the Emperor had failed to do by violence. Datus walked in front of the mutilated Venus. Then with a sudden spring he tore the baton out of the hand of one of his guardians, leaped upon the pedestal, and showered his blows upon the lovely marble woman. With a crack and a dull thud her right arm dropped to the ground. Another fierce blow and the left had followed. Flaccus danced and screamed with horror, while his servants dragged the raving iconoclast from his impassive victim. Domitian's brutal laughter echoed through the hall.

"Well, friend, what think you now?" he cried. "Are you wiser than your Emperor? Can you indeed tame your Christian with kindness?"

Emilius Flaccus wiped the sweat from his brow. "He is yours, great Caesar. Do with him as you will."

"Let him be at the gladiators' entrance of the circus an hour before the games begin," said the Emperor. "Now, Emilius, the night has been a merry one. My Ligurian galley waits by the river quay. Come, cool your head with a spin to Ostia ere the business of State calls you to the Senate."

Giant Maximin

I: The Coming of Maximin

MANY ARE THE STRANGE vicissitudes of history. Greatness has often sunk to the dust, and has tempered itself to its new surrounding. Smallness has risen aloft, has flourished for a time, and then has sunk once more. Rich monarchs have become poor monks, brave conquerors have lost their manhood, eunuchs and women have overthrown armies and kingdoms. Surely there is no situation which the mind of man can invent which has not taken shape and been played out upon the world stage. But of all the strange careers and of all the wondrous happenings, stranger than Charles in his monastery, or Justin on his throne, there stands the case of Giant Maximin, what he attained, and how he attained it. Let me tell the sober facts of history, tinged only by that colouring to which the more austere historians could not condescend. It is a record as well as a story.

In the heart of Thrace some ten miles north of the Rhodope mountains, there is a valley which is named Harpessus, after the stream which runs down it. Through this valley lies the main road from the east to the west, and along the road, returning from an expedition against the Alani, there marched, upon the fifth day of the month of June in the year 210, a small but compact Roman army. It consisted of three legions—the Jovian, the Cappadocian, and the men of Hercules. Ten turmae of Gallic cavalry led the van, whilst the rear was covered by a regiment of Batavian Horse Guards, the immediate attendants of the Emperor Septimus Severus who had conducted the campaign in person. The peasants who lined the low hills which fringed the valley looked with indifference upon the long files of dusty, heavily-burdened infantry, but they broke into murmurs of delight at the gold-faced cuirasses and high brazen horse-hair helmets of the guardsmen, applauding their stalwart figures, their martial bearing, and the stately black chargers which they rode. A soldier might know that it was the little weary men with their short swords, their heavy pikes over their shoulders, and their square shields slung upon their backs, who were the real terror of the enemies of the Empire, but to the eyes of the wondering Thracians it was this troop of glittering Apollos who bore Rome's victory upon their banners, and upheld the throne of the purple-togaed prince who rode before them.

Among the scattered groups of peasants who looked on from a respectful distance at this military pageant, there were two men who attracted much attention from those who stood immediately around them. The one was commonplace enough—a little grey-headed man, with uncouth dress and a frame which was bent and warped by a long life of arduous toil, goat-driving and wood-chopping among the mountains. It was the appearance of his youthful companion which had drawn the amazed observation of the bystanders. In stature he was such a giant as is seen but once or twice in each generation of mankind. Eight feet and two inches was his measure from his sandalled sole to the topmost curls of his tangled hair. Yet for all his mighty stature there was nothing heavy or clumsy in the man. His huge shoulders bore no redundant flesh, and his figure was straight and hard and supple as a young pine tree. A frayed suit of brown leather clung close to his giant body, and a cloak of undressed sheep-skin was slung from his shoulder. His bold blue eyes, shock of yellow hair and fair skin showed that he was of Gothic or northern blood, and the amazed expression upon his broad frank face as he stared at the passing troops told of a simple and uneventful life in some back valley of the Macedonian mountains.

"I fear your mother was right when she advised that we keep you at home," said the old man anxiously. "Tree-cutting and wood-carrying will seem but dull work after such a sight as this."

"When I see mother next it will be to put a golden torque round her neck," said the young giant. "And you, daddy; I will fill your leather pouch with gold pieces before I have done."

The old man looked at his son with startled eyes. "You would not leave us, Theckla! What could we do without you?"

"My place is down among yonder men," said the young man. "I was not born to drive goats and carry logs, but to sell this manhood of mine in the best market. There is my market in the Emperor's own Guard. Say nothing, daddy, for my mind is set, and if you weep now it will be to laugh hereafter. I will to great Rome with the soldiers."

The daily march of the heavily laden Roman legionary was fixed at twenty miles; but on this afternoon, though only half the distance had been accomplished, the silver trumpets blared out their welcome news that a camp was to be formed. As the men broke their ranks, the reason of their light march was announced by the decurions. It was the birthday of Geta, the younger son of the Emperor, and in his honour there would be games and a double ration of wine. But the iron discipline of the Roman army required that under all circumstances certain duties should be performed, and foremost among them that the camp should be made secure. Laying down their arms in the order of their ranks, the soldiers seized their spades and axes, and worked rapidly and joyously until sloping vallum and gaping fossa girdled them round, and gave them safe refuge against a night attack. Then in noisy, laughing, gesticulating crowds they gathered in their thousands round the grassy arena where the sports were to be held. A long green hillside sloped down to a level plain, and on this gentle incline the army lay watching the strife of the chosen athletes who contended before them. They stretched themselves in the glare of the sunshine, their heavy tunics thrown off, and their naked limbs sprawling, wine-cups an baskets of fruit and cakes circling amongst them, enjoying rest and peace as only those can to whom it comes so rarely.

The five-mile race was over, and had been won as usual by Decurion Brennus, the crack long-distance champion of the Herculians. Amid the yells of the Jovians, Capellus of the corps had carried off both the long and the high jump. Big Brebix the Gaul had out-thrown the long guardsman Serenus with the fifty pound stone. Now, as the sun sank towards the western ridge, and turned the Harpessus to a riband of gold, they had come to the final of the wrestling, where the pliant Greek, whose name is lost in the nickname of "Python," was tried out against the bull-necked Lictor of the military police, a hairy Hercules, whose heavy hand had in the way of duty oppressed many of the spectators.

As the two men, stripped save for their loin-cloths, approached the wrestling-ring, cheers and counter-cheers burst from their adherents, some favouring the Lictor for his Roman blood, some the Greek from their own private grudge. And then, of a sudden, the cheering died, heads were turned towards the slope away from the arena, men stood up and peered and pointed, until finally, in a strange hush, the whole great assembly had forgotten the athletes, and were watching a single man walking swiftly towards them down the green curve of the hill. This huge solitary figure, with the oaken club in his hand, the shaggy fleece flapping from his great shoulders, and the setting sun gleaming upon a halo of golden hair, might have been the tutelary god of the fierce and barren mountains from which he had issued. Even the Emperor rose from his chair and gazed with open-eyed amazement at the extraordinary being who approached him.

The man, whom we already know as Theckla the Thracian, paid no heed to the attention which he had aroused, but strode onwards, stepping as lightly as a deer, until he reached the fringe of the soldiers. Amid their open ranks he picked his way, sprang over the ropes which guarded the arena, and advanced towards the Emperor, until a spear at his breast warned him that he must go no nearer. Then he sunk upon his right knee and called out some words in the Gothic speech.

"Great Jupiter! Whoever saw such a body of a man!" cried the Emperor. "What says he? What is amiss with the fellow? Whence comes he, and what is his name?"

An interpreter translated the Barbarian's answer. "He says, great Caesar, that he is of good blood, and sprung by a Gothic father from a woman of the Alani. He says that his name is Theckla, and that he would fain carry a sword in Caesar's service."

The Emperor smiled. "Some post could surely be found for such a man, were it but as janitor at the Palatine Palace," said he to one of the Prefects. "I would fain see him walk even as he is through the forum. He would turn the heads of half the women in Rome. Talk to him, Crassus. You know his speech."

The Roman officer turned to the giant. "Caesar says that you are to come with him, and he will make you the servant at his door."

The Barbarian rose, and his fair cheeks flushed with resentment.

"I will serve Caesar as a soldier," said he, "but I will be house-servant to no man-not even to him. If Caesar would see what manner of man I am, let him put one of his guardsmen up against me."

"By the shade of Milo this is a bold fellow!" cried the Emperor. "How say you, Crassus? Shall he make good his words?"

"By your leave, Caesar," said the blunt soldier, "good swordsmen are too rare in these days that we should let them slay each other for sport. Perhaps if the Barbarian would wrestle a fall—"

"Excellent!" cried the Emperor. "Here is the Python, and here Varus the Lictor, each stripped for the bout. Have a look at them, Barbarian, and see which you would choose. What does he say? He would take them both? Nay then he is either the king of wrestlers or the king of boasters, and we shall soon see which. Let him have his way, and he has himself to thank if he comes out with a broken neck."

There was some laughter when the peasant tossed his sheep-skin mantle to the ground and, without troubling to remove his leather tunic, advanced towards the two wrestlers; but it became uproarious when with a quick spring he seized the Greek under one arm and the Roman under the other, holding them as in a vice. Then with a terrific effort he tore them both from the ground, carried them writhing and kicking round the arena, and finally walking up to the Emperor's throne, threw his two athletes down in front of him. Then, bowing to Caesar, the huge Barbarian withdrew, and laid his great bulk down among the ranks of the applauding soldiers, whence he watched with stolid unconcern the conclusion of the sports.

It was still daylight, when the last event had been decided, and the soldiers returned to the camp. The Emperor Severus had ordered his horse, and in the company of Crassus, his favourite prefect, rode down the winding pathway which skirts the Harpessus, chatting over the future dispersal of the army. They had ridden for some miles when Severus, glancing behind him, was surprised to see a huge figure which trotted lightly along at the very heels of his horse.

"Surely this is Mercury as well as Hercules that we have found among the Thracian mountains," said he with a smile. "Let us see how soon our Syrian horses can out-distance him."

The two Romans broke into a gallop, and did not draw rein until a good mile had been covered at the full pace of their splendid chargers. Then they turned and looked back; but there, some distance off, still running with a lightness and a spring which spoke of iron muscles and inexhaustible endurance, came the great Barbarian. The Roman Emperor waited until the athlete had come up to them.

"Why do you follow me?" he asked. "It is my hope, Caesar, that I may always follow you." His flushed face as he spoke was almost level with that of the mounted Roman.

"By the god of war, I do not know where in all the world I could find such a servant!" cried the Emperor. "You shall be my own body-guard, the one nearest to me of all."

The giant fell upon his knee. "My life and strength are yours," he said. "I ask no more than to spend them for Caesar."

Crassus had interpreted this short dialogue. He now turned to the Emperor.

"If he is indeed to be always at your call, Caesar, it would be well to give the poor Barbarian some name which your lips can frame. Theckla is as uncouth and craggy a word as one of his native rocks."

The Emperor pondered for a moment. "If I am to have the naming of him," said he, "then surely I shall call him Maximus, for there is not such a giant upon earth."

"Hark you," said the Prefect. "The Emperor has deigned to give you a Roman name, since you have come into his service. Henceforth you are no longer Theckla, but you are Maximus. Can you say it after me?"

"Maximin," repeated the Barbarian, trying to catch the Roman word.

The Emperor laughed at the mincing accent. "Yes, yes, Maximin let it be. To all the world you are Maximin, the body-guard of Severus. When we have reached Rome, we will soon see that your dress shall correspond with your office. Meanwhile march with the guard until you have my further orders."

So it came about that as the Roman army resumed its march next day, and left behind it the fair valley of the Harpessus, a huge recruit, clad in brown leather, with a rude sheep-skin floating from his shoulders, marched beside the Imperial troop. But far away in the wooden farm-house of a distant Macedonian valley two old country folk wept salt tears, and prayed to the gods for the safety of their boy who had turned his face to Rome.

II: The Rise of Giant Maximin

Exactly twenty-five years had passed since the day that Theckla the huge Thracian peasant had turned into Maximin the Roman guardsman. They had not been good years for Rome. Gone for ever were the great Imperial days of the Hadrians and the Trajans. Gone also the golden age of the two Antonines, when the highest were for once the most worthy and most wise. It had been an epoch of weak and cruel men. Severus, the swarthy African, a stark grim man, had died in far away York, after fighting all the winter with the Caledonian Highlanders—a race who have ever since worn the martial garb of the Romans. His son, known only by his slight-ing nick-name of Caracalla, had reigned during six years of insane lust and cruelty, before the knife of an angry soldier avenged the dignity of the Roman name. The nonentity Macrinus had filled the dangerous throne for a single year before he also met a bloody end, and made room for the most grotesque of all monarchs, the unspeakable Heliogabalus with his foul mind and his painted face. He in turn was cut to pieces by the soldiers, and Severus Alexander, a gentle youth, scarce seventeen years of age, had been thrust into his place. For thirteen years now he had ruled, striving with some success to put some virtue and stability into the rotting Empire, but raising many fierce enemies as he did so-enemies whom he had not the strength nor the wit to hold in check.

And Giant Maximin—what of him? He had carried his eight feet of manhood through the lowlands of Scotland, and the passes of the Grampians. He had seen Severus pass away, and had soldiered with his son. He had fought in Armenia, in Dacia, and in Germany. They had made him a centurion upon the field when with his hands he plucked out one by one the stockades of a northern village, and so cleared a path for the stormers. His strength had been the jest and the admiration of the soldiers. Legends about him had spread through the army and were the common gossip round the camp fires—of his duel with the German axeman on the Island of the Rhine, and of the blow with his fist which broke the leg of a Scythian's horse. Gradually he had won his way upwards, until now, after quarter of a century's service he was tribune of the fourth legion and superintendent of recruits for the whole army. The young soldier who had come under the glare of Maximin's eyes, or had been lifted up with one huge hand while he was cuffed by the other, had his first lesson from him in the discipline of the service.

It was nightfall in the camp of the fourth legion upon the Gallic shore of the Rhine. Across the moonlit water, amid the thick forests which stretched away to the dim horizon, lay the wild untamed German tribes. Down on the river bank the light gleamed upon the helmets of the Roman sentinels who kept guard along the river. Far away a red point rose and fell in the darkness—a watch-fire of the enemy upon the further shore.

Outside his tent, beside some smouldering logs, Giant Maximin was seated, a dozen of his officers around him. He had changed much since the day when we first met him in the Valley of the Harpessus. His huge frame was as erect as ever, and there was no sign of diminution of his strength. But he had aged none the less. The yellow tangle of hair was gone, worn down by the ever-pressing helmet. The fresh young face was drawn and hardened, with austere lines wrought by trouble and privation. The nose was more hawk-like, the eyes more cunning, the expression more cynical and more sinister. In his youth, a child would have run to his arms. Now it would shrink screaming from his gaze. That was what twenty-five years with the eagles had done for Theckla the Thracian peasant.

He was listening now—for he was a man of few words—to the chatter of his centurions. One of them, Balbus the Sicilian, had been to the main camp at Mainz, only four miles away, and had seen the Emperor Alexander arrive that very day from Rome. The rest were eager at the news, for it was a time of unrest, and the rumour of great changes was in the air.

"How many had he with him?" asked Labienus, a black-browed veteran from the south of Gaul. "I'll wager a month's pay that he was not so trustful as to come alone among his faithful legions."

"He had no great force," replied Balbus. "Ten or twelve cohorts of the Praetorians and a handful of horse."

"Then indeed his head is in the lion's mouth," cried Sulpicius, a hot-headed youth from the African Pentapolis. "How was he received?"

"Coldly enough. There was scarce a shout as he came down the line."

"They are ripe for mischief," said Labienus. "And who can wonder, when it is we soldiers who uphold the Empire upon our spears, while the lazy citizens at Rome reap all of our sowing. Why cannot a soldier have what a soldier gains? So long as they throw us our denarius a day, they think that they have done with us."

"Aye," croaked a grumbling old greybeard. "Our limbs, our blood, our lives—what do they care so long as the Barbarians are held off, and they are left in peace to their feastings and their circus? Free bread, free wine, free games—everything for the loafer at Rome. For us the frontier guard and a soldier's fare."

Maximin gave a deep laugh. "Old Plancus talks like that," said he; "but we know that for all the world he would not change his steel plate for a citizen's gown. You've earned the kennel, old hound, if you wish it. Go and gnaw your bone and growl in peace."

"Nay, I am too old for change. I will follow the eagle till I die. And yet I had rather die in serving a soldier master than a long-gowned Syrian who comes of a stock where the women are men and the men are women."

There was a laugh from the circle of soldiers, for sedition and mutiny were rife in the camp, and even the old centurion's outbreak could not draw a protest. Maximin raised his great mastiff head and looked at Balbus.

"Was any name in the mouths of the soldiers?" he asked in a meaning voice.

There was a hush for the answer. The sigh of the wind among the pines and the low lapping of the river swelled out louder in the silence. Balbus looked hard at his commander.

"Two names were whispered from rank to rank," said he. "One was Ascenius Pollio, the General. The other was—"

The fiery Sulpicius sprang to his feet waving a glowing brand above his head.

"Maximinus!" he yelled, "Imperator Maximinus Augustus!"

Who could tell how it came about? No one had thought of it an hour before. And now it sprang in an instant to full accomplishment. The shout of the frenzied young African had scarcely rung through the darkness when from the tents, from the watch-fires, from the sentries, the answer came pealing back: "Ave, Maximinus! Ave Maximinus Augustus!" From all sides men came rushing, half-clad, wild-eyed, their eyes staring, their mouths agape, flaming wisps of straw or flaring torches above their heads. The giant was caught up by scores of hands, and sat enthroned upon the bull-necks of the legionaries. "To the camp!" they yelled. "To the camp! Hail! Hail to the soldier Caesar!"

That same night Severus Alexander, the young Syrian Emperor, walked outside his Praetorian camp, accompanied by his friend Licinius Probus, the Captain of the Guard. They were talking gravely of the gloomy faces and seditious bearing of the soldiers. A great foreboding of evil weighed heavily upon the Emperor's heart, and it was reflected upon the stern bearded face of his companion.

"I like it not," said he. "It is my counsel, Caesar, that with the first light of morning we make our way south once more."

"But surely," the Emperor answered, "I could not for shame turn my back upon the danger. What have they against me? How have I harmed them that they should forget their vows and rise upon me?"

"They are like children who ask always for something new. You heard the murmur as you rode along the ranks. Nay, Caesar, fly tomorrow, and your Praetorians will see that you are not pursued. There may be some loyal cohorts among the legions, and if we join forces—"

A distant shout broke in upon their conversation—a low continued roar, like the swelling tumult of a sweeping wave. Far down the road upon which they stood there twinkled many moving lights, tossing and sinking as they rapidly advanced, whilst the hoarse tumultuous bellowing broke into articulate words, the same tremendous words, a thousand-fold repeated. Licinius seized the Emperor by the wrist and dragged him under the cover of some bushes.

"Be still, Caesar! For your life be still!" he whispered. "One word and we are lost!"

Crouching in the darkness, they saw that wild procession pass, the rushing screaming figures, the tossing arms, the bearded, distorted faces, now scarlet and now grey, as the brandished torches waxed or waned. They heard the rush of many feet, the clamour of hoarse voices, the clang of metal upon metal. And then suddenly, above them all, they saw a vision of a monstrous man, a huge bowed back, a savage face, grim hawk eyes, that looked out over the swaying shields. It was seen for an instant in a smoke-fringed circle of fire, and then it had swept on into the night.

"Who is he?" stammered the Emperor, clutching at his guardsman's sleeve. "They call him Caesar."

"It is surely Maximin the Thracian peasant." In the darkness the Praetorian officer looked with strange eyes at his master.

"It is all over, Caesar. Let us fly your tent."

But even as they went a second shout had broken forth tenfold louder than the first. If the one had been the roar of the oncoming wave, the other

41

was the full turmoil of the tempest. Twenty thousand voices from the camp had broken into one wild shout which echoed through the night, until the distant Germans round their watch-fires listened in wonder and alarm.

"Ave!" cried the voices. "Ave Maximinus Augustus!"

High upon their bucklers stood the giant, and looked round him at the great floor of upturned faces below. His own savage soul was stirred by the clamour, but only his gleaming eyes spoke of the fire within. He waved his hand to the shouting soldiers as the huntsman waves to the leaping pack. They passed him up a coronet of oak leaves, and clashed their swords in homage as he placed it on his head. And then there came a swirl in the crowd before him, a little space was cleared, and there knelt an officer in the Praetorian garb, blood upon his face, blood upon his bared forearm, blood upon his naked sword. Licinius too had gone with the tide.

"Hail, Caesar, hail!" he cried, as he bowed his head before the giant. "I come from Alexander. He will trouble you no more."

III: *The Fall of Maximin*

For three years the soldier Emperor had been upon the throne. His palace had been his tent, and his people had been the legionaries. With them he was supreme; away from them he was nothing. He had gone with them from one frontier to the other. He had fought against Dacians, Sarmatians, and once again against the Germans. But Rome knew nothing of him, and all her turbulence rose against a master who cared so little for her or her opinion that he never deigned to set foot within her walls. There were cabals and conspiracies against the absent Caesar. Then his heavy hand fell upon them, and they were cuffed, even as the young soldiers had been who passed under his discipline. He knew nothing, and cared as much for consuls, senates, and civil laws. His own will and the power of the sword were the only forces which he could understand. Of commerce and the arts he was as ignorant as when he left his Thracian home. The whole vast Empire was to him a huge machine for producing the money by which the legions were to be rewarded. Should he fail to get that money, his fellow soldiers would bear him a grudge. To watch their interests they had raised him upon their shields that night. If city funds had to be plundered or temples desecrated, still the money must be got. Such was the point of view of Giant Maximin.

But there came resistance, and all the fierce energy of the man, all the hardness which had given him the leadership of hard men, sprang forth to quell it. From his youth he had lived amidst slaughter. Life and death were cheap things to him. He struck savagely at all who stood up to him, and when they hit back, he struck more savagely still. His giant shadow lay black across the Empire from Britain to Syria. A strange subtle vindictiveness became also apparent in him. Omnipotence ripened every fault and swelled it into crime. In the old days he had been rebuked for his roughness. Now a sullen dangerous anger arose against those who had rebuked him. He sat by the hour with his craggy chin between his hands, and his elbows resting on his knees, while he recalled all the misadventures, all the vexations of his early youth, when Roman wits had shot their little satires upon his bulk and his ignorance. He could not write, but his son Verus placed the names upon his tablets, and they were sent to the Governor of Rome. Men who had long forgotten their offence were called suddenly to make most bloody reparation.

A rebellion broke out in Africa, but was quelled by his lieutenant. But the mere rumour of it set Rome in a turmoil. The Senate found something of its ancient spirit. So did the Italian people. They would not be for ever bullied by the legions. As Maximin approached from the frontier, with the sack of rebellious Rome in his mind, he was faced with every sign of a national resistance. The countryside was deserted, the farms abandoned, the fields cleared of crops and cattle. Before him lay the walled town of Aquileia. He flung himself fiercely upon it, but was met by as fierce a resistance. The walls could not be forced, and yet there was no food in the country round for his legions. The men were starving and dissatisfied. What did it matter to them who was Emperor? Maximin was no better than themselves. Why should they call down the curse of the whole Empire upon their heads by upholding him? He saw their sullen faces and their averted eyes, and he knew that the end had come.

That night he sat with his son Verus in his tent, and he spoke softly and gently as the youth had never heard him speak before. He had spoken thus in old days with Paullina, the boy's mother; but she had been dead these many years, and all that was soft and gentle in the big man had passed away with her. Now her spirit seemed very near him, and his own was tempered by its presence.

"I would have you go back to the Thracian mountains," he said. "I have tried both, boy, and I can tell you that there is no pleasure which power can bring which can equal the breath of the wind and the smell of the kine upon a summer morning. Against you they have no quarrel. Why should they mishandle you? Keep far from Rome and the Romans. Old Eudoxus has money, and to spare. He awaits you with two horses outside the camp. Make for the valley of the Harpessus, lad. It was thence that your father came, and there you will find his kin. Buy and stock a homestead, and keep yourself far from the paths of greatness and of danger. God keep you, Verus, and send you safe to Thrace."

When his son had kissed his hand and had left him, the Emperor drew his robe around him and sat long in thought. In his slow brain he revolved the past—his early peaceful days, his years with Severus, his memories of Britain, his long campaigns, his strivings and battlings, all leading to that mad night by the Rhine. His fellow soldiers had loved him then. And now he had read death in their eyes. How had he failed them? Others he might have wronged, but they at least had no complaint against him. If he had his time again, he would think less of them and more of his people, he would try to win love instead of fear, he would live for peace and not for war. If he had his time again! But there were shuffling Steps, furtive whispers, and the low rattle of arms outside his tent. A bearded face looked in at him, a swarthy African face that he knew well. He laughed, and, bearing his arm, he took his sword from the table beside him.

"It is you, Sulpicius," said he. "You have not come to cry 'Ave Imperator Maximin!' as once by the camp fire. You are tired of me, and by the gods I am tired of you, and glad to be at the end of it. Come and have done with it, for I am minded to see how many of you I can take with me when I go."

They clustered at the door of the tent, peeping over each other's shoulders, and none wishing to be the first to close with that laughing, mocking giant. But something was pushed forward upon a spear point, and as he saw it, Maximin groaned and his sword sank to the earth.

"You might have spared the boy," he sobbed. "He would not have hurt you. Have done with it then, for I will gladly follow him."

So they closed upon him and cut and stabbed and thrust, until his knees gave way beneath him and he dropped upon the floor.

"The tyrant is dead!" they cried. "The tyrant is dead," and from all the camp beneath them and from the walls of the beleaguered city the joyous cry came echoing back, "He is dead, Maximin is dead!"

I sit in my study, and upon the table before me lies a denarius of Maximin, as fresh as when the triumvir of the Temple of Juno Moneta sent it from the mint. Around it are recorded his resounding titles—Imperator Maximinus, Pontifex Maximus, Tribunitia potestate, and the rest. In the centre is the impress of a great craggy head, a massive jaw, a rude fighting face, a contracted forehead. For all the pompous roll of titles it is a peasant's face, and I see him not as the Emperor of Rome, but as the great Thracian boor who strode down the hillside on that far-distant summer day when first the eagles beckoned him to Rome.

The Coming of the Huns

IN THE MIDDLE of the fourth century the state of the Christian religion
was a scandal and a disgrace. Patient, humble, and long-suffering in ad-
versity, it had become positive, aggressive, and unreasonable with success.
Paganism was not yet dead, but it was rapidly sinking, finding its most
faithful supporters among the conservative aristocrats of the best families
on the one hand, and among those benighted villagers on the other who
gave their name to the expiring creed. Between these two extremes the
great majority of reasonable men had turned from the conception of many
gods to that of one, and had rejected for ever the beliefs of their forefathers. But with the vices of polytheism they had also abandoned its virtues,
among which toleration and religious good humour had been conspicu-
ous. The strenuous earnestness of the Christians had compelled them to
examine and define every point of their own theology; but as they had no
central authority by which such definitions could be checked, it was not
long before a hundred heresies had put forward their rival views, while the
same earnestness of conviction led the stronger bands of schismatics to
endeavour, for conscience sake, to force their views upon the weaker, and
thus to cover the Eastern world with confusion and strife.

Alexandria, Antioch, and Constantinople were centres of theologi-
cal warfare. The whole north of Africa, too, was rent by the strife of the
Donatists, who upheld their particular schism by iron flails and the war-
cry of "Praise to the Lord!" But minor local controversies sank to nothing
when compared with the huge argument of the Catholic and the Arian,
which rent every village in twain, and divided every household from the
cottage to the palace. The rival doctrines of the Homoousian and of the
Homoiousian, containing metaphysical differences so attenuated that they
could hardly be stated, turned bishop against bishop and congregation

45

against congregation. The ink of the theologians and the blood of the fanatics were spilled in floods on either side, and gentle followers of Christ were horrified to find that their faith was responsible for such a state of riot and bloodshed as had never yet disgraced the religious history of the world. Many of the more earnest among them, shocked and scandalized, slipped away to the Libyan Desert, or to the solitude of Pontus, there to await in self-denial and prayer that second coming which was supposed to be at hand. Even in the deserts they could not escape the echo of the distant strife, and the hermits themselves scowled fiercely from their dens at passing travellers who might be contaminated by the doctrines of Athanasius or of Arius.

Such a hermit was Simon Melas, of whom I write. A Trinitarian and a Catholic, he was shocked by the excesses of the persecution of the Arians, which could be only matched by the similar outrages with which these same Arians in the day of their power avenged their treatment on their brother Christians. Weary of the whole strife, and convinced that the end of the world was indeed at hand, he left his home in Constantinople and travelled as far as the Gothic settlements in Dacia, beyond the Danube, in search of some spot where he might be free from the never-ending disputes. Still journeying to the north and east, he crossed the river which we now call the Dneister, and there, finding a rocky hill rising from an immense plain, he formed a cell near its summit, and settled himself down to end his life in self-denial and meditation. There were fish in the stream, the country teemed with game, and there was an abundance of wild fruits, so that his spiritual exercises were not unduly interrupted by the search of sustenance for his mortal frame.

In this distant retreat he expected to find absolute solitude, but the hope was in vain. Within a week of his arrival, in an hour of worldly curiosity, he explored the edges of the high rocky hill upon which he lived. Making his way up to a cleft, which was hung with olives and myrtles, he came upon a cave in the opening of which sat an aged man, white-bearded, white-haired, and infirm—a hermit like himself. So long had this stranger been alone that he had almost forgotten the use of his tongue; but at last, words coming more freely, he was able to convey the information that his name was Paul of Nicopolis, that he was a Greek citizen, and that he also had come out into the desert for the saving of his soul, and to escape from the contamination of heresy.

"Little I thought, brother Simon," said he, "that I should ever find any one else who had come so far upon the same holy errand. In all these years, and they are so many that I have lost count of them, I have never seen a man, save indeed one or two wandering shepherds far out upon yonder plain."

From where they sat, the huge steppe, covered with waving grass and gleaming with a vivid green in the sun, stretched away as level and as unbroken as the sea, to the eastern horizon. Simon Melas stared across it with curiosity.

"Tell me, brother Paul," said he, "you who have lived here so long— what lies at the further side of that plain?"

The old man shook his head. "There is no further side to the plain," said he. "It is the earth's boundary, and stretches away to eternity. For all these years I have sat beside it, but never once have I seen anything come across it. It is manifest that if there had been a further side there would certainly at some time have come some traveller from that direction. Over the great river yonder is the Roman post of Tyras; but that is a long day's journey from here, and they have never disturbed my meditations."

"On what do you meditate, brother Paul?"

"At first I meditated on many sacred mysteries; but now, for twenty years, I have brooded continually on the nature of the Logos. What is your view upon that vital matter, brother Simon?"

"Surely," said the younger man, "there can be no question as to that. The Logos is assuredly but a name used by St. John to signify the Deity."

The old hermit gave a hoarse cry of fury, and his brown, withered face was convulsed with anger. Seizing the huge cudgel which he kept to beat off the wolves, he shook it murderously at his companion.

"Out with you! Out of my cell!" he cried. "Have I lived here so long to have it polluted by a vile Trinitarian—a follower of the rascal Athanasius? Wretched idolater, learn once for all, that the Logos is in truth an emanation from the Deity, and in no sense equal or co-eternal with Him! Out with you, I say, or I will dash out your brains with my staff!"

It was useless to reason with the furious Arian, and Simon withdrew in sadness and wonder, that at this extreme verge of the known earth the spirit of religious strife should still break upon the peaceful solitude of the wilderness. With hanging head and heavy heart he made his way down the valley, and climbed up once more to his own cell, which lay at the crown of the hill, with the intention of never again exchanging visits with his Arian neighbour.

Here, for a year, dwelt Simon Melas, leading a life of solitude and prayer. There was no reason why any one should ever come to this outermost point of human habitation. Once a young Roman officer—Caius Crassus—rode out a day's journey from Tyras, and climbed the hill to have speech with the anchorite. He was of an equestrian family, and still held his belief in the old dispensation. He looked with interest and surprise, but also with some disgust, at the ascetic arrangements of that humble abode.

"Whom do you please by living in such a fashion?" he asked.

"We show that our spirit is superior to our flesh," Simon answered. "If we fare badly in this world, we believe that we shall reap an advantage in the world to come."

The centurion shrugged his shoulders. "There are philosophers among our people, Stoics and others, who have the same idea. When I was in the Herulian Cohort of the Fourth Legion we were quartered in Rome itself, and I saw much of the Christians, but I could never learn anything from them which I had not heard from my own father, whom you, in your arrogance, would call a Pagan. It is true that we talk of numerous gods; but for many years we have not taken them very seriously. Our thoughts upon virtue and duty and a noble life are the same as your own."

Simon Melas shook his head.

"If you have not the holy books," said he, "then what guide have you to direct your steps?"

"If you will read our philosophers, and above all the divine Plato, you will find that there are other guides who may take you to the same end. Have you by chance read the book which was written by our Emperor Marcus Aurelius? Do you not discover there every virtue which man could have, although he knew nothing of your creed? Have you considered, also, the words and actions of our late Emperor Julian, with whom I served my first campaign when he went out against the Persians? Where could you find a more perfect man than he?"

"Such talk is unprofitable, and I will have no more of it," said Simon, sternly. "Take heed while there is time, and embrace the true faith; for the end of the world is at hand, and when it comes there will be no mercy for those who have shut their eyes to the light." So saying, he turned back once more to his praying-stool and to his crucifix, while the young Roman walked in deep thought down the hill, and mounting his horse, rode off to his distant post. Simon watched him until his brazen helmet was but a bead of light on the western edge of the great plain; for this was the first human face that he had seen in all this long year, and there were times when his heart yearned for the voices and the faces of his kind.

So another year passed, and save for the chance of weather and the slow change of the seasons, one day was as another. Every morning, when Simon opened his eyes, he saw the same grey line ripening into red in the furthest east, until the bright rim pushed itself above that far-off horizon across which no living creature had ever been known to come. Slowly the sun swept across the huge arch of the heavens, and as the shadows shifted from the black rocks which jutted upward from above his cell, so did the hermit regulate his terms of prayer and meditation. There was nothing on earth to draw his eye, or to distract his mind, for the grassy plain below was as void from month to month as the heaven above. So the long hours passed, until the red rim slipped down on the further side, and the day ended in the same pearl-grey shimmer with which it had begun. Once two ravens circled for some days round the lonely hill, and once a white fish-eagle came from the Dneister and screamed above the hermit's head. Sometimes red dots were seen on the green plain where the antelopes grazed, and often a wolf howled in the darkness from the base of the rocks. Such was the uneventful life of Simon Melas the anchorite, until there came the day of wrath.

It was in the late spring of the year 375 that Simon came out from his cell, his gourd in his hand, to draw water from the spring. Darkness had closed in, the sun had set, but one last glimmer of rosy light rested upon a rocky peak, which jutted forth from the hill, on the further side from the hermit's dwelling. As Simon came forth from under his ledge, the gourd dropped from his hand, and he stood gazing in amazement.

On the opposite peak a man was standing, his outline black in the fading light. He was a strange almost a deformed figure, short-statured, round-backed, with a large head, no neck, and a long rod jutting out from between his shoulders. He stood with his face advanced, and his body bent, peering very intently over the plain to the westward. In a moment he was gone, and the lonely black peak showed up hard and naked against the faint eastern glimmer. Then the night closed down, and all was black once more.

Simon Melas stood long in bewilderment, wondering who this stranger could be. He had heard, as had every Christian, of those evil spirits which were wont to haunt the hermits in the Thebaid and on the skirts of the Ethiopian waste. The strange shape of this solitary creature, its dark outline and prowling, intent attitude, suggestive rather of a fierce, rapacious beast than of a man, all helped him to believe that he had at last encountered one of those wanderers from the pit, of whose existence, in those days of robust faith, he had no more doubt than of his own. Much of the night he spent in prayer, his eyes glancing continually at the low arch of his cell door, with its curtain of deep purple wrought with stars. At any instant some crouching monster, some homed abomination, might peer in upon him; and he clung with frenzied appeal to his crucifix, as his human weakness quailed at the thought. But at last his fatigue overcame his fears, and falling upon his couch of dried grass, he slept until the bright daylight brought him to his senses.

It was later than was his wont, and the sun was far above the horizon. As he came forth from his cell, he looked across at the peak of rock, but it stood there bare and silent. Already it seemed to him that that strange dark figure which had startled him so was some dream, some vision of the twilight. His gourd lay where it had fallen, and he picked it up with the intention of going to the spring. But suddenly he was aware of something new. The whole air was throbbing with sound. From all sides it came, rumbling, indefinite, an inarticulate mutter, low, but thick and strong, rising, falling, reverberating among the rocks, dying away into vague whispers, but always there. He looked round at the blue, cloudless sky in bewilderment. Then he scrambled up the rocky pinnacle above him, and sheltering himself in its shadow, he stared out over the plain. In his wildest dream he had never imagined such a sight.

The whole vast expanse was covered with horse-men, hundreds and thousands and tens of thousands, all riding slowly and in silence, out of the unknown east. It was the multitudinous beat of their horses' hoofs which caused that low throbbing in his ears. Some were so close to him as he looked down upon them that he could see clearly their thin wiry horses, and the strange humped figures of the swarthy riders, sitting forward on the withers, shapeless bundles, their short legs hanging stirrupless, their bodies balanced as firmly as though they were part of the beast. In those nearest he could see the bow and the quiver, the long spear and the short sword, with the coiled lasso behind the rider, which told that this was no helpless horde of wanderers, but a formidable army upon the march. His eyes passed on from them and swept further and further, but still to the very horizon, which quivered with movement, there was no end to this monstrous cavalry. Already the vanguard was far past the island of rock upon which he dwelt, and he could now understand that in front of this vanguard were single scouts who guided the course of the army, and that it was one of these whom he had seen the evening before.

All day, held spell-bound by this wonderful sight, the hermit crouched in the shadow of the rocks, and all day the sea of horsemen rolled onward over the plain beneath. Simon had seen the swarming quays of Alexandria, he had watched the mob which blocked the hippodrome of Constantinople, yet never had he imagined such a multitude as now defiled beneath his eyes, coming from that eastern skyline which had been the end of his world. Sometimes the dense streams of horsemen were broken by droves of brood-mares and foals, driven along by mounted guards; sometimes there were herds of cattle; sometimes there were lines of waggons with skin canopies above them; but then once more, after every break, came the horsemen, the horsemen, the hundreds and the thousands and the tens of thousands, slowly, ceaselessly, silently drifting from the east to the west.

The long day passed, the light waned, and the shadows fell; but still the great broad stream was flowing by.

But the night brought a new and even stranger sight. Simon had marked bundles of faggots upon the backs of many of the led horses, and now he saw their use. All over the great plain, red pin-points gleamed through the darkness, which grew and brightened into flickering columns of flame. So far as he could see both to east and west the fires extended, until they were but points of light in the furthest distance. White stars shone in the vast heavens above, red ones in the great plain below. And from every side rose the low, confused murmur of voices, with the lowing of oxen and the neighing of horses.

Simon had been a soldier and a man of affairs before ever he forsook the world, and the meaning of all that he had seen was clear to him. History told him how the Roman world had ever been assailed by fresh swarms of Barbarians, coming from the outer darkness, and that the Eastern Empire had already, in its fifty years of existence since Constantine had moved the capital of the world to the shores of the Bosphorus, been tormented in the same way. Gepidae and Heruli, Ostrogoths and Sarmatians, he was familiar with them all. What the advanced sentinel of Europe had seen from this lonely outlying hill, was a fresh swarm breaking in upon the Empire, distinguished only from the others by its enormous, incredible size and by the strange aspect of the warriors who composed it. He alone of all civilized men knew of the approach of this dreadful shadow, sweeping like a heavy storm-cloud from the unknown depths of the east. He thought of the little Roman posts along the Dneister, of the ruined Dacian wall of Trajan behind them, and then of the scattered, defenceless villages which lay with no thought of danger over all the open country which stretched down to the Danube. Could he but give them the alarm! Was it not, perhaps, for that very end that God had guided him to the wilderness?

Then suddenly he remembered his Arian neighbour, who dwelt in the cave beneath him. Once or twice during the last year he had caught a glimpse of his tall, bent figure hobbling round to examine the traps which he laid for quails and partridges. On one occasion they had met at the brook; but the old theologian waved him away, as if he were a leper. What did he think now of this strange happening? Surely their differences might be forgotten at such a moment. He stole down the side of the hill, and made his way to his fellow-hermit's cave.

But there was a terrible silence as he approached it. His heart sank at that deadly stillness in the little valley. No glimmer of light came from the cleft in the rocks. He entered and called, but no answer came back. Then, with flint, steel, and the dry grass which he used for tinder, he struck a spark, and blew it into a blaze. The old hermit, his white hair dabbled with crimson, lay sprawling across the floor. The broken crucifix, with which his head had been beaten in, lay in splinters across him. Simon had dropped on his knees beside him, straightening his contorted limbs, and muttering the office for the dead, when the thud of a horse's hoofs was heard ascending the little valley which led to the hermit's cell. The dry grass had burned down, and Simon crouched trembling in the darkness, pattering prayers to the Virgin that his strength might be upheld.

It may have been that the newcomer had seen the gleam of the light, or it may have been that he had heard from his comrades of the old man whom they had murdered, and that his curiosity had led him to the spot. He stopped his horse outside the cave, and Simon, lurking in the shadows within, had a fair view of him in the moonlight. He slipped from his saddle, fastened the bridle to a root, and then stood peering through the opening of the cell. He was a very short, thick man, with a dark face, which was gashed with three cuts upon either side. His small eyes were sunk deep in his head, showing like black holes in the heavy, flat, hairless face. His legs were short and very bandy, so that he waddled uncouthly as he walked.

Simon crouched in the darkest angle, and he gripped in his hand that same knotted cudgel which the dead theologian had once raised against him. As that hideous stooping head advanced into the darkness of the cell, he brought the staff down upon it with all the strength of his right arm, and then, as the stricken savage fell forward upon his face, he struck madly again and again, until the shapeless figure lay limp and still. One roof covered the first slain of Europe and of Asia.

Simon's veins were throbbing and quivering with the unwonted joy of action. All the energy stored up in those years of repose came in a flood at this moment of need. Standing in the darkness of the cell, he saw, as in a map of fire, the outlines of the great Barbaric host, the line of the river, the position of the settlements, the means by which they might be warned. Silently he waited in the shadow until the moon had sunk. Then he flung himself upon the dead man's horse, guided it down the gorge, and set forth at a gallop across the plain.

There were fires on every side of him, but he kept clear of the rings of light. Round each he could see, as he passed, the circle of sleeping warriors, with the long lines of picketed horses. Mile after mile and league after league stretched that huge encampment. And then, at last, he had reached the open plain which led to the river, and the fires of the invaders were but a dull smoulder against the black eastern sky. Ever faster and faster he sped across the steppe, like a single fluttered leaf which whirls before the storm. Even as the dawn whitened the sky behind him, it gleamed also upon the broad river in front, and he flogged his weary horse through the shallows, until he plunged into its full yellow tide.

So it was that, as the young Roman centurion—Caius Crassus—made his morning round in the fort of Tyras he saw a single horseman, who rode towards him from the river. Weary and spent, drenched with water and caked with dirt and sweat, both horse and man were at the last stage of their endurance. With amazement the Roman watched their progress, and recognized in the ragged, swaying figure, with flying hair and staring eyes, the hermit of the eastern desert. He ran to meet him, and caught him in his arms as he reeled from the saddle.

"What is it, then?" he asked. "What is your news?"

But the hermit could only point at the rising sun. "To arms!" he croaked. "To arms! The day of wrath is come!" And as he looked, the Roman saw—far across the river—a great dark shadow, which moved slowly over the distant plain.

The Last of the Legions

PONTUS, THE ROMAN VICEROY, sat in the atrium of his palatial villa by the Thames, and he looked with perplexity at the scroll of papyrus which he had just unrolled. Before him stood the messenger who had brought it, a swarthy little Italian, whose black eyes were glazed with want of sleep, and his olive features darker still from dust and sweat. The viceroy was looking fixedly at him, yet he saw him not, so full was his mind of this sudden and most unexpected order. To him it seemed as if the solid earth had given way beneath his feet. His life and the work of his life had come to irremediable ruin.

"Very good," he said at last in a hard dry voice, "you can go."

The man saluted and staggered out of the hall.

A yellow-haired British major-domo came forward for orders.

"Is the General there?"

"He is waiting, your excellency."

"Then show him in, and leave us together."

A few minutes later Licinius Crassus, the head of the British military establishment, had joined his chief. He was a large bearded man in a white civilian toga, hemmed with the Patrician purple. His rough, bold features, burned and seamed and lined with the long African wars, were shadowed with anxiety as he looked with questioning eyes at the drawn, haggard face of the viceroy.

"I fear, your excellency, that you have had bad news from Rome."

"The worst, Crassus. It is all over with Britain. It is a question whether even Gaul will be held."

"Saint Albus save us! Are the orders precise?"

"Here they are, with the Emperor's own seal."

"But why? I had heard a rumour, but it had seemed too incredible."

54

"So had I only last week, and had the fellow scourged for having spread it. But here it is as clear as words can make it: 'Bring every man of the Legions by forced marches to the help of the Empire. Leave not a cohort in Britain.' These are my orders."

"But the cause?"

"They will let the limbs wither so that the heart be stronger. The old German hive is about to swarm once more. There are fresh crowds of Barbarians from Dacia and Scythia. Every sword is needed to hold the Alpine passes. They cannot let three legions lie idle in Britain."

The soldier shrugged his shoulder's.

"When the legions go no Roman would feel that his life was safe here. For all that we have done, it is none the less the truth that it is no country of ours, and that we hold it as we won it by the sword."

"Yes, every man, woman, and child of Latin blood must come with us to Gaul. The galleys are already waiting at Portus Dubris. Get the orders out, Crassus, at once. As the Valerian legion falls back from the Wall of Hadrian it can take the northern colonists with it. The Jovians can bring in the people from the west, and the Batavians can escort the easterns if they will muster at Camboricum. You will see to it." He sank his face for a moment in his hands. "It is a fearsome thing," said he, "to tear up the roots of so goodly a tree."

"To make more space for such a crop of weeds," said the soldier bitterly. "My God, what will be the end of these poor Britons! From ocean to ocean there is not a tribe which will not be at the throat of its neighbour when the last Roman Lictor has turned his back. With these hot-headed Silures it is hard enough now to keep the swords in their sheaths."

"The kennel might fight as they chose among themselves until the best hound won," said the Roman Governor. "At least the victor would keep the arts and the religion which we have brought them, and Britain would be one land. No, it is the bear from the north and the wolves from oversea, the painted savage from beyond the walls and the Saxon pirate from over the water, who will succeed to our rule. Where we saved, they will slay; where we built, they will burn; where we planted, they will ravage. But the die is cast, Crassus. You will carry out the orders."

"I will send out the messengers within an hour. This very morning there has come news that the Barbarians are through the old gap in the wall, and their outriders as far south as Vinovia." The Governor shrugged his shoulders. "These things concern us no longer," said he. Then a bitter smile broke upon his aquiline clean-shaven face. "Whom think you that I see in audience this morning?"

"Nay, I know not."

"Caradoc and Regnus, and Celticus the Icenian, who, like so many of the richer Britons, have been educated at Rome, and who would lay before me their plans as to the ruling of this country."

"And what is their plan?"

"That they themselves should do it." The Roman soldier laughed. "Well, they will have their will," said he, as he saluted and turned upon his heel. "Farewell, your excellency. There are hard days coming for you and for me."

An hour later the British deputation was ushered into the presence of the Governor. They were good steadfast men, men who with a whole heart, and at some risk to themselves, had taken up their country's cause, so far as they could see it. At the same time, they well knew that under the mild and beneficent rule of Rome it was only when they passed from words to deeds that their backs or their necks would be in danger. They stood now, earnest and a little abashed, before the throne of the viceroy. Celticus was a swarthy black-bearded little Iberian. Caradoc and Regnus were tall middle-aged men of the fair flaxen British type. All three were dressed in the draped yellow toga after the Latin fashion, instead of in the bracae and tunic which distinguished their more insular fellow-countrymen.

"Well?" asked the Governor.

"We are here," said Celticus boldly, "as the spokesmen of a great number of our fellow-countrymen, for the purpose of sending our petition through you to the Emperor and to the Roman Senate, that we may urge upon them the policy of allowing us to govern this country after our own ancient fashion." He paused, as if awaiting some outburst as an answer to his own temerity; but the Governor merely nodded his head as a sign that he should proceed. "We had laws of our own before ever Caesar set foot in Britain, which have served their purpose since first our forefathers came from the land of Ham. We are not a child among the nations, but our history goes back in our own traditions—further even than that of Rome, and we are galled by this yoke which you have laid upon us."

"Are not our laws just?" asked the Governor.

"The code of Caesar is just, but it is always the code of Caesar. Our own laws were made for our own uses and our own circumstances, and we would fain have them again."

"You speak Roman as if you had been bred in the Forum; you wear a Roman toga; your hair is filleted in Roman fashion—are not these the gifts of Rome?"

"We would take all the learning and all the arts that Rome or Greece could give, but we would still be Britain, and ruled by Britons."

The viceroy smiled. "By the rood of Saint Helena," said he, "had you spoken thus to some of my heathen ancestors, there would have been an end to your politics. That you have dared to stand before my face and say as much is a proof for ever of the gentleness of our rule. But I would reason with you for a moment upon this your request. You know well that this land has never been one kingdom, but was always under many chiefs and many tribes, who have made war upon each other. Would you in very truth have it so again?"

"Those were in the evil pagan days, the days of the Druid and the oak-grove, your excellency. But now we are held together by a gospel of peace."

The viceroy shook his head. "If all the world were of the same way of thinking, then it would be easier," said he. "It may be that this blessed doctrine of peace will be little help to you when you are face to face with strong men who still worship the god of war. What would you do against the Picts of the north?"

"Your excellency knows that many of the bravest legionaries are of British blood. These are our defence."

"But discipline, man, the power to command, the knowledge of war, the strength to act—it is in these things that you would fail. Too long have you leaned upon the crutch."

"The times may be hard, but when we have gone through them, Britain will be herself again."

"Nay, she will be under a different and a harsher master," said the Roman. "Already the pirates swarm upon the eastern coast. Were it not for our Roman Count of the Saxon shore they would land tomorrow. I see the day when Britain may, indeed, be one; but that will be because you and your fellows are either dead or are driven into the mountains of the west. All goes into the melting-pot, and if a better Albion should come forth from it, it will be after ages of strife, and neither you nor your people will have part or lot in it."

Regnus, the tall young Celt, smiled. "With the help of God and our own right arms we should hope for a better end," said he. "Give us but the chance, and we will bear the brunt."

"You are as men that are lost," said the viceroy sadly. "I see this broad land, with its gardens and orchards, its fair villas and its walled towns, its bridges and its roads, all the work of Rome. Surely it will pass even as a dream, and these three hundred years of settled order will leave no trace behind. For learn that it will indeed be as you wish, and that this very day the orders have come to me that the legions are to go."

The three Britons looked at each other in amazement. Their first impulse was towards a wild exultation, but reflection and doubt followed close upon its heels.

"This is indeed wondrous news," said Celticus. "This is a day of days to the motherland. When do the legions go, your excellency, and what troops will remain behind for our protection?"

"The legions go at once," said the viceroy. "You will doubtless rejoice to hear that within a month there will be no Roman soldier in the island, nor, indeed, a Roman of any sort, age, or sex, if I can take them with me."

The faces of the Britons were shadowed, and Caradoc, a grave and thoughtful man, spoke for the first time.

"But this is over sudden, your excellency," said he. "There is much truth in what you have said about the pirates. From my villa near the fort of Anderida I saw eighty of their galleys only last week, and I know well that they would be on us like ravens on a dying ox. For many years to come it would not be possible for us to hold them off."

The viceroy shrugged his shoulders. "It is your affair now," said he. "Rome must look to herself."

The last traces of joy had passed from the faces of the Britons. Suddenly the future had started up clearly before them, and they quailed at the prospect.

"There is a rumour in the market-place," said Celticus, "that the northern Barbarians are through the gap in the wall. Who is to stop their progress?"

"You and your fellows," said the Roman.

Clearer still grew the future, and there was terror in the eyes of the spokesmen as they faced it.

"But, your excellency, if the legions should go at once, we should have the wild Scots at York, and the Northmen in the Thames within the month. We can build ourselves up under your shield, and in a few years it would be easier for us; but not now, your excellency, not now."

"Tut, man; for years you have been clamouring in our ears and raising the people. Now you have got what you asked. What more would you have? Within the month you will be as free as were your ancestors before Caesar set foot upon your shore."

"For God's sake, your excellency, put our words out of your head. The matter had not been well considered. We will send to Rome. We will ride post-haste ourselves. We will fall at the Emperor's feet. We will kneel before the Senate and beg that the legions remain."

The Roman proconsul rose from his chair and motioned that the audience was at an end.

"You will do what you please," said he. "I and my men are for Italy."

And even as he said, so was it, for before the spring had ripened into summer, the troops were clanking down the via Aurelia on their way to the Ligurian passes, whilst every road in Gaul was dotted with the carts and the waggons which bore the Brito-Roman refugees on their weary journey to their distant country. But ere another summer had passed Celticus was dead, for he was flayed alive by the pirates and his skin nailed upon the door of a church near Caistor. Regnus, too, was dead, for he was tied to a tree and shot with arrows when the painted men came to the sacking of Isca. Caradoc only was alive, but he was a slave to Elda the red Caledonian, and his wife was mistress to Mordred the wild chief of the western Cymri. From the ruined wall in the north to Vectis in the south blood and ruin and ashes covered the fair land of Britain. And after many days it came out fairer than ever, but, even as the Roman had said, neither the Britons nor any men of their blood came into the heritage of that which had been their own.

The First Cargo

"EX OVO OMNIA"

When you left Briton with your legion, my dear Crassus, I promised that I would write to you from time to time when a messenger chanced to be going to Rome, and keep you informed as to anything of interest which might occur in this country. Personally, I am very glad that I remained behind when the troops and so many of our citizens left, for though the living is rough and the climate is infernal, still by dint of the three voyages which I have made for amber to the Baltic, and the excellent prices which I obtained for it here, I shall soon be in a position to retire, and to spend my old age under my own fig tree, or even perhaps to buy a small villa at Baiae or Posuoli, where I could get a good sun-bath after the continued fogs of this accursed island. I picture myself on a little farm, and I read the Georgics as a preparation; but when I hear the rain falling and the wind howling, Italy seems very far away.

In my previous letter, I let you know how things were going in this country. The poor folk, who had given up all soldiering during the centuries that we guarded them, are now perfectly helpless before these Picts and Scots, tattooed Barbarians from the north, who overrun the whole country and do exactly what they please. So long as they kept to the north, the people in the south, who are the most numerous, and also the most civilized of the Britons, took no heed of them; but now the rascals have come as far as London, and the lazy folk in these parts have had to wake up. Vortigern, the king, is useless for anything but drink or women, so he sent across to the Baltic to get over some of the North Germans, in the hope that they would come and help him. It is bad enough to have a bear in your house, but it does not seem to me to mend matters if you call in a pack of ferocious wolves as well. However, nothing better could be devised, so an invitation was sent and very promptly accepted. And it is here that your humble friend appears upon the scene. In the course of my amber trading I had learned the Saxon speech, and so I was sent down in all haste to the Kentish shore that I might be there when our new allies came. I arrived there on the very day when their first vessel appeared, and it is of my adventures that I wish to tell you. It is perfectly clear to me that the landing of these warlike Germans in England will prove to be an event of historical importance, and so your inquisitive mind will not feel wearied if I treat the matter in some detail.

It was, then, upon the day of Mercury, immediately following the Feast of Our Blessed Lord's Ascension, that I found myself upon the south bank of the river Thames, at the point where it opens into a wide estuary. There is an island there named Thanet, which was the spot chosen for the landfall of our visitors. Sure enough, I had no sooner ridden up than there was a great red ship, the first as it seems of three, coming in under full sail. The white horse, which is the ensign of these rovers, was hanging from her topmast, and she appeared to be crowded with men. The sun was shining brightly, and the great scarlet ship, with snow-white sails and a line of gleaming shields slung over her side, made as fair a picture on that blue expanse as one would wish to see.

I pushed off at once in a boat, because it had been arranged that none of the Saxons should land until the king had come down to speak with their leaders. Presently I was under the ship, which had a gilded dragon in the bows, and a tier of oars along either side. As I looked up, there was a row of helmeted heads looking down at me, and among them I saw, to my great surprise and pleasure, that of Eric the Swart, with whom I do business at Venta every year. He greeted me heartily when I reached the deck, and became at once my guide, friend, and counsellor. This helped me greatly with these Barbarians, for it is their nature that they are very cold and aloof unless one of their own number can vouch for you, after which they are very hearty and hospitable. Try as they will, they find it hard, however, to avoid a certain suggestion of condescension, and in the baser sort, of contempt, when they are dealing with a foreigner.

It was a great stroke of luck meeting Eric, for he was able to give me some idea of how things stood before I was shown into the presence of Kenna, the leader of this particular ship. The crew, as I learned from him, was entirely made up of three tribes or families—those of Kenna, of Lanc, and of Hasta. Each of these tribes gets its name by putting the letters "ing" after the name of the chief, so that the people on board would describe themselves as Kennings, Lancings, and Hastings. I observed in the Baltic that the villages were named after the family who lived in them, each keeping to itself, so that I have no doubt if these fellows get a footing on shore, we shall see settlements with names like these rising up among the British towns.

The greater part of the men were sturdy fellows with red, yellow, or brown hair, mostly the latter. To my surprise, I saw several women among them. Eric, in answer to my question, explained that they always take their women with them so far as they can, and that instead of finding them an incumbrance as our Roman dames would be, they look upon them as helpmates and advisers. Of course, I remembered afterwards that our excellent and accurate Tacitus has remarked upon this characteristic of the Germans. All laws in the tribes are decided by votes, and a vote has not yet been given to the women, but many are in favour of it, and it is thought that woman and man may soon have the same power in the State, though many of the women themselves are opposed to such an innovation. I observed to Eric that it was fortunate there were several women on board, as they could keep each other company; but he answered that the wives of chiefs had no desire to know the wives of the inferior officers, and that both of them combined against the more common women, so that any companionship was out of the question. He pointed as he spoke to Editha, the wife of Kenna, a red-faced, elderly woman, who walked among the others, her chin in the air, taking no more notice than if they did not exist.

Whilst I was talking to my friend Eric, a sudden altercation broke out upon the deck, and a great number of the men paused in their work, and flocked towards the spot with faces which showed that they were deeply interested in the matter. Eric and I pushed our way among the others, for I was very anxious to see as much as I could of the ways and manners of these Barbarians. A quarrel had broken out about a child, a little blue-eyed fellow with curly yellow hair, who appeared to be greatly amused by the hubbub of which he was the cause. On one side of him stood a white-bearded old man, of very majestic aspect, who signified by his gestures that he claimed the lad for himself, while on the other was a thin, earnest, anxious person, who strongly objected to the boy being taken from him. Eric whispered in my ear that the old man was the tribal high priest, who was the official sacrificer to their great god Woden, whilst the other was a man who took somewhat different views, not upon Woden, but upon the means by which he should be worshipped. The majority of the crew were on the side of the old priest; but a certain number, who liked greater liberty of worship, and to invent their own prayers instead of always repeating the official ones, followed the lead of the younger man. The difference was too deep and too old to be healed among the grown men, but each had a great desire to impress their view upon the children. This was the reason why these two were now so furious with each other, and the argument between them ran so high that several of their followers on either side had drawn the short saxes, or knives from which their name of Saxon is derived, when a burly, red-headed man pushed his way through the throng, and in a voice of thunder brought the controversy to an end.

"You priests, who argue about the things which no man can know, are more trouble aboard this ship than all the dangers of the sea," he cried. "Can you not be content with worshipping Woden, over which we are all agreed, and not make so much of those small points upon which we may differ? If there is all this fuss about the teaching of the children, then I shall forbid either of you to teach them, and they must be content with as much as they can learn from their mothers."

The two angry teachers walked away with discontented faces; and Kenna—for it was he who spoke—ordered that a whistle should be sounded, and that the crew should assemble. I was pleased with the free bearing of these people, for though this was their greatest chief, they showed none of the exaggerated respect which soldiers of a legion might show to the Praetor, but met him on a respectful equality, which showed how highly they rated their own manhood.

From our Roman standard, his remarks to his men would seem very wanting in eloquence, for there were no graces nor metaphors to be found in them, and yet they were short, strong and to the point. At any rate it was very clear that they were to the minds of his hearers. He began by reminding them that they had left their own country because the land was all taken up, and that there was no use returning there, since there was no place where they could dwell as free and independent men. This island of Britain was but sparsely inhabited, and there was a chance that every one of them would be able to found a home of his own.

"You, Whitta," he said, addressing some of them by name, "you will found a Whitting hame, and you, Bucka, we shall see you in a Bucking hame, where your children, and your children's children will bless you for the broad acres which your valour will have gained for them." There was no word of glory or of honour in his speech, but he said that he was aware that they would do their duty, on which they all struck their swords upon their shields so that the Britons on the beach could hear the clang. Then, his eyes falling upon me, he asked me whether I was the messenger from Vortigern, and on my answering, he bid me follow him into his cabin, where Lanc and Hasta the other chiefs were waiting for a council.

Picture me, then, my dear Crassus, in a very low-roofed cabin, with these three huge Barbarians seated round me. Each was clad in some sort of saffron tunic, with chain-mail shirts over it, and helmets with the horns of oxen on either side, laid upon the table before them. Like most of the Saxon chiefs, their beards were shaved, but they wore their hair long and their huge light-coloured moustaches drooped down on to their shoulders. They are gentle, slow, and somewhat heavy in their bearing, but I can well fancy that their fury is the more terrible when it does arise.

Their minds seem to be of a very practical and positive nature, for they at once began to ask me a series of questions upon the numbers of the Britons, the resources of the kingdom, the conditions of its trade, and other such subjects. They then set to work arguing over the information which I had given, and became so absorbed in their own contention that I believe there were times when they forgot my presence. Everything, after due discussion, was decided between them by vote, the one who found himself in the minority always submitting, though sometimes with a very bad grace. Indeed, on one occasion Lanc, who usually differed from the others, threatened to refer the matter to the general vote of the whole crew. There was a constant conflict in the point of view; for whereas Kenna and Hasta were anxious to extend the Saxon power, and to make it greater in the eyes of the world, Lanc was of opinion that they should give less thought to conquest and more to the comfort and advancement of their followers. At the same time it seemed to me that really Lanc was the more combative of the three; so much so that, even in time of peace, he could not forego this contest with his own brethren. Neither of the others seemed very fond of him, for they were each, as was easy to see, proud of their chieftainship, and anxious to use their authority, referring continually to those noble ancestors from whom it was derived; while Lanc, though he was equally well born, took the view of the common men upon every occasion, claiming that the interests of the many were superior to the privileges of the few. In a word, Crassus, if you could imagine a free-booting Gracchus on one side, and two piratical Patricians upon the other, you would understand the effect which my companions produced upon me.

There was one peculiarity which I observed in their conversation which soothed me very much. I am fond of these Britons, among whom I have spent so much of my life, and I wish them well. It was very pleasing, therefore, to notice that these men insisted upon it in their conversation that the whole object of their visit was the good of the Islanders. Any prospect of advantage to themselves was pushed into the background. I was not clear that these professions could be made to agree with the speech in which Kenna had promised a hundred hides of land to every man on the ship; but on my making this remark, the three chiefs seemed very surprised and hurt by my suspicions, and explained very plausibly that, as the Britons needed them as a guard, they could not aid them better than by settling on the soil, and so being continually at hand in order to help them. In time, they said, they hoped to raise and train the natives to such a point that they would be able to look after themselves. Lanc spoke with some degree of eloquence upon the nobleness of the mission which they had undertaken, and the others clattered their cups of mead (a jar of that unpleasant drink was on the table) in token of their agreement.

I observed also how much interested, and how very earnest and intolerant these Barbarians were in the matter of religion. Of Christianity they knew nothing, so that although they were aware that the Britons were Christians, they had not a notion of what their creed really was. Yet without examination they started by taking it for granted that their own worship of Woden was absolutely right, and that therefore this other creed must be absolutely wrong. "This vile religion," "This sad superstition," and "This grievous error," were among the phrases which they used towards it. Instead of expressing pity for any one who had been misinformed upon so serious a question, their feelings were those of anger, and they declared most earnestly that they would spare no pains to set the matter right, fingering the hilts of their long broad-swords as they said so.

Well, my dear Crassus, you will have had enough of me and of my Saxons. I have given you a short sketch of these people and their ways. Since I began this letter, I have visited the two other ships which have come in, and as I find the same characteristics among the people on board them, I cannot doubt that they lie deeply in the race. For the rest, they are brave, hardy, and very pertinacious in all that they undertake; whereas the Britons, though a great deal more spirited, have not the same steadiness of purpose, their quicker imaginations suggesting always some other course, and their more fiery passions being succeeded by reaction. When I looked from the deck of the first Saxon ship, and saw the swaying excited multitude of Britons on the beach, contrasting them with the intent, silent men who stood beside me, it seemed to me more than ever dangerous to call in such allies. So strongly did I feel it that I turned to Kenna, who was also looking towards the beach.

"You will own this island before you have finished," said I.

His eyes sparkled as he gazed. "Perhaps," he cried; and then suddenly collecting himself and thinking that he had said too much, he added—

"A temporary occupation—nothing more."

The Home-Coming

IN THE SPRING OF THE YEAR 528, a small brig used to run as a passenger boat between Chalcedon on the Asiatic shore and Constantinople. On the morning in question, which was that of the feast of Saint George, the vessel was crowded with excursionists who were bound for the great city in order to take part in the religious and festive celebrations which marked the festival of the Megalo-martyr, one of the most choice occasions in the whole vast hagiology of the Eastern Church. The day was fine and the breeze light, so that the passengers in their holiday mood were able to enjoy without a qualm the many objects of interest which marked the approach to the greatest and most beautiful capital in the world.

On the right, as they sped up the narrow strait, there stretched the Asiatic shore, sprinkled with white villages and with numerous villas peeping out from the woods which adorned it. In front of them, the Prince's Islands, rising as green as emeralds out of the deep sapphire blue of the Sea of Marmora, obscured for the moment the view of the capital. As the brig rounded these, the great city burst suddenly upon their sight, and a murmur of admiration and wonder rose from the crowded deck. Tier above tier it rose, white and glittering, a hundred brazen roofs and gilded statues gleaming in the sun, with high over all the magnificent shining cupola of Saint Sophia. Seen against a cloudless sky, it was the city of a dream-too delicate, too airily lovely for earth.

In the prow of the small vessel were two travellers of singular appearance. The one was a very beautiful boy, ten or twelve years of age, swarthy, clear-cut, with dark, curling hair and vivacious black eyes, full of intelligence and of the joy of living. The other was an elderly man, gaunt-faced and grey-bearded, whose stern features were lit up by a smile as he observed the excitement and interest with which his young companion viewed the beautiful distant city and the many vessels which thronged the narrow strait.

"See! see!" cried the lad. "Look at the great red ships which sail out from yonder harbour. Surely, your holiness, they are the greatest of all ships in the world."

The old man, who was the abbot of the monastery of Saint Nicephorus in Antioch, laid his hand upon the boy's shoulder.

"Be wary, Leon, and speak less loudly, for until we have seen your mother we should keep ourselves secret. As to the red galleys they are indeed as large as any, for they are the Imperial ships of war, which come forth from the harbour of Theodosius. Round yonder green point is the Golden Horn, where the merchant ships are moored. But now, Leon, if you follow the line of buildings past the great church, you will see a long row of pillars fronting the sea. It marks the Palace of the Caesars."

The boy looked at it with fixed attention. "And my mother is there," he whispered.

"Yes, Leon, your mother the Empress Theodora and her husband the great Justinian dwell in yonder palace."

The boy looked wistfully up into the old man's face.

"Are you sure, Father Luke, that my mother will indeed be glad to see me?"

The abbot turned away his face to avoid those questioning eyes.

"We cannot tell, Leon. We can only try. If it should prove that there is no place for you, then there is always a welcome among the brethren of Saint Nicephorus."

"Why did you not tell my mother that we were coming, Father Luke? Why did you not wait until you had her command?"

"At a distance, Leon, it would be easy to refuse you. An Imperial messenger would have stopped us. But when she sees you, Leon—your eyes, so like her own, your face, which carries memories of one whom she loved—then, if there be a woman's heart within her bosom, she will take you into it. They say that the Emperor can refuse her nothing. They have no child of their own. There is a great future before you, Leon. When it comes, do not forget the poor brethren of Saint Nicephorus, who took you in when you had no friend in the world."

The old abbot spoke cheerily, but it was easy to see from his anxious countenance that the nearer he came to the capital the more doubtful did his errand appear. What had seemed easy and natural from the quiet cloisters of Antioch became dubious and dark now that the golden domes of Constantinople glittered so close at hand. Ten years before, a wretched woman, whose very name was an offence throughout the eastern world where she was as infamous for her dishonour as famous for her beauty, had come to the monastery gate, and had persuaded the monks to take charge of her infant son, the child of her shame. There he had been ever since. But she, Theodora, the harlot, returning to the capital, had by the strangest turn of Fortune's wheel caught the fancy and finally the enduring love of Justinian the heir to the throne. Then on the death of his uncle Justin, the young man had become the greatest monarch upon the earth, and had raised Theodora to be not only his wife and Empress, but to be absolute ruler with powers equal to and independent of his own. And she, the polluted one, had risen to the dignity, had cut herself sternly away from all that related to her past life, and had shown signs already of being a great Queen, stronger and wiser than her husband, but fierce, vindictive, and unbending, a firm support to her friends, but a terror to her foes. This was the woman to whom the Abbot Luke of Antioch was bringing Leon, her forgotten son. If ever her mind strayed back to the days when, abandoned by her lover Ecebolus, the Governor of the African Pentapolis, she had made her way on foot through Asia Minor, and left her infant with the monks, it was only to persuade herself that the brethren cloistered far from the world would never identify Theodora the Empress with Theodora the dissolute wanderer, and that the fruits of her sin would be for ever concealed from her Imperial husband.

The little brig had now rounded the point of the Acropolis, and the long blue stretch of the Golden Horn lay before it. The high wall of Theodosius lined the whole harbour, but a narrow verge of land had been left between it and the water's edge to serve as a quay. The vessel ran alongside near the Neorion Gate, and the passengers, after a short scrutiny from the group of helmeted guards who lounged beside it, were allowed to pass through into the great city.

The abbot, who had made several visits to Constantinople upon the business of his monastery, walked with the assured step of one who knows his ground; while the boy, alarmed and yet pleased by the rush of people, the roar and glitter of passing chariots, and the vista of magnificent buildings, held tightly to the loose gown of his guide, while staring eagerly about him in every direction. Passing through the steep and narrow streets which led up from the water, they emerged into the open space which surrounds the magnificent pile of Saint Sophia, the great church begun by Constantine, hallowed by Saint Chrysostom, and now the seat of the Patriarch, and the very centre of the Eastern Church. Only with many crossings and genuflections did the pious abbot succeed in passing the revered shrine of his religion, and hurried on to his difficult task.

Having passed Saint Sophia, the two travellers crossed the marble-paved Augusteum, and saw upon their right the gilded gates of the hippodrome through which a vast crowd of people was pressing, for though the morning had been devoted to the religious ceremony, the afternoon was given over to secular festivities. So great was the rush of the populace that the two strangers had some difficulty in disengaging themselves from the stream and reaching the huge arch of black marble which formed the outer gate of the palace. Within they were fiercely ordered to halt by a gold-crested and magnificent sentinel who laid his shining spear across their breasts until his superior officer should give them permission to pass. The abbot had been warned, however, that all obstacles would give way if he mentioned the name of Basil the eunuch, who acted as chamberlain of the palace and also as Parakimomen—a high office which meant that he slept at the door of the Imperial bed-chamber. The charm worked wonderfully, for at the mention of that potent name the Protosphathaire, or Head of the Palace Guards, who chanced to be upon the spot, immediately detached one of his soldiers with instructions to convoy the two strangers into the presence of the chamberlain.

Passing in succession a middle guard and an inner guard, the travellers came at last into the palace proper, and followed their majestic guide from chamber to chamber, each more wonderful than the last. Marbles and gold, velvet and silver, glittering mosaics, wonderful carvings, ivory screens, curtains of Armenian tissue and of Indian silk, damask from Arabia, and amber from the Baltic—all these things merged themselves in the minds of the two simple provincials, until their eyes ached and their senses reeled before the blaze and the glory of this, the most magnificent of the dwellings of man. Finally, a pair of curtains, crusted with gold, were parted, and their guide handed them over to a negro mute who stood within. A heavy, fat, brown-skinned man, with a large, flabby, hairless face was pacing up and down the small apartment, and he turned upon them as they entered with an abominable and threatening smile. His loose lips and pendulous cheeks were those of a gross old woman, but above them there shone a pair of dark malignant eyes, full of fierce intensity of observation and judgment.

"You have entered the palace by using my name," he said. "It is one of my boasts that any of the populace can approach me in this way. But it is not fortunate for those who take advantage of it without due cause." Again he smiled a smile which made the frightened boy cling tightly to the loose serge skirts of the abbot.

But the ecclesiastic was a man of courage. Undaunted by the sinister appearance of the great chamberlain, or by the threat which lay in his words, he laid his hand upon his young companion's shoulder and faced the eunuch with a confidential smile.

"I have no doubt, your excellency," said he, "that the importance of my mission has given me the right to enter the palace. The only thing which troubles me is whether it may not be so important as to forbid me from broaching it to you, or indeed, to anybody save the Empress Theodora, since it is she only whom it concerns."

The eunuch's thick eyebrows bunched together over his vicious eyes.

"You must make good those words," he said. "If my gracious master— the ever-glorious Emperor Justinian—does not disdain to take me into his most intimate confidence in all things, it would be strange if there were any subject within your knowledge which I might not hear. You are, as I gather from your garb and bearing, the abbot of some Asiatic monastery?"

"You are right, your excellency, I am the abbot of the Monastery of St. Nicephorus in Antioch. But I repeat that I am assured that what I have to say is for the ear of the Empress Theodora only."

The eunuch was evidently puzzled, and his curiosity aroused by the old man's persistence. He came nearer, his heavy face thrust forward, his flabby brown hands, like two sponges, resting upon the table of yellow jasper before him.

"Old man," said he, "there is no secret which concerns the Empress which may not be told to me. But if you refuse to speak, it is certain that you will never see her. Why should I admit you, unless I know your errand? How should I know that you are not a Manichean heretic with a poniard in your bosom, longing for the blood of the mother of the Church?"

The abbot hesitated no longer. "If there be a mistake in the matter, then on your head be it," said he. "Know then that this lad Leon is the son of Theodora the Empress, left by her in our monastery within a month of his birth ten years ago. This papyrus which I hand you will show you that what I say is beyond all question or doubt."

The eunuch Basil took the paper, but his eyes were fixed upon the boy, and his features showed a mixture of amazement at the news that he had received, and of cunning speculation as to how he could turn it to profit.

"Indeed, he is the very image of the Empress," he muttered; and then, with sudden suspicion, "Is it not the chance of this likeness which has put the scheme into your head, old man?"

"There is but one way to answer that," said the abbot. "It is to ask the Empress herself whether what I say is not true, and to give her the glad tidings that her boy is alive and well."

The tone of confidence, together with the testimony of the papyrus, and the boy's beautiful face, removed the last shadow of doubt from the eunuch's mind. Here was a great fact; but what use could he make of it? Above all, what advantage could he draw from it? He stood with his fat chin in his hand, turning it over in his cunning brain.

"Old man," said he at last, "to how many have you told this secret?"

"To no one in the whole world," the other answered. "There is Deacon Bardas at the monastery and myself. No one else knows anything."

"You are sure of this?"

"Absolutely certain."

The eunuch had made up his mind. If he alone of all men in the palace knew of this event, he would have a powerful hold over his masterful mistress. He was certain that Justinian the Emperor knew nothing of this. It would be a shock to him. It might even alienate his affections from his wife. She might care to take precautions to prevent him from knowing. And if he, Basil the eunuch, was her confederate in those precautions, then how very close it must draw him to her. All this flashed through his mind as he stood, the papyrus in his hand, looking at the old man and the boy.

"Stay here," said he. "I will be with you again." With a swift rustle of his silken robes he swept from the chamber.

A few minutes had elapsed when a curtain at the end of the room was pushed aside, and the eunuch, reappearing, held it back, doubling his unwieldy body into a profound obeisance as he did so. Through the gap came a small alert woman, clad in golden tissue, with a loose outer mantle and shoes of the Imperial purple. That colour alone showed that she could be none other than the Empress; but the dignity of her carriage, the fierce authority of her magnificent dark eyes, and the perfect beauty of her haughty face, all proclaimed that it could only be that Theodora who, in spite of her lowly origin, was the most majestic as well as the most maturely lovely of all the women in her kingdom. Gone now were the buffoon tricks which the daughter of Acacius the bearward had learned in the amphitheatre; gone too was the light charm of the wanton, and what was left was the worthy mate of a great king, the measured dignity of one who was every inch an empress.

Disregarding the two men, Theodora walked up to the boy, placed her two white hands upon his shoulders, and looked with a long questioning gaze, a gaze which began with hard suspicion and ended with tender recognition, into those large lustrous eyes which were the very reflection of her own. At first the sensitive lad was chilled by the cold intent question of the look; but as it softened, his own spirit responded, until suddenly, with a cry of "Mother! mother!" he cast himself into her arms, his hands locked round her neck, his face buried in her bosom. Carried away by the sudden natural outburst of emotion, her own arms tightened round the lad's figure, and she strained him for an instant to her heart. Then, the strength of the Empress gaining instant command over the temporary weakness of the mother, she pushed him back from her, and waved that they should leave her to herself. The slaves in attendance hurried the two visitors from the room. Basil the eunuch lingered, looking down at his mistress, who had thrown herself upon a damask couch, her lips white and her bosom heaving with the tumult of her emotion. She glanced up and met the chancellor's crafty gaze, her woman's instinct reading the threat that lurked within it.

"I am in your power," she said. "The Emperor must never know of this."

"I am your slave," said the eunuch, with his ambiguous smile. "I am an instrument in your hand. If it is your will that the Emperor should know nothing, then who is to tell him?"

"But the monk, the boy? What are we to do?"

"There is only one way for safety," said the eunuch.

She looked at him with horrified eyes. His spongy hands were pointing down to the floor. There was an underground world to this beautiful palace, a shadow that was ever close to the light, a region of dimly-lit passages, of shadowed corners, of noiseless, tongueless slaves, of sudden, sharp screams in the darkness. To this the eunuch was pointing.

A terrible struggle rent her breast. The beautiful boy was hers, flesh of her flesh, bone of her bone. She knew it beyond all question or doubt. It was her one child, and her whole heart went out to him. But Justinian! She knew the Emperor's strange limitations. Her career in the past was forgotten. He had swept it all aside by special Imperial decree published throughout the Empire, as if she were new-born through the power of his will, and her association with his person. But they were childless, and this sight of one which was not his own would cut him to the quick. He could dismiss her infamous past from his mind, but if it took the concrete shape of this beautiful child, then how could he wave it aside as if it had never been? All her instincts and her intimate knowledge of the man told her that even her charm, and her influence might fail under such circumstances to save her from ruin. Her divorce would be as easy to him as her elevation had been. She was balanced upon a giddy pinnacle, the highest in the world, and yet the higher the deeper the fall. Everything that earth could give was now at her feet. Was she to risk the losing of it all—for what? For a weakness which was unworthy of an Empress, for a foolish new-born spasm of love, for that which had no existence within her in the morning? How could she be so foolish as to risk losing such a substance for such a shadow?

"Leave it to me," said the brown watchful face above her.

"Must it be—death?"

"There is no real safety outside. But if your heart is too merciful, then by the loss of sight and speech—"

She saw in her mind the white-hot iron approaching those glorious eyes, and she shuddered at the thought.

"No, no! Better death than that!"

"Let it be death then. You are wise, great Empress, for there only is real safety and assurance of silence."

"And the monk?"

"Him also."

"But the Holy Synod? He is a tonsured priest. What would the Patriarch do?"

"Silence his babbling tongue. Then let them do what they will. How are we of the palace to know that this conspirator, taken with a dagger in his sleeve, is really what he says?"

Again she shuddered and shrank down among the cushions.

"Speak not of it, think not of it," said the eunuch. "Say only that you leave it in my hands. Nay, then, if you cannot say it, do but nod your head, and I take it as your signal."

In that moment there flashed before Theodora's mind a vision of all her enemies, of all those who envied her rise, of all whose hatred and contempt would rise into a clamour of delight could they see the daughter of the bearward hurled down again into that abyss from which she had been dragged. Her face hardened, her lips tightened, her little hands clenched in the agony of her thought. "Do it!" she said.

In an instant, with a terrible smile, the messenger of death hurried from the room. She groaned aloud, and buried herself yet deeper amid the silken cushions, clutching them frantically with convulsed and twitching hands.

The eunuch wasted no time, for this deed, once done, he became— save for some insignificant monk in Asia Minor, whose fate would soon be sealed—the only sharer of Theodora's secret, and therefore the only person who could curb and bend that most imperious nature. Hurrying into the chamber where the visitors were waiting, he gave a sinister signal, only too well known in those iron days. In an instant the black mutes in attendance seized the old man and the boy, pushing them swiftly down a passage and into a meaner portion of the palace, where the heavy smell of luscious cooking proclaimed the neighbourhood of the kitchens. A side corridor led to a heavily-barred iron door, and this in turn opened upon a steep flight of stone steps, feebly illuminated by the glimmer of wall lamps. At the head and foot stood a mute sentinel like an ebony statue, and below, along the dusky and forbidding passages from which the cells opened, a succession of niches in the wall were each occupied by a similar guardian. The unfortunate visitors were dragged brutally down a number of stone-flagged and dismal corridors until they descended another long stair which led so deeply into the earth that the damp feeling in the heavy air and the drip of water all round showed that they had come down to the level of the sea. Groans and cries, like those of sick animals, from the various grated doors which they passed showed how many there were who spent their whole lives in this humid and poisonous atmosphere.

At the end of this lowest passage was a door which opened into a single large vaulted room. It was devoid of furniture, but in the centre was a large and heavy wooden board clamped with iron. This lay upon a rude stone parapet, engraved with inscriptions beyond the wit of the eastern scholars, for this old well dated from a time before the Greeks founded Byzantium, when men of Chaldea and Phoenicia built with huge unmortared blocks, far below the level of the town of Constantine. The door was closed, and the eunuch beckoned to the slaves that they should remove the slab which covered the well of death. The frightened boy screamed and clung to the abbot, who, ashy-pale and trembling, was pleading hard to melt the heart of the ferocious eunuch.

"Surely, surely, you would not slay the innocent boy!" he cried. "What has he done? Was it his fault that he came here? I alone—I and Deacon Bardas—are to blame. Punish us, if some one must indeed be punished. We are old. It is today or tomorrow with us. But he is so young and so beautiful, with all his life before him. Oh, sir! oh, your excellency, you would not have the heart to hurt him!"

He threw himself down and clutched at the eunuch's knees, while the boy sobbed piteously and cast horror-stricken eyes at the black slaves who were tearing the wooden slab from the ancient parapet beneath. The only answer which the chamberlain gave to the frantic pleadings of the abbot was to take a stone which lay on the coping of the well and toss it in. It could be heard clattering against the old, damp, mildewed walls, until it fell with a hollow boom into some far distant subterranean pool. Then he again motioned with his hands, and the black slaves threw themselves upon the boy and dragged him away from his guardian. So shrill was his clamour that no one heard the approach of the Empress. With a swift rush she had entered the room, and her arms were round her son.

"It shall not be! It cannot be!" she cried. "No, no, my darling! my darling! they shall do you no hurt. I was mad to think of it—mad and wicked to dream of it. Oh, my sweet boy! To think that your mother might have had your blood upon her head!"

The eunuch's brows were gathered together at this failure of his plans, at this fresh example of feminine caprice.

"Why kill them, great lady, if it pains your gracious heart?" said he. "With a knife and a branding iron they can be disarmed for ever."

She paid no attention to his words. "Kiss me, Leon!" she cried. "Just once let me feel my own child's soft lips rest upon mine. Now again! No, no more, or I shall weaken for what I have still to say and still to do. Old man, you are very near a natural grave, and I cannot think from your venerable aspect that words of falsehood would come readily to your lips. You have indeed kept my secret all these years, have you not?"

"I have in very truth, great Empress. I swear to you by Saint Nicephorus, patron of our house, that, save old Deacon Bardas, there is none who knows."

"Then let your lips still be sealed. If you have kept faith in the past, I see no reason why you should be a babbler in the future. And you, Leon"—she bent her wonderful eyes with a strange mixture of sternness and of love upon the boy, "can I trust you? Will you keep a secret which could never help you, but would be the ruin and downfall of your mother?"

"Oh, mother, I would not hurt you! I swear that I will be silent."

"Then I trust you both. Such provision will be made for your monastery and for your own personal comforts as will make you bless the day you came to my palace. Now you may go. I wish never to see you again. If I did, you might find me in a softer mood, or in a harder, and the one would lead to my undoing, the other to yours. But if by whisper or rumour I have reason to think that you have failed me, then you and your monks and your monastery will have such an end as will be a lesson for ever to those who would break faith with their Empress."

"I will never speak," said the old abbot; "neither will Deacon Bardas; neither will Leon. For all three I can answer. But there are others—these slaves, the chancellor. We may be punished for another's fault."

"Not so," said the Empress, and her eyes were like flints. "These slaves are voiceless; nor have they any means to tell those secrets which they know. As to you, Basil—" She raised her white hand with the same deadly gesture which he had himself used so short a time before. The black slaves were on him like hounds on a stag.

"Oh, my gracious mistress, dear lady, what is this? What is this? You cannot mean it!" he screamed, in his high, cracked voice. "Oh, what have I done? Why should I die?"

"You have turned me against my own. You have goaded me to slay my own son. You have intended to use my secret against me. I read it in your eyes from the first. Cruel, murderous villain, taste the fate which you have yourself given to so many others. This is your doom. I have spoken."

The old man and the boy hurried in horror from the vault. As they glanced back they saw the erect inflexible, shimmering, gold-clad figure of the Empress. Beyond they had a glimpse of the green-scummed lining of the well, and of the great red open mouth of the eunuch, as he screamed and prayed while every tug of the straining slaves brought him one step nearer to the brink. With their hands over their ears they rushed away, but even so they heard that last woman-like shriek, and then the heavy plunge far down in the dark abysses of the earth.

The Red Star

THE HOUSE OF THEODOSIUS, the famous eastern merchant, was in the best part of Constantinople at the Sea Point which is near the Church of Saint Demetrius. Here he would entertain in so princely a fashion that even the Emperor Maurice had been known to come privately from the neighbouring Bucoleon palace in order to join in the revelry. On the night in question, however, which was the fourth of November in the year of our Lord 630, his numerous guests had retired early, and there remained only two intimates, both of them successful merchants like himself, who sat with him over their wine on the marble verandah of his house, whence on the one side they could see the lights of the shipping in the Sea of Marmora, and on the other the beacons which marked out the course of the Bosphorus. Immediately at their feet lay a narrow strait of water, with the low, dark loom of the Asiatic hills beyond. A thin haze hid the heavens, but away to the south a single great red star burned sullenly in the darkness.

The night was cool, the light was soothing, and the three men talked freely, letting their minds drift back into the earlier days when they had staked their capital, and often their lives, on the ventures which had built up their present fortunes. The host spoke of his long journeys in North Africa, the land of the Moors; how he had travelled, keeping the blue sea ever upon his right, until he had passed the ruins of Carthage, and so on and ever on until a great tidal ocean beat upon a yellow strand before him, while on the right he could see the high rock across the waves which marked the Pillars of Hercules. His talk was of dark-skinned bearded men, of lions, and of monstrous serpents. Then Demetrius, the Cilician, an austere man of sixty, told how he also had built up his mighty wealth. He spoke of a journey over the Danube and through the country of the fierce Huns, until he and his friends had found themselves in the mighty forest of Germany, on the shores of the great river which is called the Elbe. His stories were of huge men, sluggish of mind, but murderous in their cups, of sudden midnight broils and nocturnal flights, of villages buried in dense woods, of bloody heathen sacrifices, and of the bears and wolves who haunted the forest paths. So the two elder men capped each other's stories and awoke each other's memories, while Manuel Ducas, the young merchant of gold and ostrich feathers, whose name was already known all over the Levant, sat in silence and listened to their talk. At last, however, they called upon him also for an anecdote, and leaning his cheek upon his elbow, with his eyes fixed upon the great red star which burned in the south, the younger man began to speak.

"It is the sight of that star which brings a story into my mind," said he. "I do not know its name. Old Lascaris the astronomer would tell me if I asked, but I have no desire to know. Yet at this time of the year I always look out for it, and I never fail to see it burning in the same place. But it seems to me that it is redder and larger than it was.

"It was some ten years ago that I made an expedition into Abyssinia, where I traded to such good effect that I set forth on my return with more than a hundred camel-loads of skins, ivory, gold, spices, and other African produce. I brought them to the sea-coast at Arsinoe, and carried them up the Arabian Gulf in five of the small boats of the country. Finally, I landed near Saba, which is a starting-point for caravans, and, having assembled my camels and hired a guard of forty men from the wandering Arabs, I set forth for Macoraba. From this point, which is the sacred city of the idolaters of those parts, one can always join the large caravans which go north twice a year to Jerusalem and the sea-coast of Syria.

"Our route was a long and weary one. On our left hand was the Arabian Gulf, lying like a pool of molten metal under the glare of day, but changing to blood-red as the sun sank each evening behind the distant African coast. On our right was a monstrous desert which extends, so far as I know, across the whole of Arabia and away to the distant kingdom of the Persians. For many days we saw no sign of life save our own long, straggling line of laden camels with their tattered, swarthy guardians. In these deserts the soft sand deadens the footfall of the animals, so that their silent progress day after day through a scene which never changes, and which is itself noiseless, becomes at last like a strange dream. Often as I rode behind my caravan, and gazed at the grotesque figures which bore my wares in front of me, I found it hard to believe that it was indeed reality, and that it was I, I, Manuel Ducas, who lived near the Theodosian Gate of Constantinople, and shouted for the Green at the hippodrome every Sunday afternoon, who was there in so strange a land and with such singular comrades.

"Now and then, far out at sea, we caught sight of the white triangular sails of the boats which these people use, but as they are all pirates, we were very glad to be safely upon shore. Once or twice, too, by the water's edge we saw dwarfish creatures-one could scarcely say if they were men or monkeys—who burrow for homes among the seaweed, drink the pools of brackish water, and eat what they can catch. These are the fish-eaters, the Ichthyophagi, of whom old Herodotus talks—surely the lowest of all the human race. Our Arabs shrank from them with horror, for it is well known that, should you die in the desert, these little people will settle on you like carrion crows, and leave not a bone unpicked. They gibbered and croaked and waved their skinny arms at us as we passed, knowing well that they could swim far out to sea if we attempted to pursue them; for it is said that even the sharks turn with disgust from their foul bodies.

"We had travelled in this way for ten days, camping every evening at the vile wells which offered a small quantity of abominable water. It was our habit to rise very early and to travel very late, but to halt during the intolerable heat of the afternoon, when, for want of trees, we would crouch in the shadow of a sandhill, or, if that were wanting, behind our own camels and merchandise, in order to escape from the insufferable glare of the sun. On the seventh day we were near the point where one leaves the coast in order to strike inland to Macoraba. We had concluded our midday halt, and were just starting once more, the sun still being so hot that we could hardly bear it, when, looking up, I saw a remarkable sight. Standing on a hillock to our right there was a man about forty feet high, holding in his hand a spear which was the size of the mast of a large ship. You look surprised, my friends, and you can therefore imagine my feelings when I saw such a sight. But my reason soon told me that the object in front of me was really a wandering Arab, whose form had been enormously magnified by the strange distorting effects which the hot air of the desert is able to cause.

"However, the actual apparition caused more alarm to my companions than the imagined one had to me, for with a howl of dismay they shrank together into a frightened group, all pointing and gesticulating as they gazed at the distant figure. I then observed that the man was not alone, but that from all the sandhills a line of turbaned heads was gazing down upon us. The chief of the escort came running to me, and informed me of the cause of their terror, which was that they recognized, by some peculiarity of their headgear, that these men belonged to the tribe of the Dilwas, the most ferocious and unscrupulous of the Bedouin, who had evidently laid an ambuscade for us at this point with the intention of seizing our caravan. When I thought of all my efforts in Abyssinia, of the length of my journey and of the dangers and fatigues which I had endured, I could not bear to think of this total disaster coming upon me at the last instant and robbing me not only of my profits, but also of my original outlay. It was evident, however, that the robbers were too numerous for us to attempt to defend ourselves, and that we should be very fortunate if we escaped with our lives. Sitting upon a packet, therefore, I commended my soul to our blessed Saint Helena, while I watched with despairing eyes the stealthy and menacing approach of the Arab robbers.

"It may have been our own good fortune, or it may have been the handsome offering of beeswax candles—four to the pound—which I had mentally vowed to the blessed Helena, but at that instant I heard a great outcry of joy from among my own followers. Standing up on the packet that I might have a better view, I was overjoyed to see a long caravan—five hundred camels at least-with a numerous armed guard coming along the route from Macoraba. It is, I need not tell you, the custom of all caravans to combine their forces against the robbers of the desert, and with the aid of these newcomers we had become the stronger party. The marauders recognized it at once, for they vanished as if their native sands had swallowed them. Running up to the summit of a sandhill, I was just able to catch a glimpse of a dust-cloud whirling away across the yellow plain, with the long necks of their camels, the flutter of their loose garments, and the gleam of their spears breaking out from the heart of it. So vanished the marauders.

"Presently I found, however, that I had only exchanged one danger for another. At first I had hoped that this new caravan might belong to some Roman citizen, or at least to some Syrian Christian, but I found that it was entirely Arab. The trading Arabs who are settled in the numerous towns of Arabia are, of course, very much more peaceable than the Bedouin of the wilderness, those sons of Ishmael of whom we read in Holy Writ. But the Arab blood is covetous and lawless, so that when I saw several hundred of them formed in a semi-circle round our camels, looking with greedy eyes at my boxes of precious metals and my packets of ostrich feathers, I feared the worst.

"The leader of the new caravan was a man of dignified bearing and remarkable appearance. His age I would judge to be about forty. He had aquiline features, a noble black beard, and eyes so luminous, so searching, and so intense that I cannot remember in all my wanderings to have seen any which could be compared with them. To my thanks and salutations he returned a formal bow, and stood stroking his beard and looking in silence at the wealth which had suddenly fallen into his power. A murmur from his followers showed the eagerness with which they awaited the order to fall upon the plunder, and a young ruffian, who seemed to be on intimate terms with the leader, came to his elbow and put the desires of his companions into words.

"'Surely, oh Revered One,' said he, 'these people and their treasure have been delivered into our hands. When we return with it to the holy place, who of all the Koraish will fail to see the finger of God which has led us?'

"But the leader shook his head. 'Nay, Ali, it may not be,' he answered. 'This man is, as I judge, a citizen of Rome, and we may not treat him as though he were an idolater.'

"'But he is an unbeliever,' cried the youth, fingering a great knife which hung in his belt. 'Were I to be the judge, he would lose not only his merchandise, but his life also, if he did not accept the faith.'

"The older man smiled and shook his head. 'Nay, Ali; you are too hotheaded,' said he, 'seeing that there are not as yet three hundred faithful in the world, our hands would indeed be full if we were to take the lives and property of all who are not with us. Forget not, dear lad, that charity and honesty are the very nose-ring and halter of the true faith.'

"'Among the faithful,' said the ferocious youth.

"'Nay, towards every one. It is the law of Allah. And yet'—here his countenance darkened, and his eyes shone with a most sinister light—'the day may soon come when the hour of grace is past, and woe, then, to those who have not hearkened! Then shall the sword of Allah be drawn, and it shall not be sheathed until the harvest is reaped. First it shall strike the idolaters on the day when my own people and kinsmen, the unbelieving Koraish, shall be scattered, and the three hundred and sixty idols of the Caaba thrust out upon the dungheaps of the town. Then shall the Caaba be the home and temple of one God only who brooks no rival on earth or in heaven.'

"The man's followers had gathered round him, their spears in their hands, their ardent eyes fixed upon his face, and their dark features convulsed with such fanatic enthusiasm as showed the hold which he had upon their love and respect.

"'We shall be patient,' said he; 'but some time next year, the year after, the day may come when the great angel Gabriel shall bear me the message that the time of words has gone by, and that the hour of the sword has come. We are few and weak, but if it is His will, who can stand against us? Are you of Jewish faith, stranger?' he asked.

"I answered that I was not.

"'The better for you,' he answered, with the same furious anger in his swarthy face. 'First shall the idolaters fall, and then the Jews, in that they have not known those very prophets whom they had themselves foretold. Then last will come the turn of the Christians, who follow indeed a true Prophet, greater than Moses or Abraham, but who have sinned in that they have confounded a creature with the Creator. To each in turn—idolater, Jew, and Christian—the day of reckoning will come.'

"The ragamuffins behind him all shook their spears as he spoke. There was no doubt about their earnestness, but when I looked at their tattered dresses and simple arms, I could not help smiling to think of their ambitious threats, and to picture what their fate would be upon the day of battle before the battle-axes of our Imperial Guards, or the spears of the heavy cavalry of the Armenian Themes. However, I need not say that I was discreet enough to keep my thoughts to myself, as I had no desire to be the first martyr in this fresh attack upon our blessed faith.

"It was now evening, and it was decided that the two caravans should camp together—an arrangement which was the more welcome as we were by no means sure that we had seen the last of the marauders. I had invited the leader of the Arabs to have supper with me, and after a long exercise of prayer with his followers he came to join me, but my attempt at hospitality was thrown away, for he would not touch the excellent wine which I had unpacked for him, nor would he eat any of my dainties, contenting himself with stale bread, dried dates, and water. After this meal we sat alone by the smouldering fire, the magnificent arch of the heavens above us of that deep, rich blue with those gleaming, clear-cut stars which can only be seen in that dry desert air. Our camp lay before us, and no sound reached our ears save the dull murmur of the voices of our companions and the occasional shrill cry of a jackal among the sandhills around us. Face to face I sat with this strange man, the glow of the fire beating upon his eager and imperious features and reflecting from his passionate eyes. It was the strangest vigil, and one which will never pass from my recollection. I have spoken with many wise and famous men upon my travels, but never with one who left the impression of this one.

"And yet much of his talk was unintelligible to me, though, as you are aware, I speak Arabian like an Arab. It rose and fell in the strangest way. Sometimes it was the babble of a child, sometimes the incoherent raving of a fanatic, sometimes the lofty dreams of a prophet and philosopher. There were times when his stories of demons, of miracles, of dreams, and of omens, were such as an old woman might tell to please the children of an evening. There were others when, as he talked with shining face of his converse with angels, of the intentions of the Creator, and the end of the universe, I felt as if I were in the company of some one more than mortal, some one who was indeed the direct messenger of the Most High.

"There were good reasons why he should treat me with such confidence. He saw in me a messenger to Constantinople and to the Roman Empire. Even as Saint Paul had brought Christianity to Europe, so he hoped that I might carry his doctrines to my native city. Alas! be the doctrines what they may, I fear that I am not the stuff of which Pauls are made. Yet he strove with all his heart during that long Arabian night to bring me over to his belief. He had with him a holy book, written, as he said, from the dictation of an angel, which he carried in tablets of bone in the nose-bag of a camel. Some chapters of this he read me; but, though the precepts were usually good, the language seemed wild and fanciful. There were times when I could scarce keep my countenance as I listened to him. He planned out his future movements, and indeed, as he spoke, it was hard to remember that he was only the wandering leader of an Arab caravan, and not one of the great ones of the earth.

"'When God has given me sufficient power, which will be within a few years,' said he, 'I will unite all Arabia under my banner. Then I will spread my doctrine over Syria and Egypt. When this has been done, I will turn to Persia, and give them the choice of the true faith or the sword. Having taken Persia, it will be easy then to overrun Asia Minor, and so to make our way to Constantinople.'

"I bit my lip to keep from laughing. 'And how long will it be before your victorious troops have reached the Bosphorus?' I asked.

"'Such things are in the hands of God, whose servants we are,' said he. 'It may be that I shall myself have passed away before these things are accomplished, but before the days of our children are completed, all that I have now told you will come to pass. Look at that star,' he added, pointing to a beautiful clear planet above our heads. 'That is the symbol of Christ. See how serene and peaceful it shines, like His own teaching and the memory of His life. Now,' he added, turning his outstretched hand to a dusky red star upon the horizon—the very one on which we are gazing now—'that is my star, which tells of wrath, of war, of a scourge upon sinners. And yet both are indeed stars, and each does as Allah may ordain.'

"Well, that was the experience which was called to my mind by the sight of this star tonight. Red and angry, it still broods over the south, even as I saw it that night in the desert. Somewhere down yonder that man is working and striving. He may be stabbed by some brother fanatic or slain in a tribal skirmish. If so, that is the end. But if he lives, there was that in his eyes and in his presence which tells me that Mahomet the son of Abdallah—for that was his name—will testify in some noteworthy fashion to the faith that is in him."

Part Two

The Silver Mirror

JAN. 3.—This affair of White and Wotherspoon's accounts proves to be a gigantic task. There are twenty thick ledgers to be examined and checked. Who would be a junior partner? However, it is the first big bit of business which has been left entirely in my hands. I must justify it. But it has to be finished so that the lawyers may have the result in time for the trial. Johnson said this morning that I should have to get the last figure out before the twentieth of the month. Good Lord! Well, have at it, and if human brain and nerve can stand the strain, I'll win out at the other side. It means office-work from ten to five, and then a second sitting from about eight to one in the morning. There's drama in an accountant's life. When I find myself in the still early hours, while all the world sleeps, hunting through column after column for those missing figures which will turn a respected alderman into a felon, I understand that it is not such a prosaic profession after all.

On Monday I came on the first trace of defalcation. No heavy game hunter ever got a finer thrill when first he caught sight of the trail of his quarry. But I look at the twenty ledgers and think of the jungle through which I have to follow him before I get my kill. Hard work—but rare sport, too, in a way! I saw the fat fellow once at a City dinner, his red face glowing above a white napkin. He looked at the little pale man at the end of the table. He would have been pale too if he could have seen the task that would be mine.

JAN. 6.—What perfect nonsense it is for doctors to prescribe rest when rest is out of the question! Asses! They might as well shout to a man who has a pack of wolves at his heels that what he wants is absolute quiet. My figures must be out by a certain date; unless they are so, I shall lose the chance of my lifetime, so how on earth am I to rest? I'll take a week or so after the trial.

Perhaps I was myself a fool to go to the doctor at all. But I get nervous and highly-strung when I sit alone at my work at night. It's not a pain—only a sort of fullness of the head with an occasional mist over the eyes. I thought perhaps some bromide, or chloral, or something of the kind might do me good. But stop work? It's absurd to ask such a thing. It's like a long-distance race. You feel queer at first and your heart thumps and your lungs pant, but if you have only the pluck to keep on, you get your second wind. I'll stick to my work and wait for my second wind. If it never comes—all the same, I'll stick to my work. Two ledgers are done, and I am well on in the third. The rascal has covered his tracks well, but I pick them up for all that.

JAN. 9.—I had not meant to go to the doctor again. And yet I have had to. "Straining my nerves, risking a complete breakdown, even endangering my sanity." That's a nice sentence to have fired off at one. Well, I'll stand the strain and I'll take the risk, and so long as I can sit in my chair and move a pen I'll follow the old sinner's slot.

By the way, I may as well set down here the queer experience which drove me this second time to the doctor. I'll keep an exact record of my symptoms and sensations, because they are interesting in themselves—"a curious psycho-physiological study," says the doctor—and also because I am perfectly certain that when I am through with them they will all seem blurred and unreal, like some queer dream betwixt sleeping and waking. So now, while they are fresh, I will just make a note of them, if only as a change of thought after the endless figures.

There's an old silver-framed mirror in my room. It was given me by a friend who had a taste for antiquities, and he, as I happen to know, picked it up at a sale and had no notion where it came from. It's a large thing—three feet across and two feet high—and it leans at the back of a side-table on my left as I write. The frame is flat, about three inches across, and very old; far too old for hall-marks or other methods of determining its age. The glass part projects, with a bevelled edge, and has the magnificent reflecting power which is only, as it seems to me, to be found in very old mirrors. There's a feeling of perspective when you look into it such as no modern glass can ever give.

The mirror is so situated that as I sit at the table I can usually see nothing in it but the reflection of the red window curtains. But a queer thing happened last night. I had been working for some hours, very much against the grain, with continual bouts of that mistiness of which I had complained. Again and again I had to stop and clear my eyes. Well, on one of these occasions I chanced to look at the mirror. It had the oddest appearance. The red curtains which should have been reflected in it were no longer there, but the glass seemed to be clouded and steamy, not on the surface, which glittered like steel, but deep down in the very grain of it. This opacity, when I stared hard at it, appeared to slowly rotate this way and that, until it was a thick white cloud swirling in heavy wreaths. So real and solid was it, and so reasonable was I, that I remember turning, with the idea that the curtains were on fire. But everything was deadly still in the room—no sound save the ticking of the clock, no movement save the slow gyration of that strange woolly cloud deep in the heart of the old mirror.

Then, as I looked, the mist, or smoke, or cloud, or whatever one may call it, seemed to coalesce and solidify at two points quite close together, and I was aware, with a thrill of interest rather than of fear, that these were two eyes looking out into the room. A vague outline of a head I could see—a woman's by the hair, but this was very shadowy. Only the eyes were quite distinct; such eyes—dark, luminous, filled with some passionate emotion, fury or horror, I could not say which. Never have I seen eyes which were so full of intense, vivid life. They were not fixed upon me, but stared out into the room. Then as I sat erect, passed my hand over my brow, and made a strong conscious effort to pull myself together, the dim head faded into the general opacity, the mirror slowly cleared, and there were the red curtains once again.

A sceptic would say, no doubt, that I had dropped asleep over my figures, and that my experience was a dream. As a matter of fact, I was never more vividly awake in my life. I was able to argue about it even as I looked at it, and to tell myself that it was a subjective impression—a chimera of the nerves—begotten by worry and insomnia. But why this particular shape? And who is the woman, and what is the dreadful emotion which I read in those wonderful brown eyes? They come between me and my work. For the first time I have done less than the daily tally which I had marked out. Perhaps that is why I have had no abnormal sensations tonight. Tomorrow I must wake up, come what may.

JAN. II.—All well, and good progress with my work. I wind the net, coil after coil, round that bulky body. But the last smile may remain with him if my own nerves break over it. The mirror would seem to be a sort of barometer which marks my brain-pressure. Each night I have observed that it had clouded before I reached the end of my task.

Dr. Sinclair (who is, it seems, a bit of a psychologist) was so interested in my account that he came round this evening to have a look at the mirror. I had observed that something was scribbled in crabbed old characters upon the metal-work at the back. He examined this with a lens, but could make nothing of it. "Sanc. X. Pal." was his final reading of it, but that did not bring us any farther. He advised me to put it away into another room; but, after all, whatever I may see in it is, by his own account only a symptom. It is in the cause that the danger lies. The twenty ledgers—not the silver mirror—should be packed away if I could only do it. I'm at the eighth now, so I progress.

JAN. 13.— Perhaps it would have been wiser after all if I had packed away the mirror. I had an extraordinary experience with it last night. And yet I find it so interesting, so fascinating, that even now I will keep it in its place. What on earth is the meaning of it all?

I suppose it was about one in the morning, and I was closing my books preparatory to staggering off to bed, when I saw her there in front of me. The stage of mistiness and development must have passed unobserved, and there she was in all her beauty and passion and distress, as clear-cut as if she were really in the flesh before me. The figure was small, but very distinct—so much so that every feature, and every detail of dress, are stamped in my memory. She is seated on the extreme left of the mirror. A sort of shadowy figure crouches down beside her—I can dimly discern that it is a man—and then behind them is cloud, in which I see figures—figures which move. It is not a mere picture upon which I look. It is a scene in life, an actual episode. She crouches and quivers. The man beside her cowers down. The vague figures make abrupt movements and gestures. All my fears were swallowed up in my interest. It was maddening to see so much and not to see more.

But I can at least describe the woman to the smallest point. She is very beautiful and quite young—not more than five-and-twenty, I should judge. Her hair is of a very rich brown, with a warm chestnut shade fining into gold at the edges. A little flat-pointed cap comes to an angle in front, and is made of lace edged with pearls. The forehead is high, too high perhaps for perfect beauty; but one would not have it otherwise, as it gives a touch of power and strength to what would otherwise be a softly feminine face. The brows are most delicately curved over heavy eyelids, and then come those wonderful eyes—so large, so dark, so full of over-mastering emotion, of rage and horror, contending with a pride of self-control which holds her from sheer frenzy! The cheeks are pale, the lips white with agony, the chin and throat most exquisitely rounded. The figure sits and leans forward in the chair, straining and rigid, cataleptic with horror. The dress is black velvet, a jewel gleams like a flame in the breast, and a golden crucifix smoulders in the shadow of a fold. This is the lady whose image still lives in the old silver mirror. What dire deed could it be which has left its impress there, so that now, in another age, if the spirit of a man be but worn down to it, he may be conscious of its presence?

One other detail: On the left side of the skirt of the black dress was, as I thought at first, a shapeless bunch of white ribbon. Then, as I looked more intently or as the vision defined itself more clearly, I perceived what it was. It was the hand of a man, clenched and knotted in agony, which held on with a convulsive grasp to the fold of the dress. The rest of the crouching figure was a mere vague outline, but that strenuous hand shone clear on the dark background, with a sinister suggestion of tragedy in its frantic clutch. The man is frightened-horribly frightened. That I can clearly discern. What has terrified him so? Why does he grip the woman's dress? The answer lies amongst those moving figures in the background. They have brought danger both to him and to her. The interest of the thing fascinated me. I thought no more of its relation to my own nerves. I stared and stared as if in a theatre. But I could get no farther. The mist thinned. There were tumultuous movements in which all the figures were vaguely concerned. Then the mirror was clear once more.

The doctor says I must drop work for a day, and I can afford to do so, for I have made good progress lately. It is quite evident that the visions depend entirely upon my own nervous state, for I sat in front of the mirror for an hour tonight, with no result whatever. My soothing day has chased them away. I wonder whether I shall ever penetrate what they all mean? I examined the mirror this evening under a good light, and besides the mysterious inscription "Sanc. X. Pal.," I was able to discern some signs of heraldic marks, very faintly visible upon the silver. They must be very ancient, as they are almost obliterated. So far as I could make out, they were three spear-heads, two above and one below. I will show them to the doctor when he calls tomorrow.

JAN. 14.—Feel perfectly well again, and I intend that nothing else shall stop me until my task is finished. The doctor was shown the marks on the mirror and agreed that they were armorial bearings. He is deeply in-terested in all that I have told him, and cross-questioned me closely on the details. It amuses me to notice how he is torn in two by conflicting desires—the one that his patient should lose his symptoms, the other that the medium—for so he regards me—should solve this mystery of the past. He advised continued rest, but did not oppose me too violently when I declared that such a thing was out of the question until the ten remaining ledgers have been checked.

JAN. 17.—For three nights I have had no experiences—my day of rest has borne fruit. Only a quarter of my task is left, but I must make a forced march, for the lawyers are clamouring for their material. I will give them enough and to spare. I have him fast on a hundred counts. When they realize what a slippery, cunning rascal he is, I should gain some credit from the case. False trading accounts, false balance-sheets, dividends drawn from capital, losses written down as profits, suppression of working expenses, manipulation of petty cash—it is a fine record!

JAN. 18.—Headaches, nervous twitches, mistiness, fullness of the temples—all the premonitions of trouble, and the trouble came sure enough. And yet my real sorrow is not so much that the vision should come as that it should cease before all is revealed.

But I saw more tonight. The crouching man was as visible as the lady whose gown he clutched. He is a little swarthy fellow, with a black-pointed beard. He has a loose gown of damask trimmed with fur. The prevailing tints of his dress are red. What a fright the fellow is in, to be sure! He cowers and shivers and glares back over his shoulder. There is a small knife in his other hand, but he is far too tremulous and cowed to use it. Dimly now I begin to see the figures in the background. Fierce faces, bearded and dark, shape themselves out of the mist. There is one terrible creature, a skeleton of a man, with hollow cheeks and eyes sunk in his head. He also has a knife in his hand. On the right of the woman stands a tall man, very young, with flaxen hair, his face sullen and dour. The beautiful woman looks up at him in appeal. So does the man on the ground. This youth seems to be the arbiter of their fate. The crouching man draws closer and hides himself in the woman's skirts. The tall youth bends and tries to drag her away from him. So much I saw last night before the mirror cleared. Shall I never know what it leads to and whence it comes? It is not a mere imagination, of that I am very sure. Somewhere, some time, this scene has been acted, and this old mirror has reflected it. But when—where?

JAN. 20.—My work draws to a close, and it is time. I feel a tenseness within my brain, a sense of intolerable strain, which warns me that something must give. I have worked myself to the limit. But tonight should be the last night. With a supreme effort I should finish the final ledger and complete the case before I rise from my chair. I will do it. I will.

FEB. 7.—I did. My God, what an experience! I hardly know if I am strong enough yet to set it down.

Let me explain in the first instance that I am writing this in Dr. Sinclair's private hospital some three weeks after the last entry in my diary. On the night of January 20 my nervous system finally gave way, and I remembered nothing afterwards until I found myself three days ago in this home of rest. And I can rest with a good conscience. My work was done before I went under. My figures are in the solicitors' hands. The hunt is over.

And now I must describe that last night. I had sworn to finish my work, and so intently did I stick to it, though my head was bursting, that I would never look up until the last column had been added. And yet it was fine self-restraint, for all the time I knew that wonderful things were happening in the mirror. Every nerve in my body told me so. If I looked up there was an end of my work. So I did not look up till all was finished. Then, when at last with throbbing temples I threw down my pen and raised my eyes, what a sight was there!

The mirror in its silver frame was like a stage, brilliantly lit, in which a drama was in progress. There was no mist now. The oppression of my nerves had wrought this amazing clarity. Every feature, every movement, was as clear-cut as in life. To think that I, a tired accountant, the most prosaic of mankind, with the account-books of a swindling bankrupt before me, should be chosen of all the human race to look upon such a scene!

It was the same scene and the same figures, but the drama had advanced a stage. The tall young man was holding the woman in his arms. She strained away from him and looked up at him with loathing in her face. They had torn the crouching man away from his hold upon the skirt of her dress. A dozen of them were round him—savage men, bearded men. They hacked at him with knives. All seemed to strike him together. Their arms rose and fell. The blood did not flow from him-it squirted. His red dress was dabbled in it. He threw himself this way and that, purple upon crimson, like an over-ripe plum. Still they hacked, and still the jets shot from him. It was horrible—horrible! They dragged him kicking to the door. The woman looked over her shoulder at him and her mouth gaped. I heard nothing, but I knew that she was screaming. And then, whether it was this nerve-racking vision before me, or whether, my task finished, all the overwork of the past weeks came in one crushing weight upon me, the room danced round me, the floor seemed to sink away beneath my feet, and I remembered no more. In the early morning my landlady found me stretched senseless before the silver mirror, but I knew nothing myself until three days ago I awoke in the deep peace of the doctor's nursing home.

FEB. 9.—Only today have I told Dr. Sinclair my full experience. He had not allowed me to speak of such matters before. He listened with an absorbed interest. "You don't identify this with any well-known scene in history?" he asked, with suspicion in his eyes. I assured him that I knew nothing of history. "Have you no idea whence that mirror came and to whom it once belonged?" he continued. "Have you?" I asked, for he spoke with meaning. "It's incredible," said he, "and yet how else can one explain it? The scenes which you described before suggested it, but now it has gone beyond all range of coincidence. I will bring you some notes in the evening."

LATER.—He has just left me. Let me set down his words as closely as I can recall them. He began by laying several musty volumes upon my bed.

"These you can consult at your leisure," said he. "I have some notes here which you can confirm. There is not a doubt that what you have seen is the murder of Rizzio by the Scottish nobles in the presence of Mary, which occurred in March, 1566. Your description of the woman is accurate. The high forehead and heavy eyelids combined with great beauty could hardly apply to two women. The tall young man was her husband, Darnley. Rizzio, says the chronicle, 'was dressed in a loose dressing-gown of furred damask, with hose of russet velvet.' With one hand he clutched Mary's gown, with the other he held a dagger. Your fierce, hollow-eyed man was Ruthven, who was new-risen from a bed of sickness. Every detail is exact."

"But why to me?" I asked, in bewilderment. "Why of all the human race to me?"

"Because you were in the fit mental state to receive the impression. Because you chanced to own the mirror which gave the impression."

"The mirror! You think, then, that it was Mary's mirror—that it stood in the room where the deed was done?"

"I am convinced that it was Mary's mirror. She had been Queen of France. Her personal property would be stamped with the Royal arms. What you took to be three spear-heads were really the lilies of France."

"And the inscription?"

"'Sanc. X. Pal.' You can expand it into Sanctae Crucis Palatium. Some one has made a note upon the mirror as to whence it came. It was the Palace of the Holy Cross."

"Holyrood!" I cried.

"Exactly. Your mirror came from Holyrood. You have had one very singular experience, and have escaped. I trust that you will never put yourself into the way of having such another."

The Blighting of Sharkey

SHARKEY, THE ABOMINABLE SHARKEY, was out again. After two years of the Coromandel coast, his black barque of death, *The Happy Delivery*, was prowling off the Spanish Main, while trader and fisher flew for dear life at the menace of that patched fore-topsail, rising slowly over the violet rim of the tropical sea.

As the birds cower when the shadow of the hawk falls athwart the field, or as the jungle folk crouch and shiver when the coughing cry of the tiger is heard in the night-time, so through all the busy world of ships, from the whalers of Nantucket to the tobacco ships of Charleston, and from the Spanish supply ships of Cadiz to the sugar merchants of the Main, there spread the rumour of the black curse of the ocean.

Some hugged the shore, ready to make for the nearest port, while others struck far out beyond the known lines of commerce, but none were so stout-hearted that they did not breathe more freely when their passengers and cargoes were safe under the guns of some mothering fort.

Through all the islands there ran tales of charred derelicts at sea, of sudden glares seen afar in the night-time, and of withered bodies stretched upon the sand of waterless Bahama Keys. All the old signs were there to show that Sharkey was at his bloody game once more.

These fair waters and yellow-rimmed, palm-nodding islands are the traditional home of the sea rover. First it was the gentleman adventurer, the man of family and honour, who fought as a patriot, though he was ready to take his payment in Spanish plunder.

Then, within a century, his debonnaire figure had passed to make room for the buccaneers, robbers pure and simple, yet with some organized code of their own, commanded by notable chieftains, and taking in hand great concerted enterprises.

They, too, passed with their fleets and their sacking of cities, to make room for the worst of all, the lonely outcast pirate, the bloody Ishmael of the seas, at war with the whole human race. This was the vile brood which the early eighteenth century had spawned forth, and of them all there was none who could compare in audacity, wickedness, and evil repute with the unutterable Sharkey.

It was early in May, in the year 1720, that *The Happy Delivery* lay with her fore-yard aback some five leagues west of the Windward Passage, waiting to see what rich, helpless craft the trade-wind might bring down to her.

Three days she had lain there, a sinister black speck, in the centre of the great sapphire circle of the ocean. Far to the south-east the low blue hills of Hispaniola showed up on the skyline.

Hour by hour as he waited without avail, Sharkey's savage temper had risen, for his arrogant spirit chafed against any contradiction, even from Fate itself. To his quartermaster, Ned Galloway, he had said that night, with his odious neighing laugh, that the crew of the next captured vessel should answer to him for having kept him waiting so long.

The cabin of the pirate barque was a good-sized room, hung with much tarnished finery, and presenting a strange medley of luxury and disorder. The panelling of carved and polished sandal-wood was blotched with foul smudges and chipped with bullet-marks fired in some drunken revelry.

Rich velvets and laces were heaped upon the brocaded settees, while metal-work and pictures of great price filled every niche and corner, for anything which caught the pirate's fancy in the sack of a hundred vessels was thrown haphazard into his chamber. A rich, soft carpet covered the floor, but it was mottled with wine-stains and charred with burned tobacco.

Above, a great brass hanging-lamp threw a brilliant yellow light upon this singular apartment, and upon the two men who sat in their shirt-sleeves with the wine between them, and the cards in their hands, deep in a game of piquet. Both were smoking long pipes, and the thin blue reek filled the cabin and floated through the skylight above them, which, half opened, disclosed a slip of deep violet sky spangled with great silver stars.

Ned Galloway, the quartermaster, was a huge New England wastrel, the one rotten branch upon a goodly Puritan family tree. His robust limbs and giant frame were the heritage of a long line of God-fearing ancestors, while his black savage heart was all his own. Bearded to the temples, with fierce blue eyes, a tangled lion's mane of coarse, dark hair, and huge gold rings in his ears, he was the idol of the women in every waterside hell from the Tortugas to Maracaibo on the Main. A red cap, a blue silken shirt, brown velvet breeches with gaudy knee-ribbons, and high sea-boots made up the costume of the rover Hercules.

A very different figure was Captain John Sharkey. His thin, drawn, clean-shaven face was corpse-like in its pallor, and all the suns of the Indies could but turn it to a more deathly parchment tint. He was part bald, with a few lank locks of tow-like hair, and a steep, narrow forehead. His thin nose jutted sharply forth, and near-set on either side of it were those filmy blue eyes, red-rimmed like those of a white bull-terrier, from which strong men winced away in fear and loathing. His bony hands, with long, thin fingers which quivered ceaselessly like the antennae of an insect, were toying constantly with the cards and the heap of gold moidores which lay before him. His dress was of some sombre drab material, but, indeed, the men who looked upon that fearsome face had little thought for the costume of its owner.

The game was brought to a sudden interruption, for the cabin door was swung rudely open, and two rough fellows—Israel Martin, the boatswain, and Red Foley, the gunner—rushed into the cabin. In an instant Sharkey was on his feet with a pistol in either hand and murder in his eyes.

"Sink you for villains!" he cried. "I see well that if I do not shoot one of you from time to time you will forget the man I am. What mean you by entering my cabin as though it were a Wapping alehouse?"

"Nay, Captain Sharkey," said Martin, with a sullen frown upon his brick-red face, "it is even such talk as this which has set us by the ears. We have had enough of it."

"And more than enough," said Red Foley, the gunner. "There be no mates aboard a pirate craft, and so the boatswain, the gunner, and the quarter-master are the officers."

"Did I gainsay it?" asked Sharkey with an oath.

"You have miscalled us and mishandled us before the men, and we scarce know at this moment why we should risk our lives in fighting for the cabin and against the foc'sle."

Sharkey saw that something serious was in the wind. He laid down his pistols and leaned back in his chair with a flash of his yellow fangs.

"Nay, this is sad talk," said he, "that two stout fellows who have emptied many a bottle and cut many a throat with me, should now fall out over nothing. I know you to be roaring boys who would go with me against the devil himself if I bid you. Let the steward bring cups and drown all unkindness between us."

"It is no time for drinking, Captain Sharkey," said Martin. "The men are holding council round the mainmast, and may be aft at any minute. They mean mischief, Captain Sharkey, and we have come to warn you."

Sharkey sprang for the brass-handled sword which hung from the wall.

"Sink them for rascals!" he cried. "When I have gutted one or two of them they may hear reason."

But the others barred his frantic way to the door.

"There are forty of them under the lead of Sweetlocks, the master," said Martin, "and on the open deck they would surely cut you to pieces. Here within the cabin it may be that we can hold them off at the points of our pistols."

He had hardly spoken when there came the tread of many heavy feet upon the deck. Then there was a pause with no sound but the gentle lipping of the water against the sides of the pirate vessel. Finally, a crashing blow as from a pistol-butt fell upon the door, and an instant afterwards Sweetlocks himself, a tall, dark man, with a deep red birthmark blazing upon his cheek, strode into the cabin. His swaggering air sank somewhat as he looked into those pale and filmy eyes.

"Captain Sharkey," said he, "I come as spokesman of the crew."

"So I have heard, Sweetlocks," said the captain, softly. "I may live to rip you the length of your vest for this night's work."

"That is as it may be, Captain Sharkey," the master answered, "but if you will look up you will see that I have those at my back who will not see me mishandled."

"Cursed if we do!" growled a deep voice from above, and glancing upwards the officers in the cabin were aware of a line of fierce, bearded, sun-blackened faces looking down at them through the open skylight.

"Well, what would you have?" asked Sharkey. "Put it in words, man, and let us have an end of it."

"The men think," said Sweetlocks, "that you are the devil himself, and that there will be no luck for them whilst they sail the sea in such company. Time was when we did our two or three craft a day, and every man had women and dollars to his liking, but now for a long week we have not raised a sail, and save for three beggarly sloops, have taken never a vessel since we passed the Bahama Bank. Also, they know that you killed Jack Bartholomew, the carpenter, by beating his head in with a bucket, so that each of us goes in fear of his life. Also, the rum has given out, and we are hard put to it for liquor. Also, you sit in your cabin whilst it is in the articles that you should drink and roar with the crew. For all these reasons it has been this day in general meeting decreed—"

Sharkey had stealthily cocked a pistol under the table, so it may have been as well for the mutinous master that he never reached the end of his discourse, for even as he came to it there was a swift patter of feet upon the deck, and a ship lad, wild with his tidings, rushed into the room.

"A craft!" he yelled. "A great craft, and close aboard us!"

In a flash the quarrel was forgotten, and the pirates were rushing to quarters. Sure enough, surging slowly down before the gentle trade-wind, a great full-rigged ship, with all sail set, was close beside them.

It was clear that she had come from afar and knew nothing of the ways of the Caribbean Sea, for she made no effort to avoid the low, dark craft which lay so close upon her bow, but blundered on as if her mere size would avail her.

So daring was she, that for an instant the Rovers, as they flew to loose the tackles of their guns, and hoisted their battle-lanterns, believed that a man-of-war had caught them napping.

But at the sight of her bulging, portless sides and merchant rig a shout of exultation broke from amongst them, and in an instant they had swung round their fore-yard, and darting alongside they had grappled with her and flung a spray of shrieking, cursing ruffians upon her deck.

Half a dozen seamen of the night-watch were cut down where they stood, the mate was felled by Sharkey and tossed overboard by Ned Galloway, and before the sleepers had time to sit up in their berths, the vessel was in the hands of the pirates.

The prize proved to be the full-rigged ship *Portobello*—Captain Hardy, master—bound from London to Kingston in Jamaica, with a cargo of cotton goods and hoop-iron.

Having secured their prisoners, all huddled together in a dazed, distracted group, the pirates spread over the vessel in search of plunder, handing all that was found to the giant quartermaster, who in turn passed it over the side of *The Happy Delivery* and laid it under guard at the foot of her mainmast.

The cargo was useless, but there were a thousand guineas in the ship's strong-box, and there were some eight or ten passengers, three of them wealthy Jamaica merchants, all bringing home well-filled boxes from their London visit.

When all the plunder was gathered, the passengers and crew were dragged to the waist, and under the cold smile of Sharkey each in turn was thrown over the side—Sweetlocks standing by the rail and ham-stringing them with his cutlass as they passed over, lest some strong swimmer should rise in judgment against them. A portly, grey-haired woman, the wife of one of the planters, was among the captives, but she also was thrust screaming and clutching over the side.

"Mercy, you hussy!" neighed Sharkey, "you are surely a good twenty years too old for that."

The captain of the *Portobello*, a hale, blue-eyed grey-beard, was the last upon the deck. He stood, a thick-set resolute figure, in the glare of the lanterns, while Sharkey bowed and smirked before him.

"One skipper should show courtesy to another," said he, "and sink me if Captain Sharkey would be behind in good manners! I have held you to the last, as you see, where a brave man should be; so now, my bully, you have seen the end of them, and may step over with an easy mind."

"So I shall, Captain Sharkey," said the old seaman, "for I have done my duty so far as my power lay. But before I go over I would say a word in your ear."

"If it be to soften me, you may save your breath. You have kept us waiting here for three days, and curse me if one of you shall live!"

"Nay, it is to tell you what you should know. You have not yet found what is the true treasure aboard of this ship."

"Not found it? Sink me, but I will slice your liver, Captain Hardy, if you do not make good your words! Where is this treasure you speak of?"

"It is not a treasure of gold, but it is a fair maid, which may be no less welcome."

"Where is she, then? And why is she not with the others?"

"I will tell you why she is not with the others. She is the only daughter of the Count and Countess Ramirez, who are amongst those whom you have murdered. Her name is Inez Ramirez, and she is of the best blood of Spain, her father being Governor of Chagre, to which he was now bound. It chanced that she was found to have formed an attachment, as maids will, to one far beneath her in rank aboard this ship; so her parents, being people of great power, whose word is not to be gainsaid, constrained me to confine her close in a special cabin aft of my own. Here she was held straitly, all food being carried to her, and she allowed to see no one. This I tell you as a last gift, though why I should make it to you I do not know, for indeed you are a most bloody rascal, and it comforts me in dying to think that you will surely be gallow's-meat in this world, and hell's-meat in the next."

At the words he ran to the rail, and vaulted over into the darkness, praying as he sank into the depths of the sea, that the betrayal of this maid might not be counted too heavily against his soul.

The body of Captain Hardy had not yet settled upon the sand forty fathoms deep before the pirates had rushed along the cabin gangway. There, sure enough, at the further end, was a barred door, overlooked in their previous search. There was no key, but they beat it in with their gun-stocks, whilst shriek after shriek came from within. In the light of their outstretched lanterns they saw a young woman, in the very prime and fullness of her youth, crouching in a corner, her unkempt hair hanging to the ground, her dark eyes glaring with fear, her lovely form straining away in horror from this inrush of savage blood-stained men. Rough hands seized her, she was jerked to her feet, and dragged with scream on scream to where John Sharkey awaited her. He held the light long and fondly to her face, then, laughing loudly, he bent forward and left his red hand-print upon her cheek.

"'Tis the Rover's brand, lass, that he marks his ewes. Take her to the cabin and use her well. Now, hearties, get her under water, and out to our luck once more."

Within an hour the good ship *Portobello* had settled down to her doom, till she lay beside her murdered passengers upon the Caribbean sand, while the pirate barque, her deck littered with plunder, was heading northward in search of another victim.

There was a carouse that night in the cabin of *The Happy Delivery*, at which three men drank deep. They were the captain, the quartermaster, and Baldy Stable, the surgeon, a man who had held the first practice in Charleston, until, misusing a patient, he fled from justice, and took his skill over to the pirates. A bloated fat man he was, with a creased neck and a great shining scalp, which gave him his name. Sharkey had put for the moment all thought of the mutiny out of his head, knowing that no animal is fierce when it is over-fed, and that whilst the plunder of the great ship was new to them he need fear no trouble from his crew. He gave himself up, therefore, to the wine and the riot, shouting and roaring with his boon companions. All three were flushed and mad, ripe for any devilment, when the thought of the woman crossed the pirate's evil mind. He yelled to the negro steward that he should bring her on the instant.

Inez Ramirez had now realized it all—the death of her father and mother, and her own position in the hands of their murderers. Yet calmness had come with the knowledge, and there was no sign of terror in her proud, dark face as she was led into the cabin, but rather a strange, firm set of the mouth and an exultant gleam of the eyes, like one who sees great hopes in the future. She smiled at the pirate captain as he rose and seized her by the waist.

"Fore God! this is a lass of spirit," cried Sharkey, passing his arm round her. "She was born to be a Rover's bride. Come, my bird, and drink to our better friendship."

"Article Six!" hiccoughed the doctor. "All *bona robas* in common."

"Aye! we hold you to that, Captain Sharkey," said Galloway. "It is so writ in Article Six."

"I will cut the man into ounces who comes betwixt us!" cried Sharkey, as he turned his fish-like eyes from one to the other. "Nay, lass, the man is not born that will take you from John Sharkey. Sit here upon my knee, and place your arm round me so. Sink me, if she has not learned to love me at sight! Tell me, my pretty, why you were so mishandled and laid in the bilboes aboard yonder craft?"

The woman shook her head and smiled. "No Inglese—no Inglese," she lisped. She had drunk off the bumper of wine which Sharkey held to her, and her dark eyes gleamed more brightly than before. Sitting on Sharkey's knee, her arm encircled his neck, and her hand toyed with his hair, his ear, his cheek. Even the strange quartermaster and the hardened surgeon felt a horror as they watched her, but Sharkey laughed in his joy. "Curse me, if she is not a lass of metal!" he cried, as he pressed her to him and kissed her unresisting lips.

But a strange intent look of interest had come into the surgeon's eyes as he watched her, and his face set rigidly, as if a fearsome thought had entered his mind. There stole a grey pallor over his bull face, mottling all the red of the tropics and the flush of the wine.

"Look at her hand, Captain Sharkey!" he cried. "For the Lord's sake, look at her hand!"

Sharkey stared down at the hand which had fondled him. It was of a strange dead pallor, with a yellow shiny web betwixt the fingers. All over it was a white fluffy dust, like the flour of a new-baked loaf. It lay thick on Sharkey's neck and cheek. With a cry of disgust he flung the woman from his lap; but in an instant, with a wild-cat bound, and a scream of triumphant malice, she had sprung at the surgeon, who vanished yelling under the table. One of her clawing hands grasped Galloway by the beard, but he tore himself away, and snatching a pike, held her off from him as she gibbered and mowed with the blazing eyes of a maniac.

The black steward had run in on the sudden turmoil, and among them they forced the mad creature back into a cabin and turned the key upon her. Then the three sank panting into their chairs, and looked with eyes of horror upon each other. The same word was in the mind of each, but Galloway was the first to speak it.

"A leper!" he cried. "She has us all, curse her!"

"Not me," said the surgeon; "she never laid her finger on me."

"For that matter," cried Galloway, "it was but my beard that she touched. I will have every hair of it off before morning."

"Dolts that we were!" the surgeon shouted, beating his head with his hand. "Tainted or no, we shall never know a moment's peace till the year is up and the time of danger past. 'Fore God, that merchant skipper has left his mark on us, and pretty fools we were to think that such a maid would be quarantined for the cause he gave. It is easy to see now that her corruption broke forth in the journey, and that save throwing her over they had no choice but to board her up until they should come to some port with a lazarette."

Sharkey had sat leaning back in his chair with a ghastly face while he listened to the surgeon's words. He mopped himself with his red handkerchief, and wiped away the fatal dust with which he was smeared.

"What of me?" he croaked. "What say you, Baldy Stable? Is there a chance for me? Curse you for a villain! speak out, or I will drub you within an inch of your life, and that inch also! Is there a chance for me, I say?"

But the surgeon shook his head. "Captain Sharkey," said he, "it would be an ill deed to speak you false. The taint is on you. No man on whom the leper scales have rested is ever clean again."

Sharkey's head fell forward on his chest, and he sat motionless, stricken by this great and sudden horror, looking with his smouldering eyes into his fearsome future. Softly the mate and the surgeon rose from their places, and stealing out from the poisoned air of the cabin, came forth into the freshness of the early dawn, with the soft, scent-laden breeze in their faces and the first red feathers of cloud catching the earliest gleam of the rising sun as it shot its golden rays over the palm-clad ridges of distant Hispaniola.

That morning a second council of the Rovers was held at the base of the mainmast, and a deputation chosen to see the captain. They were approaching the after-cabins when Sharkey came forth, the old devil in his eyes, and his bandolier with a pair of pistols over his shoulder.

"Sink you all for villains!" he cried, "Would you dare to cross my hawse? Stand out, Sweetlocks, and I will lay you open! Here, Galloway, Martin, Foley, stand by me and lash the dogs to their kennel!"

But his officers had deserted him, and there was none to come to his aid. There was a rush of the pirates. One was shot through the body, but an instant afterwards Sharkey had been seized and was triced to his own mainmast. His filmy eyes looked round from face to face, and there was none who felt the happier for having met them.

"Captain Sharkey," said Sweetlocks, "you have mishandled many of us, and you have now pistolled John Masters, besides killing Bartholomew, the carpenter, by braining him with a bucket. All this might have been forgiven you, in that you have been our leader for years, and that we have signed articles to serve under you while the voyage lasts. But now we have heard of this bona roba on board, and we know that you are poisoned to the marrow, and that while you rot there will be no safety for any of us, but that we shall all be turned into filth and corruption. Therefore, John Sharkey, we Rovers of *The Happy Delivery*, in council assembled, have decreed that while there be yet time, before the plague spreads, you shall be set adrift in a boat to find such a fate as Fortune may be pleased to send you."

John Sharkey said nothing, but slowly circling his head, he cursed them all with his baleful gaze. The ship's dinghy had been lowered, and he with his hands still tied, was dropped into it on the bight of a rope.

"Cast her off!" cried Sweetlocks.

"Nay, hold hard a moment, Master Sweetlocks!" shouted one of the crew. "What of the wench? Is she to bide aboard and poison us all?"

"Send her off with her mate!" cried another, and the Rovers roared their approval. Driven forth at the end of pikes, the girl was pushed towards the boat. With all the spirit of Spain in her rotting body she flashed triumphant glances on her captors. "Perros! Perros Ingleses! Lepero, Lepero!" she cried in exultation, as they thrust her over into the boat.

"Good luck, captain! God speed you on your honeymoon!" cried a chorus of mocking voices, as the painter was unloosed, and *The Happy Delivery*, running full before the trade-wind, left the little boat astern, a tiny dot upon the vast expanse of the lonely sea.

Extract from the log of H.M. fifty-gun ship *Hecate* in her cruise off the American Main.

"JAN. 26, 1721.—This day, the junk having become unfit for food, and five of the crew down with scurvy, I ordered that we send two boats ashore at the nor'-western point of Hispaniola, to seek for fresh fruit, and perchance shoot some of the wild oxen with which the island abounds.

"7 P.M.—The boats have returned with good store of green stuff and two bullocks. Mr. Woodruff, the master, reports that near the landing-place at the edge of the forest was found the skeleton of a woman, clad in European dress, of such sort as to show that she may have been a person of quality. Her head had been crushed by a great stone which lay beside her. Hard by was a grass hut, and signs that a man had dwelt therein for some time, as was shown by charred wood, bones and other traces. There is a rumour upon the coast that Sharkey, the bloody pirate, was marooned in these parts last year, but whether he has made his way into the interior, or whether he has been picked up by some craft, there is no means of knowing. If he be once again afloat, then I pray that God send him under our guns."

The Marriage of the Brigadier

I AM SPEAKING, my friends, of days which are long gone by, when I had scarcely begun to build up that fame which has made my name so familiar. Among the thirty officers of the Hussars of Conflans there was nothing to indicate that I was superior in any way to the others. I can well imagine how surprised they would all have been had they realized that young Lieutenant Etienne Gerard was destined for so glorious a career, and would live to command a brigade and to receive from the Emperor's own hands that cross which I can show you any time that you do me the honour to visit me in my little cottage. You know, do you not, the little white-washed cottage with the vine in front, in the field beside the Garonne?

People have said of me that I have never known what fear was. No doubt you have heard them say it. For many years, out of a foolish pride, I have let the saying pass. And yet now, in my old age, I can afford to be honest. The brave man dares to be frank. It is only the coward who is afraid to make admissions. So I tell you now that I also am human; that I also have felt my skin grow cold, and my hair rise; that I have even known what it was to run away until my limbs could scarce support me. It shocks you to hear it? Well, some day it may comfort you, when your own courage has reached its limits, to know that even Etienne Gerard has known what it was to be afraid. I will tell you now how this experience befell me, and also how it brought me a wife.

For the moment France was at peace, and we, the Hussars of Conflans, were in camp all that summer a few miles from the town of Les Andelys in Normandy. It is not a very gay place by itself, but we of the Light Cavalry make all places gay which we visit, and so we passed our time very pleasantly. Many years and many scenes have dulled my remembrance, but still the name Les Andelys brings back to me a huge ruined castle, great orchards of apple trees, and above all, a vision of the lovely maidens of Normandy. They were the very finest of their sex, as we may be said to have been of ours, and so we were well met in that sweet sunlit summer. Ah, the youth, the beauty, the valour, and then the dull, dead years that blurr them all! There are times when the glorious past weighs on my heart like lead. No, sir, no wine can wash away such thoughts, for they are of the spirit and the soul. It is only the gross body which responds to wine, but if you offer it for that, then I will not refuse it.

Now of all the maidens who dwelt in those parts there was one who was so superior in beauty and in charm that she seemed to be very specially marked out for me. Her name was Marie Ravon, and her people, the Ravons, were of yeoman stock who had farmed their own land in those parts since the days when Duke William went to England. If I close my eyes now, I see her as she then was, her cheeks, dusky like moss roses; her hazel eyes, so gentle and yet so full of spirit; her hair of that deepest black which goes most fitly with poetry and with passion; her finger as supple as a young birch tree in the wind. Ah! how she swayed away from me when first I laid my arm round it, for she was full of fire and pride, ever evading, ever resisting, fighting to the last that her surrender might be the more sweet. Out of a hundred and forty women—But who can compare where all are so near perfection!

You will wonder why it should be, if this maiden was so beautiful, that I should be left without a rival. There was a very good reason, my friends, for I so arranged it that my rivals were in the hospital. There was Hippolyte Lesoeur, he visited them for two Sundays; but if he lives, I dare swear that he still limps from the bullet which lodges in his knee. Poor Victor also—up to his death at Austerlitz he wore my mark. Soon it was understood that if I could not win Marie, I should at least have a fair field in which to try. It was said in our camp that it was safer to charge a square of unbroken infantry than to be seen too often at the farmhouse of the Ravons.

Now let me be precise for a moment. Did I wish to marry Marie? Ah! my friends, marriage is not for a Hussar. Today he is in Normandy; tomorrow he is in the hills of Spain or in the bogs of Poland. What shall he do with a wife? Would it be fair to either of them? Can it be right that his courage should be blunted by the thought of the despair which his death would bring, or is it reasonable that she should be left fearing lest every post should bring her the news of irreparable misfortune? A Hussar can but warm himself at the fire, and then hurry onwards, too happy if he can but pass another fire from which some comfort may come. And Marie, did she wish to marry me? She knew well that when our silver trumpets blew the march it would be over the grave of our married life. Better far to hold fast to her own people and her own soil, where she and her husband could dwell for ever amid the rich orchards and within sight of the great Castle of Le Galliard. Let her remember her Hussar in her dreams, but let her waking days be spent in the world as she finds it. Meanwhile we pushed such thoughts from our minds, and gave ourselves up to a sweet companionship, each day complete in itself with never a thought of the morrow. It is true that there were times when her father, a stout old gentleman with a face like one of his own apples, and her mother, a thin anxious woman of the country, gave me hints that they would wish to be clearer as to my intentions; but in their hearts they each knew well that Etienne Gerard was a man of honour, and that their daughter was very safe as well as very happy in his keeping. So the matter stood until the night of which I speak.

It was the Sunday evening, and I had ridden over from the camp. There were several of our fellows who were visiting the village, and we all left our horses at the inn. Thence I had to walk to the Ravons, which was only separated by a single very large field extending to the very door. I was about to start when the landlord ran after me. "Excuse me, lieutenant," said he, "it is farther by the road, and yet I should advise you to take it."

"It is a mile or more out of my way."

"I know it. But I think that it would be wiser," and he smiled as he spoke.

"And why?" I asked.

"Because," said he, "the English bull is loose in the field."

If it were not for that odious smile, I might have considered it. But to hold a danger over me and then to smile in such a fashion was more than my proud temper could bear. I indicated by a gesture what I thought of the English bull.

"I will go by the shortest way," said I.

I had no sooner set my foot in the field than I felt that my spirit had betrayed me into rashness. It was a very large square field, and as I came further out into it I felt like the cockle-shell which ventures out from land and sees no port save that from which it has issued. There was a wall on every side of the field save that from which I had come. In front of me was the farmhouse of the Ravons, with wall extending to right and left. A back door opened upon the field, and there were several windows, but all were barred, as is usual in the Norman farms. I pushed on rapidly to the door, as being the only harbour of safety, walking with dignity as befits a soldier, and yet with such speed as I could summon. From the waist upwards I was unconcerned and even debonnaire. Below, I was swift and alert.

I had nearly reached the middle of the field when I perceived the creature. He was rooting about with his fore feet under a large beech tree which lay upon my right hand. I did not turn my head, nor would the by-stander have detected that I took notice of him, but my eye was watching him with anxiety. It may have been that he was in a contented mood, or it may have been that he was arrested by the nonchalance of my bearing, but he made no movement in my direction. Reassured, I fixed my eyes upon the open window of Marie's bed-chamber, which was immediately over the back door, in the hope that those dear, tender, dark eyes, were survey-ing me from behind the curtains. I flourished my little cane, loitered to pick a primrose, and sang one of our devil-may-care choruses in order to insult this English beast, and to show my love how little I cared for dan-ger when it stood between her and me. The creature was abashed by my fearlessness, and so, pushing open the back door, I was able to enter the farmhouse in safety and in honour.

And was it not worth the danger? Had all the bulls of Castile guarded the entrance, would it not still have been worth it? Ah, the hours, the sunny hours, which can never come back, when our youthful feet seemed scarce to touch the ground, and we lived in a sweet dreamland of our own creation! She honoured my courage, and she loved me for it. As she lay with her flushed cheek pillowed against the silk of my dolman, look-ing up at me with her wondering eyes, shining with love and admiration, she marvelled at the stories in which I gave her some pictures of the true character of her lover.

"Has your heart never failed you? Have you never known the feeling of fear?" she asked. I laughed at such a thought. What place could fear have in the mind of a Hussar? Young as I was, I had given my proofs. I told her how I had led my squadron into a square of Hungarian Grenadiers. She shuddered as she embraced me. I told her also how I had swum my horse over the Danube at night with a message for Davoust. To be frank, it was not the Danube, nor was it so deep that I was compelled to swim, but when one is twenty and in love, one tells a story as best one can. Many such stories I told her, while her dear eyes grew more and more amazed.

"Never in my dreams, Etienne," said she, "did I believe that so brave a man existed. Lucky France that has such a soldier, lucky Marie that has such a lover!"

You can think how I flung myself at her feet as I murmured that I was the luckiest of all—I who had found some one who could appreciate and understand.

It was a charming relationship, too infinitely sweet and delicate for the interference of coarser minds. But you can understand that the parents imagined that they also had their duty to do. I played dominoes with the old man, and I wound wool for his wife, and yet they could not be led to believe that it was from love of them that I came thrice a week to their farm. For some time an explanation was inevitable, and that night it came. Marie, in delightful mutiny, was packed off to her room, and I faced the old people in the parlour as they plied me with questions upon my prospects and my intentions.

"One way or the other," they said, in their blunt country fashion. "Let us hear that you are betrothed to Marie, or let us never see your face again."

I spoke of my honour, my hopes, and my future, but they remained immovable upon the present. I pleaded my career, but they in their selfish way would think of nothing but their daughter. It was indeed a difficult position in which I found myself. On the one hand, I could not forsake my Marie; on the other, what would a young Hussar do with marriage? At last, hard pressed, I begged them to leave the matter, if it were only for a day.

"I will see Marie," said I, "I will see her without delay. It is her heart and her happiness which come before all else."

They were not satisfied, these grumbling old people, but they could say no more. They bade me a short good night and I departed, full of perplexity, for the inn. I came out by the same door which I had entered, and I heard them lock and bar it behind me.

I walked across the field lost in thought, with my mind entirely filled with the arguments of the old people and the skilful replies which I had made to them. What should I do? I had promised to see Marie without delay. What should I say to her when I did see her? Would I surrender to her beauty and turn my back upon my profession? If Etienne Gerard's sword were turned to a scythe, then indeed it was a bad day for the Emperor and France. Or should I harden my heart and turn away from Marie? Or was it not possible that all might be reconciled; that I might be a happy husband in Normandy but a brave soldier elsewhere? All these thoughts were buzzing in my head, when a sudden noise made me look up. The moon had come from behind a cloud, and there was the bull before me.

He had seemed a large animal beneath the beech tree, but now he appeared enormous. He was black in colour. His head was held down, and the moon shone upon two menacing and bloodshot eyes. His tail switched swiftly from side to side, and his fore feet dug into the earth. A more horrible-looking monster was never seen in a nightmare. He was moving slowly and stealthily in my direction.

I glanced behind me, and I found that in my distraction I had come a very long way from the edge of the field. I was more than half-way across it. My nearest refuge was the inn, but the bull was between me and it. Perhaps if the creature understood how little I feared him, he would make way for me. I shrugged my shoulders and made a gesture of contempt. I even whistled. The creature thought I called it, for he approached with alacrity. I kept my face boldly towards him, but I walked swiftly backwards. When one is young and active, one can almost run backwards and yet keep a brave and smiling face to the enemy. As I ran I menaced the animal with my cane. Perhaps it would have been wiser had I restrained my spirit. He regarded it as a challenge—which, indeed, was the last thing in my mind. It was a misunderstanding, but a fatal one. With a snort he raised his tail and charged.

Have you ever seen a bull charge, my friends? It is a strange sight. You think, perhaps, that he trots, or even that he gallops. No, it is worse than this. It is a succession of bounds by which he advances, each more menacing than the last. I have no fear of anything which man can do. When I deal with man, I feel that the nobility of my own attitude, the gallant ease with which I face him, will in itself go far to disarm him. What he can do, I can do, so why should I fear him? But when it is a ton of enraged beef with which you contend, it is another matter. You cannot hope to argue, to soften, to conciliate. There is no resistance possible. My proud assurance was all wasted upon the creature. In an instant my ready wit had weighed every possible course, and had determined that no one, not the Emperor himself, could hold his ground. There was but one course—to fly.

But one may fly in many ways. One may fly with dignity or one may fly in panic. I fled, I trust, like a soldier. My bearing was superb though my legs moved rapidly. My whole appearance was a protest against the position in which I was placed. I smiled as I ran—the bitter smile of the brave man who mocks his own fate. Had all my comrades surrounded the field, they could not have thought the less of me when they saw the disdain with which I avoided the bull.

But here it is that I must make my confession. When once flight commences, though it be ever so soldierly, panic follows hard upon it. Was it not so with the Guard at Waterloo? So it was that night with Etienne Gerard. After all, there was no one to note my bearing—no one save this accursed bull. If for a minute I forgot my dignity, who would be the wiser? Every moment the thunder of the hoofs and the horrible snorts of the monster drew nearer to my heels. Horror filled me at the thought of so ignoble a death. The brutal rage of the creature sent a chill to my heart. In an instant everything was forgotten. There were in the world but two creatures, the bull and I—he trying to kill me, I striving to escape. I put down my head and I ran—I ran for my life.

It was for the house of the Ravons that I raced. But even as I reached it, it flashed into my mind that there was no refuge for me there. The door was locked. The lower windows were barred. The wall was high upon either side. And the bull was nearer me with every stride. But oh, my friends, it is at that supreme moment of danger that Etienne Gerard has ever risen to his height. There was one path to safety, and in an instant I had chosen it.

I have said that the window of Marie's bedroom was above the door. The curtains were closed, but the folding sides were thrown open, and a lamp burned in the room. Young and active, I felt that I could spring high enough to reach the edge of the window sill and to draw myself out of danger. The monster was within touch of me as I sprang. Had I been unaided, I should have done what I had planned. But even as in a superb effort I rose from the earth he butted me into the air. I shot through the curtains as if I had been fired from a gun, and I dropped upon my hands and knees in the centre of the room.

There was, as it appears, a bed in the window, but I had passed over it in safety. As I staggered to my feet I turned towards it in consternation, but it was empty. My Marie sat in a low chair in the corner of the room, and her flushed cheeks showed that she had been weeping. No doubt her parents had given her some account of what had passed between us. She was too amazed to move, and could only sit looking at me with her mouth open.

"Etienne!" she gasped. "Etienne!"

In an instant I was as full of resource as ever. There was but one course for a gentleman, and I took it.

"Marie," I cried, "forgive, oh forgive the abruptness of my return! Marie, I have seen your parents tonight. I could not return to the camp without asking you whether you will make me for ever happy by promising to be my wife?"

It was long before she could speak, so great was her amazement. Then every emotion was swept away in the one great flood of her admiration.

"Oh, Etienne! my wonderful Etienne!" she cried, her arms round my neck. "Was ever such love! Was ever such a man! As you stand there, white and trembling with passion, you seem to me the very hero of my dreams. How hard you breathe, my love, and what a spring it must have been which brought you to my arms! At the instant that you came, I heard the tramp of your war-horse without."

There was nothing more to explain, and when one is newly betrothed, one finds other uses for one's lips. But there was a scurry in the passage and a pounding at the panels. At the crash of my arrival the old folk had rushed to the cellar to see if the great cider cask had toppled off the trestles, but now they were back and eager for admittance. I flung open the door, and stood with Marie's hand in mine.

"Behold your son!" I said.

Ah, the joy which I had brought to that humble household! It warms my heart still when I think of it. It did not seem too strange to them that I should fly in through the window, for who should be a hot-headed suitor if it is not a gallant Hussar? And if the door be locked, then what way is there but the window? Once more we assembled all four in the parlour, while the cobwebbed bottle was brought up and the ancient glories of the House of Ravon were unrolled before me. Once more I see the heavy-raftered room, the two old smiling faces, the golden circle of the lamp-light, and she, my Marie, the bride of my youth, won so strangely, and kept for so short a time.

It was late when we parted. The old man came with me into the hall.

"You can go by the front door or the back," said he. "The back way is the shorter."

"I think that I will take the front way," I answered. "It may be a bit longer, but it will give me the more time to think of Marie."

The Lord of Falconbridge

A Legend of the Ring

TOM CRIBB, Champion of England, having finished his active career by his two famous battles with the terrible Molineux, had settled down into the public house which was known as the Union Arms, at the corner of Panton Street in the Haymarket. Behind the bar of this hostelry there was a green baize door which opened into a large, red-papered parlour, adorned by many sporting prints and by the numerous cups and belts which were the treasured trophies of the famous prize-fighter's victorious career. In this snuggery it was the custom of the Corinthians of the day to assemble in order to discuss, over Tom Cribb's excellent wines, the matches of the past, to await the news of the present, and to arrange new ones for the future. Hither also came his brother pugilists, especially such as were in poverty or distress, for the Champion's generosity was proverbial, and no man of his own trade was ever turned from his door if cheering words or a full meal could mend his condition.

On the morning in question—August 25, 1818—there were but two men in this famous snuggery. One was Cribb himself—all run to flesh since the time seven years before, when, training for his last fight, he had done his forty miles a day with Captain Barclay over the Highland roads. Broad and deep, as well as tall, he was a little short of twenty stone in weight, but his heavy, strong face and lion eyes showed that the spirit of the prize-fighter was not yet altogether overgrown by the fat of the publican. Though it was not eleven o'clock, a great tankard of bitter ale stood upon the table before him, and he was busy cutting up a plug of black tobacco and rubbing the slices into powder between his horny fingers. For all his record of desperate battles, he looked what he was—a good-hearted, respectable householder, law-abiding and kindly, a happy and prosperous man.

His companion, however, was by no means in the same easy circumstances, and his countenance wore a very different expression. He was a tall and well-formed man, some fifteen years younger than the Champion, and recalling in the masterful pose of his face and in the fine spread of his shoulders something of the manly beauty which had distinguished Cribb at his prime. No one looking at his countenance could fail to see that he was a fighting man by profession, and any judge of the fancy, considering his six feet in height, his thirteen stone solid muscle, and his beautifully graceful build, would admit that he had started his career with advantages which, if they were only backed by the driving power of a stout heart, must carry him far. Tom Winter, or Spring—as he chose to call himself—had indeed come up from his Herefordshire home with a fine country record of local successes, which had been enhanced by two victories gained over formidable London heavy-weights. Three weeks before, however, he had been defeated by the famous Painter, and the set-back weighed heavily upon the young man's spirit.

"Cheer up, lad," said the Champion, glancing across from under his tufted eyebrows at the disconsolate face of his companion. "Indeed, Tom, you take it overhard."

The young man groaned, but made no reply. "Others have been beat before you and lived to be Champions of England. Here I sit with that very title. Was I not beat down Broadwater way by George Nicholls in 1805? What then? I fought on, and here I am. When the big Black came from America it was not George Nicholls they sent for. I say to you—fight on, and by George, I'll see you in my own shoes yet!"

Tom Spring shook his head. "Never, if I have to fight you to get there, Daddy."

"I can't keep it for ever, Tom. It's beyond all reason. I'm going to lay it down before all London at the Fives Courts next year, and it's to you that I want to hand it. I couldn't train down to it now, lad. My day's done."

"Well, Dad, I'll never bid for it till you choose to stand aside. After that, it is as it may be."

"Well, have a rest, Tom; wait for your chance, and, meantime, there's always a bed and crust for you here."

Spring struck his clenched fist on his knee. "I know, Daddy! Ever since I came up from Fownthorpe you've been as good as a father to me."

"I've an eye for a winner."

"A pretty winner! Beat in forty rounds by Ned Painter."

"You had beat him first."

"And by the Lord, I will again!"

"So you will, lad. George Nicholls would never give me another shy. Knew too much, he did. Bought a butcher's shop in Bristol with the money, and there he is to this day."

"Yes, I'll come back on Painter, but I haven't a shilling left. My backers have lost faith in me. If it wasn't for you, Daddy, I'd be in the kennel."

"Have you nothing left, Tom?"

"Not the price of a meal. I left every penny I had, and my good name as well, in the ring at Kingston. I'm hard put to it to live unless I can get another fight, and who's going to back me now?"

"Tut, man! the knowing ones will back you. You're the top of the list, for all Ned Painter. But there are other ways a man may earn a bit. There was a lady in here this morning—nothing flash, boy, a real tip-top out-and-outer with a coronet on her coach—asking after you."

"Asking after me! A lady!" The young pugilist stood up with surprise and a certain horror rising in his eyes. "You don't mean, Daddy—"

"I mean nothing but what is honest, my lad. You can lay to that!"

"You said I could earn a bit."

"So, perhaps, you can. Enough, anyhow, to tide you over your bad time. There's something in the wind there. It's to do with fightin'. She asked questions about your height, weight, and my opinion of your prospect. You can lay that my answers did you no harm."

"She ain't making a match, surely?"

"Well, she seemed to know a tidy bit about it. She asked about George Cooper, and Richmond the Black, and Tom Oliver, always comin' back to you, and wantin' to know if you were not the pick of the bunch. *And* trustworthy. That was the other point. Could she trust you? Lord, Tom, if you was a fightin' archangel you could hardly live up to the character that I've given you."

A drawer looked in from the bar. "If you please, Mr. Cribb, the lady's carriage is back again."

The Champion laid down his long clay pipe. "This way, lad," said he, plucking his young friend by the sleeve towards the side window. "Look there, now! Saw you ever a more slap-up carriage? See, too, the pair of bays—two hundred guineas apiece. Coachman, too, and footman—you'd find 'em hard to beat. There she is now, stepping out of it. Wait here, lad, till I do the honours of my house."

Tom Cribb slipped off, and young Spring remained by the window, tapping the glass nervously with his fingers, for he was a simple-minded country lad with no knowledge of women, and many fears of the traps which await the unwary in a great city. Many stories were afloat of pugilists who had been taken up and cast aside again by wealthy ladies, even as the gladiators were in decadent Rome. It was with some suspicion therefore, and considerable inward trepidation, that he faced round as a tall veiled figure swept into the room. He was much consoled, however, to observe the bulky form of Tom Cribb immediately behind her as a proof that the interview was not to be a private one. When the door was closed, the lady very deliberately removed her gloves. Then with fingers which glittered with diamonds she slowly rolled up and adjusted her heavy veil. Finally, she turned her face upon Spring.

"Is this the man?" said she.

They stood looking at each other with mutual interest, which warmed in both their faces into mutual admiration. What she saw was as fine a figure of a young man as England could show, none the less attractive for the restrained shyness of his manner and the blush which flushed his cheeks. What he saw was a woman of thirty, tall, dark, queen-like, and imperious, with a lovely face, every line and feature of which told of pride and breed, a woman born to Courts, with the instinct of command strong within her, and yet with all the softer woman's graces to temper and conceal the firmness of her soul. Tom Spring felt as he looked at her that he had never seen nor ever dreamed of any one so beautiful, and yet he could not shake off the instinct which warned him to be upon his guard. Yes, it was beautiful, this face—beautiful beyond belief. But was it good, was it kind, was it true? There was some strange subconscious repulsion which mingled with his admiration for her loveliness. As to the lady's thoughts, she had already put away all idea of the young pugilist as a man, and regarded him now with critical eyes as a machine designed for a definite purpose.

"I am glad to meet you, Mr.—Mr. Spring," said she, looking him over with as much deliberation as a dealer who is purchasing a horse. "He is hardly as tall as I was given to understand, Mr. Cribb. You said six feet, I believe?"

"So he is, ma'am, but he carries it so easy. It's only the beanstalk that looks tall. See here, I'm six foot myself, and our heads are level, except I've lost my fluff."

"What is the chest measurement?"

"Forty-three inches, ma'am."

"You certainly seem to be a very strong young man. And a game one, too, I hope?"

Young Spring shrugged his shoulders.

"It's not for me to say, ma'am."

"I can speak for that, ma'am," said Cribb. "You read the *Sporting Chronicle* for three weeks ago, ma'am. You'll see how he stood up to Ned Painter until his senses were beat out of him. I waited on him, ma'am, and I know. I could show you my waistcoat now—that would let you guess what punishment he can take."

The lady waved aside the illustration. "But he was beat," said she, coldly. "The man who beat him must be the better man."

"Saving your presence, ma'am, I think not, and outside Gentleman Jackson my judgment would stand against any in the ring. My lad here has beat Painter once, and will again, if your ladyship could see your way to find the battle-money."

The lady started and looked angrily at the Champion.

"Why do you call me that?"

"I beg pardon. It was just my way of speaking."

"I order you not to do it again."

"Very good, ma'am."

"I am here incognito. I bind you both upon your honours to make no inquiry as to who I am. If I do not get your firm promise, the matter ends here."

"Very good, ma'am. I'll promise for my own part, and so, I am sure, will Spring. But if I may be so bold, I can't help my drawers and potmen talking with your servants."

"The coachman and footman know just as much about me as you do. But my time is limited, so I must get to business. I think, Mr. Spring, that you are in want of something to do at present?"

"That is so, ma'am."

"I understand from Mr. Cribb that you are prepared to fight any one at any weight?"

"Anything on two legs," cried the Champion. "Who did you wish me to fight?" asked the young pugilist.

"That cannot concern you. If you are really ready to fight any one, then the particular name can be of no importance. I have my reasons for withholding it."

"Very good, ma'am."

"You have been only a few weeks out of training. How long would it take you to get back to your best?"

"Three weeks or a month."

"Well, then, I will pay your training expenses and two pounds a week over. Here are five pounds as a guarantee. You will fight when I consider that you are ready, and that the circumstances are favourable. If you win your fight, you shall have fifty pounds. Are you satisfied with the terms?"

"Very handsome, ma'am, I'm sure."

"And remember, Mr. Spring, I choose you, not because you are the best man—for there are two opinions about that—but because I am given to understand that you are a decent man whom I can trust. The terms of this match are to be secret."

"I understand that. I'll say nothing."

"It is a private match. Nothing more. You will begin your training tomorrow."

"Very good, ma'am."

"I will ask Mr. Cribb to train you."

"I'll do that, ma'am, with pleasure. But, by your leave, does he have anything if he loses?"

A spasm of emotion passed over the woman's face and her hands clenched white with passion.

"If he loses, not a penny, not a penny!" she cried. "He must not, shall not lose!"

"Well, ma'am," said Spring, "I've never heard of any such match. But it's true that I am down at heel, and beggars can't be choosers. I'll do just what you say. I'll train till you give the word, and then I'll fight where you tell me. I hope you'll make it a large ring."

"Yes," said she; "it will be a large ring."

"And how far from London?"

"Within a hundred miles. Have you anything else to say? My time is up."

"I'd like to ask, ma'am," said the Champion, earnestly, "whether I can act as the lad's second when the time comes. I've waited on him the last two fights. Can I give him a knee?"

"No," said the woman, sharply. Without another word she turned and was gone, shutting the door behind her. A few moments later the trim carriage flashed past the window, turned down the crowded Haymarket, and was engulfed in the traffic.

The two men looked at each other in silence.

"Well, blow my dicky, if this don't beat cockfightin'!" cried Tom Cribb at last. "Anyhow, there's the fiver, lad. But it's a rum go, and no mistake about it."

After due consultation, it was agreed that Tom Spring should go into training at the Castle Inn on Hampstead Heath, so that Cribb could drive over and watch him. Thither Spring went on the day after the interview with his patroness, and he set to work at once with drugs, dumb-bells, and breathers on the common to get himself into condition. It was hard, however, to take the matter seriously, and his good-natured trainer found the same difficulty.

"It's the baccy I miss, Daddy," said the young pugilist, as they sat together on the afternoon of the third day. "Surely there can't be any harm in my havin' a pipe?"

"Well, well, lad, it's against my conscience, but here's my box and there's a yard o' clay," said the Champion. "My word, I don't know what

Captain Barclay of Ury would have said if he had seen a man smoke when he was in trainin'! He was the man to work you! He had me down from sixteen to thirteen the second time I fought the Black."

Spring had lit his pipe and was leaning back amid a haze of blue smoke.

"It was easy for you, Daddy, to keep strict trainin' when you knew what was before you. You had your date and your place and your man. You knew that in a month you would jump the ropes with ten thousand folk round you, and carrying maybe a hundred thousand in bets. You knew also the man you had to meet, and you wouldn't give him the better of you. But it's all different with me. For all I know, this is just a woman's whim, and will end in nothing. If I was sure it was serious, I'd break this pipe before I would smoke it."

Tom Cribb scratched his head in puzzlement.

"I can make nothing of it, lad, 'cept that her money is good. Come to think of it, how many men on the list could stand up to you for half an hour? It can't be Stringer, 'cause you've beat him. Then there's Cooper; but he's up Newcastle way. It can't be him. There's Richmond; but you wouldn't need to take your coat off to beat him. There's the Gasman; but he's not twelve stone. And there's Bill Neat of Bristol. That's it, lad. The lady has taken into her head to put you up against either the Gasman or Bill Neat."

"But why not say so? I'd train hard for the Gasman and harder for Bill Neat, but I'm blowed if I can train, with any heart when I'm fightin' nobody in particular and everybody in general, same as now."

There was a sudden interruption to the speculations of the two prize-fighters. The door opened and the lady entered. As her eyes fell upon the two men her dark, handsome face flushed with anger, and she gazed at them silently with an expression of contempt which brought them both to their feet with hangdog faces. There they stood, their long, reeking pipes in their hands, shuffling and downcast, like two great rough mastiffs before an angry mistress.

"So!" said she, stamping her foot furiously. "And this is training!"

"I'm sure we're very sorry, ma'am," said the abashed Champion. "I didn't think—I never for one moment supposed—"

"That I would come myself to see if you were taking my money on false pretences? No, I dare say not. You fool!" she blazed, turning suddenly upon Tom Spring. "You'll be beat. That will be the end of it."

The young man looked up with an angry face.

"I'll trouble you not to call me names, ma'am. I've my self-respect, the same as you. I'll allow that I shouldn't have smoked when I was in trainin'. But I was saying to Tom Cribb here, just before you came in, that if you would give over treatin' us as if we were children, and if you would tell us just who it is you want me to fight, and when, and where, it would be a deal easier for me to take myself in hand."

"It's true, ma'am," said the Champion. "I know it must be either the Gasman or Bill Neat. There's no one else. So give me the office, and I'll promise to have him as fit as a trout on the day."

The lady laughed contemptuously.

"Do you think," said she, "that no one can fight save those who make a living by it?"

"By George, it's an amateur!" cried Cribb, in amazement. "But you don't surely ask Tom Spring to train for three weeks to meet a Corinthian?"

"I will say nothing more of who it is. It is no business of yours," the lady answered fiercely. "All I *do* say is, that if you do not train I will cast you aside and take some one who will. Do not think you can fool me because I am a woman. I have learned the points of the game as well as any man."

"I saw that the very first word you spoke," said Cribb.

"Then don't forget it. I will not warn you again. If I have occasion to find fault I shall choose another man."

"And you won't tell me who I am to fight?"

"Not a word. But you can take it from me that at your very best it will take you, or any man in England, all your time to master him. Now, get back this instant to your work, and never let me find you shirking it again." With imperious eyes she looked the two strong men down, and then, turning on her heel, she swept out of the room.

The Champion whistled as the door closed behind her, and mopped his brow with his red bandanna handkerchief as he looked across at his abashed companion. "My word, lad," said he, "it's earnest from this day on."

"Yes," said Tom Spring, solemnly, "it's earnest from this day on."

In the course of the next fortnight the lady made several surprise visits to see that her champion was being properly prepared for the contest which lay before him. At the most unexpected moments she would burst into the training quarters, but never again had she to complain of any slackness upon his part or that of his trainer. With long bouts of the gloves, with thirty-mile walks, with mile runs at the back of a mailcart with a bit of blood between the shafts, with interminable series of jumps with a skipping-rope, he was sweated down until his trainer was able to proudly proclaim that "the last ounce of tallow is off him and he is ready to fight for his life." Only once was the lady accompanied by any one upon these visits of inspection. Upon this occasion a tall young man was her companion. He was graceful in figure, aristocratic in his bearing, and would have been strikingly handsome had it not been for some accident which had shattered his nose and broken all the symmetry of his features. He stood in silence with moody eyes and folded arms, looking at the splendid torso of the prize-fighter as, stripped to the waist, he worked with his dumbbells.

"Don't you think he will do?" said the lady.

The young swell shrugged his shoulders. "I don't like it, *cara mia*. I can't pretend that I like it."

"You must like it, George. I have set my very heart on it."

"It is not English, you know. Lucrezia Borgia and Mediaeval Italy. Woman's love and woman's hatred are always the same, but this particular manifestation of it seems to me out of place in nineteenth-century London."

"Is not a lesson needed?"

"Yes, yes; but one would think there were other ways."

"You tried another way. What did you get out of that?"

The young man smiled rather grimly, as he turned up his cuff and looked at a puckered hole in his wrist.

"Not much, certainly," said he.

"You've tried and failed."

"Yes, I must admit it."

"What else is there? The law?"

"Good gracious, no!"

"Then it is my turn, George, and I won't be balked."

"I don't think any one is capable of balking you, *cara mia*. Certainly I, for one, should never dream of trying. But I don't feel as if I could co-operate."

"I never asked you to."

"No, you certainly never did. You are perfectly capable of doing it alone. I think, with your leave, if you have quite done with your prize-fighter, we will drive back to London. I would not for the world miss Goldoni in the Opera."

So they drifted away; he, frivolous and dilettante, she with her face as set as Fate, leaving the fighting men to their business.

And now the day came when Cribb was able to announce to his employer that his man was as fit as science could make him.

"I can do no more, ma'am. He's fit to fight for a kingdom. Another week would see him stale."

The lady looked Spring over with the eye of a connoisseur.

"I think he does you credit," she said at last. "Today is Tuesday. He will fight the day after tomorrow."

"Very good, ma'am. Where shall he go?"

"I will tell you exactly, and you will please take careful note of all that I say. You, Mr. Cribb, will take your man down to the Golden Cross Inn at Charing Cross by nine o'clock on Wednesday morning. He will take the Brighton coach as far as Tunbridge Wells, where he will alight at the Royal Oak Arms. There he will take such refreshment as you advise before a fight. He will wait at the Royal Oak Arms until he receives a message by word, or by letter, brought him by a groom in a mulberry livery. This message will give him his final instructions."

"And I am not to come?"

"No," said the lady.

"But surely, ma'am," he pleaded, "I may come as far as Tunbridge Wells? It's hard on a man to train a cove for a fight and then to leave him."

"It can't be helped. You are too well known. Your arrival would spread all over the town, and my plans might suffer. It is quite out of the question that you should come."

"Well, I'll do what you tell me, but it's main hard."

"I suppose," said Spring, "you would have me bring my fightin' shorts and my spiked shoes?"

"No; you will kindly bring nothing whatever which may point to your trade. I would have you wear just those clothes in which I saw you first, such clothes as any mechanic or artisan might be expected to wear."

Tom Cribb's blank face had assumed an expression of absolute despair.

"No second, no clothes, no shoes—it don't seem regular. I give you my word, ma'am, I feel ashamed to be mixed up in such a fight. I don't know as you can call the thing a fight where there is no second. It's just a scramble—nothing more. I've gone too far to wash my hands of it now, but I wish I had never touched it."

In spite of all professional misgivings on the part of the Champion and his pupil, the imperious will of the woman prevailed, and everything was carried out exactly as she had directed. At nine o'clock Tom Spring found himself upon the box-seat of the Brighton coach, and waved his hand in goodbye to burly Tom Cribb, who stood, the admired of a ring of waiters and ostlers, upon the doorstep of the Golden Cross. It was in the pleasant season when summer is mellowing into autumn, and the first golden patches are seen amid the beeches and the ferns. The young country-bred lad breathed more freely when he had left the weary streets of Southwark and Lewisham behind him, and he watched with delight the glorious prospect as the coach, whirled along by six dapple greys, passed by the classic grounds of Knowle, or after crossing Riverside Hill skirted the vast expanse of the Weald of Kent. Past Tonbridge School went the coach, and on through Southborough, until it wound down a steep, curving road with strange outcrops of sandstone beside it, and halted before a great hostelry, bearing the name which had been given him in his directions. He descended, entered the coffee-room, and ordered the underdone steak which his trainer had recommended. Hardly had he finished it when a servant with a mulberry coat and a peculiarly expressionless face entered the apartment.

"Beg your pardon, sir, are you Mr. Spring—Mr. Thomas Spring, of London?"

"That is my name, young man."

"Then the instructions which I had to give you are that you wait for one hour after your meal. After that time you will find me in a phaeton at the door, and I will drive you in the right direction."

The young pugilist had never been daunted by any experience which had befallen him in the ring. The rough encouragement of his backers, the surge and shouting of the multitude, and the sight of his opponent had always cheered his stout heart and excited him to prove himself worthy of being the centre of such a scene. But his loneliness and uncertainty were deadly. He flung himself down on the horse-hair couch and tried to doze, but his mind was too restless and excited. Finally he rose, and paced up and down the empty room. Suddenly he was aware of a great rubicund face which surveyed him from round the angle of the door. Its owner, seeing that he was observed, pushed forward into the room.

"I beg pardon, sir," said he, "but surely I have the honour of talking to Mr. Thomas Spring?"

"At your service," said the young man.

"Bless me! I am vastly honoured to have you under my roof! Cordery is my name, sir, landlord of this old-fashioned inn. I thought that my eyes could not deceive me. I am a patron of the ring, sir, in my own humble way, and was present at Moulsey in September last, when you beat Jack Stringer of Rawcliffe. A very fine fight, sir, and very handsomely fought, if I may make bold to say so. I have a right to an opinion, sir, for there's never been a fight for many a year in Kent or Sussex that you wouldn't find Joe Cordery at the ring-side. Ask Mr. Gregson at the Chop-house in Holborn and he'll tell you about old Joe Cordery. By the way, Mr. Spring, I suppose it is not business that has brought you down into these parts? Any one can see with half an eye that you are trained to a hair. I'd take it very kindly if you would give me the office."

It crossed Spring's mind that if he were frank with the landlord it was more than likely that he would receive more information than he could give. He was a man of his word, however, and he remembered his promise to his employer.

"Just a quiet day in the country, Mr. Cordery. That's all."

"Dear me! I had hoped there was a mill in the wind. I've a nose for these things, Mr. Spring, and I thought I had a whiff of it. But, of course, you should know best. Perhaps you will drive round with me this afternoon and view the hop-gardens—just the right time of year, sir."

Tom Spring was not very skilful in deception, and his stammering excuses may not have been very convincing to the landlord, or finally persuaded him that his original supposition was wrong. In the midst of the conversation, however, the waiter entered with the news that a phaeton was waiting at the door. The innkeeper's eyes shone with suspicion and eagerness.

"I thought you said you knew no one in these parts, Mr. Spring?"

"Just one kind friend, Mr. Cordery, and he has sent his gig for me. It's likely that I will take the night coach to town. But I'll look in after an hour or two and have a dish of tea with you."

Outside the mulberry servant was sitting behind a fine black horse in a phaeton, which had two seats in front and two behind. Tom Spring was about to climb up beside him, when the servant whispered that his directions were that he should sit behind. Then the phaeton whirled away, while the excited landlord, more convinced than ever that there was something in the wind, rushed into his stable-yard with shrieks to his ostlers, and in a very few minutes was in hot pursuit, waiting at every cross-road until he could hear tidings of a black horse and a mulberry livery.

The phaeton meanwhile drove in the direction of Crowborough. Some miles out it turned from the high-road into a narrow lane spanned by a tawny arch of beech trees. Through this golden tunnel a lady was walking, tall and graceful, her back to the phaeton. As it came abreast of her she stood aside and looked up, while the coachman pulled up the horse.

"I trust that you are at your best," said she, looking very earnestly at the prize-fighter. "How do you feel?"

"Pretty tidy, ma'am, I thank you."

"I will get up beside you, Johnson. We have some way to go. You will drive through the Lower Warren, and then take the lane which skirts the Gravel Hanger. I will tell you where to stop. Go slowly, for we are not due for twenty minutes."

Feeling as if the whole business was some extraordinary dream, the young pugilist passed through a network of secluded lanes, until the phaeton drew up at a wicket gate which led into a plantation of firs, choked with a thick undergrowth. Here the lady descended and beckoned Spring to alight.

"Wait down the lane," said she to the coachman. "We shall be some little time. Now, Mr. Spring, will you kindly follow me? I have written a letter which makes an appointment."

She passed swiftly through the plantation by a tortuous path, then over a stile, and past another wood, loud with the deep chuckling of pheasants. At the farther side was a fine rolling park, studded with oak trees, and stretching away to a splendid Elizabethan mansion, with balustraded terraces athwart its front. Across the park, and making for the wood, a solitary figure was walking.

The lady gripped the prize-fighter by the wrist. "That is your man," said she.

They were standing under the shadow of the trees, so that he was very visible to them, while they were out of his sight. Tom Spring looked hard at the man, who was still some hundreds of yards away. He was a tall, powerful fellow, clad in a blue coat with gilt buttons, which gleamed in the sun. He had white corded breeches and riding-boots. He walked with a vigorous step, and with every few strides he struck his leg with a dog-whip which hung from his wrist. There was a great suggestion of purpose and of energy in the man's appearance and bearing.

"Why, he's a gentleman!" said Spring. "Look 'ere, ma'am, this is all a bit out of my line. I've nothing against the man, and he can mean me no harm. What am I to do with him?"

"Fight him! Smash him! That is what you are here for."

Tom Spring turned on his heel with disgust. "I'm here to fight, ma'am, but not to smash a man who has no thought of fighting. It's off."

"You don't like the look of him," hissed the woman. "You have met your master."

"That is as may be. It is no job for me."

The woman's face was white with vexation and anger.

"You fool!" she cried. "Is all to go wrong at the last minute? There are fifty pounds here they are in this paper—would you refuse them?"

"It's a cowardly business. I won't do it."

"Cowardly? You are giving the man two stone, and he can beat any amateur in England."

The young pugilist felt relieved. After all, if he could fairly earn that fifty pounds, a good deal depended upon his winning it. If he could only be sure that this was a worthy and willing antagonist!

"How do you know he is so good?" he asked.

"I ought to know. I am his wife."

As she spoke she turned, and was gone like a flash among the bushes. The man was quite close now, and Tom Spring's scruples weakened as he looked at him. He was a powerful, broad-chested fellow, about thirty, with a heavy, brutal face, great thatched eyebrows, and a hard-set mouth. He could not be less than fifteen stone in weight, and he carried himself like a trained athlete. As he swung along he suddenly caught a glimpse of Spring among the trees, and he at once quickened his pace and sprang over the stile which separated them.

"Halloa!" said he, halting a few yards from him, and staring him up and down. "Who the devil are you, and where the devil did you come from, and what the devil are you doing on my property?"

His manner was even more offensive than his words. It brought a flush of anger to Spring's cheeks.

"See here, mister," said he, "civil words is cheap. You've no call to speak to me like that."

"You infernal rascal!" cried the other. "I'll show you the way out of that plantation with the toe of my boot. Do you dare to stand there on my land and talk back at me?" He advanced with a menacing face and his dog-whip half raised. "Well, are you going?" he cried, as he swung it into the air.

Tom Spring jumped back to avoid the threatened blow.

"Go slow, mister," said he. "It's only fair that you should know where you are. I'm Spring, the prize-fighter. Maybe you have heard my name."

"I thought you were a rascal of that breed," said the man. "I've had the handling of one or two of you gentry before, and I never found one that could stand up to me for five minutes. Maybe you would like to try?"

"If you hit me with that dog-whip, mister—"

"There, then!" He gave the young man a vicious cut across the shoulder. "Will that help you to fight?"

"I came here to fight," said Tom Spring, licking his dry lips. "You can drop that whip, mister, for I *will* fight. I'm a trained man and ready. But you would have it. Don't blame me."

The man was stripping the blue coat from his broad shoulders. There was a sprigged satin vest beneath it, and they were hung together on an alder branch.

"Trained are you?" he muttered. "By the Lord, I'll train you before I am through!"

Any fears that Tom Spring may have had lest he should be taking some unfair advantage were set at rest by the man's assured manner and by the splendid physique, which became more apparent as he discarded a black satin tie, with a great ruby glowing in its centre, and threw aside the white collar which cramped his thick muscular neck. He then, very deliberately, undid a pair of gold sleeve-links, and, rolling up his shirt-sleeves, disclosed two hairy and muscular arms, which would have served as a model for a sculptor.

"Come nearer the stile," said he, when he had finished. "There is more room."

The prize-fighter had kept pace with the preparations of his formidable antagonist. His own hat, coat, and vest hung suspended upon a bush. He advanced now into the open space which the other had indicated.

"Ruffianing or fighting?" asked the amateur, coolly.

"Fighting."

"Very good," said the other. "Put up your hands, Spring. Try it out."

They were standing facing one another in a grassy ring intersected by the path at the outlet of the wood. The insolent and overbearing look had passed away from the amateur's face, but a grim half-smile was on his lips and his eyes shone fiercely from under his tufted brows. From the way in which he stood it was very clear that he was a past-master at the game. Tom Spring, as he paced lightly to right and left, looking for an opening, became suddenly aware that neither with Stringer nor with the redoubtable Painter himself had he ever faced a more business-like opponent. The amateur's left was well forward, his guard low, his body leaning back from the haunches, and his head well out of danger. Spring tried a light lead at the mark, and another at the face, but in an instant his adversary was on to him with a shower of sledge-hammer blows which it took him all his time to avoid. He sprang back, but there was no getting away from that whirlwind of muscle and bone. A heavy blow beat down his guard, a second landed on his shoulder, and over went the prize-fighter with the other on the top of him. Both sprang to their feet, glared at each other, and fell into position once more.

There could be no doubt that the amateur was not only heavier, but also the harder and stronger man. Twice again he rushed Spring down, once by the weight of his blows, and once by closing and hurling him on to his back. Such falls might have shaken the fight out of a less game man, but to Tom Spring they were but incidents in his daily trade. Though bruised and winded he was always up again in an instant. Blood was trickling from his mouth, but his steadfast blue eyes told of the unshaken spirit within.

He was accustomed now to his opponent's rushing tactics, and he was ready for them. The fourth round was the same as to attack, but it was very different in defence. Up to now the young man had given way and been fought down. This time he stood his ground. As his opponent rushed in he met him with a tremendous straight hit from his left hand, delivered with the full force of his body, and doubled in effect by the momentum of the charge. So stunning was the concussion that the pugilist himself recoiled from it across the grassy ring. The amateur staggered back and leaned his shoulder on a tree-trunk, his hand up to his face.

"You'd best drop it," said Spring. "You'll get pepper if you don't."

The other gave an inarticulate curse, and spat out a mouthful of blood. "Come on!" said he.

Even now the pugilist found that he had no light task before him. Warned by his misadventure, the heavier man no longer tried to win the battle at a rush, nor to beat down an accomplished boxer as he would a country hawbuck at a village fair. He fought with his head and his feet as well as with his hands. Spring had to admit in his heart that, trained to the ring, this man must have been a match for the best. His guard was strong, his counter was like lightning, he took punishment like a man of iron, and when he could safely close he always brought his lighter antagonist to the ground with a shattering fall. But the one stunning blow which he had courted before he was taught respect for his adversary weighed heavily on him all the time. His senses had lost something of their quickness and his blows of their sting. He was fighting, too, against a man who, of all the boxers who have made their names great, was the safest, the coolest, the least likely to give anything away, or lose an advantage gained. Slowly, gradually, round by round, he was worn down by his cool, quickstepping, sharp-hitting antagonist. At last he stood exhausted, breathing hoarsely, his face, what could be seen of it, purple with his exertions. He had reached the limit of human endurance. His opponent stood waiting for him, bruised and beaten, but as cool, as ready, as dangerous as ever.

"You'd best drop it, I tell you," said he. "You're done."

But the other's manhood would not have it so. With a snarl of fury he cast his science to the winds, and rushed madly to slogging with both hands. For a moment Spring was overborne. Then he side-stepped swiftly; there was the crash of his blow, and the amateur tossed up his arms and fell all asprawl, his great limbs outstretched, his disfigured face to the sky.

For a moment Tom Spring stood looking down at his unconscious opponent. The next he felt a soft, warm hand upon his bare arm. The woman was at his elbow.

"Now is your time!" she cried, her dark eyes aflame. "Go in! Smash him!"

Spring shook her off with a cry of disgust, but she was back in an instant. "I'll make it seventy-five pounds—"

"The fight's over, ma'am. I can't touch him."

"A hundred pounds—a clear hundred! I have it here in my bodice. Would you refuse a hundred?"

He turned on his heel. She darted past him and tried to kick at the face of the prostrate man. Spring dragged her roughly away, before she could do him a mischief.

"Stand clear!" he cried, giving her a shake. "You should take shame to hit a fallen man."

With a groan the injured man turned on his side. Then he slowly sat up and passed his wet hand over his face. Finally, he staggered to his feet.

"Well," he said, shrugging his broad shoulders, "it was a fair fight. I've no complaint to make. I was Jackson's favourite pupil, but I give you best." Suddenly his eyes lit upon the furious face of the woman. "Hulloa, Betty!" he cried. "So I have you to thank. I might have guessed it when I had your letter."

"Yes, my lord," said she, with a mock curtsey. "You have me to thank. Your little wife managed it all. I lay behind those bushes, and I saw you beaten like a hound. You haven't had all that I had planned for you, but I think it will be some little time before any woman loves you for the sake of your appearance. Do you remember the words, my lord? Do you remember the words?"

He stood stunned for a moment. Then he snatched his whip from the ground, and looked at her from under his heavy brows.

"I believe you're the devil!" he cried.

"I wonder what the governess will think?" said she.

He flared into furious rage and rushed at her with his whip. Tom Spring threw himself before him with his arms out.

"It won't do, sir; I can't stand by."

The man glared at his wife over the prize-fighter's shoulder.

"So it's for dear George's sake!" he said, with a bitter laugh. "But poor, broken-nosed George seems to have gone to the wall. Taken up with a prize-fighter, eh? Found a fancy man for yourself!"

"You liar!" she gasped.

"Ha, my lady, that stings your pride, does it? Well, you shall stand together in the dock for trespass and assault. What a picture—great Lord, what a picture!"

"You wouldn't, John!"

"Wouldn't I, by—! you stay there three minutes and see if I wouldn't." He seized his clothes from the bush, and staggered off as swiftly as he could across the field, blowing a whistle as he ran.

"Quick! quick!" cried the woman. "There's not an instant to lose." Her face was livid, and she was shivering and panting with apprehension. "He'll raise the country. It would be awful—awful!"

She ran swiftly down the tortuous path, Spring following after her and dressing as he went. In a field to the right a gamekeeper, his gun in his hand, was hurrying towards the whistling. Two labourers, loading hay, had stopped their work and were looking about them, their pitchforks in their hands.

But the path was empty, and the phaeton awaited them, the horse cropping the grass by the lane-side, the driver half asleep on his perch. The woman sprang swiftly in and motioned Spring to stand by the wheel.

"There is your fifty pounds," she said, handing him a paper. "You were a fool not to turn it into a hundred when you had the chance. I've done with you now."

"But where am I to go?" asked the prize-fighter, gazing around him at the winding lanes.

"To the devil!" said she. "Drive on, Johnson!"

The phaeton whirled down the road and vanished round a curve. Tom Spring was alone.

Everywhere over the countryside he heard shoutings and whistlings. It was clear that so long as she escaped the indignity of sharing his fate his employer was perfectly indifferent as to whether he got into trouble or not. Tom Spring began to feel indifferent himself. He was weary to death, his head was aching from the blows and falls which he had received, and his feelings were raw from the treatment which he had undergone. He walked slowly some few yards down the lane, but had no idea which way to turn to reach Tunbridge Wells. In the distance he heard the baying of dogs, and he guessed that they were being set upon his track. In that case he could not hope to escape them, and might just as well await them where he was. He picked out a heavy stake from the hedge, and he sat down moodily waiting, in a very dangerous temper, for what might befall him.

But it was a friend and not a foe who came first into sight. Round the corner of the lane flew a small dog-cart, with a fast-trotting chestnut cob between the shafts. In it was seated the rubicund landlord of the Royal Oak, his whip going, his face continually flying round to glance behind him.

"Jump in, Mr. Spring jump in!" he cried, as he reined up. "They're all coming, dogs and men! Come on! Now, hud up, Ginger!" Not another word did he say until two miles of lanes had been left behind them at racing speed and they were back in safety upon the Brighton road. Then he let the reins hang loose on the pony's back, and he slapped Tom Spring with his fat hand upon the shoulder.

"Splendid!" he cried, his great red face shining with ecstasy. "Oh, Lord! but it was beautiful!"

"What!" cried Spring. "You saw the fight?"

"Every round of it! By George! to think that I should have lived to have had such a fight all to myself! Oh, but it was grand," he cried, in a frenzy of delight, "to see his lordship go down like a pithed ox and her ladyship clapping her hands behind the bush! I guessed there was something in the wind, and I followed you all the way. When you stopped, I tethered little Ginger in a grove, and I crept after you through the wood. It's as well I did, for the whole parish was up!"

But Tom Spring was sitting gazing at him in blank amazement.

"His lordship!" he gasped.

"No less, my boy. Lord Falconbridge, Chairman of the Bench, Deputy Lieutenant of the County, Peer of the Realm—that's your man."

"Good Lord!"

"And you didn't know? It's as well, for maybe you wouldn't have whacked it in as hard if you had; and, mind you, if you hadn't, he'd have beat you. There's not a man in this county could stand up to him. He takes the poachers and gipsies two and three at a time. He's the terror of the place. But you did him—did him fair. Oh, man, it was fine!"

Tom Spring was too much dazed by what he heard to do more than sit and wonder. It was not until he had got back to the comforts of the inn, and after a bath had partaken of a solid meal, that he sent for Mr. Cordery the landlord. To him he confided the whole train of events which had led up to his remarkable experience, and he begged him to throw such light as he could upon it. Cordery listened with keen interest and many chuckles to the story. Finally he left the room and returned with a frayed newspaper in his hand, which he smoothed out upon his knee.

"It's the *Pantiles Gazette*, Mr. Spring, as gossiping a rag as ever was printed. I expect there will be a fine column in it if ever it gets its prying nose into this day's doings. However, we are mum and her ladyship is mum, and, my word! his lordship is mum, though he did, in his passion, raise the hue and cry on you. Here it is, Mr. Spring, and I'll read it to you while you smoke your pipe. It's dated July of last year, and it goes like this—

"'FRACAS IN HIGH LIFE.—It is an open secret that the differences which have for some years been known to exist between Lord F—and his beautiful wife have come to a head during the last few days. His lordship's devotion to sport, and also, as it is whispered, some attentions which he has shown to a humbler member of his household, have, it is said, long alienated Lady F—'s affection. Of late she has sought consolation and friendship with a gentleman whom we will designate as Sir George W—n. Sir George, who is a famous ladykiller, and as well-proportioned a man as any in England, took kindly to the task of consoling the disconsolate fair. The upshot, however, was vastly unfortunate, both for the lady's feelings and for the gentleman's beauty. The two friends were surprised in a rendezvous near the house by Lord F—himself at the head of a party of his servants. Lord F—then and there, in spite of the shrieks of the lady, availed himself of his strength and skill to administer such punishment to the unfortunate Lothario as would, in his own parting words, prevent any woman from loving him again for the sake of his appearance. Lady F—has left his lordship and betaken herself to London, where, no doubt, she is now engaged in nursing the damaged Apollo. It is confidently expected that a duel will result from the affair, but no particulars have reached us up to the hour of going to press.'"

The landlord laid down the paper. "You've been moving in high life, Mr. Thomas Spring," said he.

The pugilist passed his hand over his battered face. "Well, Mr. Cordery," said he, "low life is good enough for me."

Out of the Running

IT WAS ON THE NORTH SIDE of Butser on the long swell of the Hampshire Downs. Beneath, some two miles away, the grey roofs and red houses of Petersfield peeped out from amid the trees which surrounded it. From the crest of the low hills downwards the country ran in low, sweeping curves, as though some green primeval sea had congealed in the midst of a ground swell and set for ever into long verdant rollers. At the bottom, just where the slope borders upon the plain, there stood a comfortable square brick farmhouse, with a grey plume of smoke floating up from the chimney. Two cowhouses, a cluster of hayricks, and a broad stretch of fields, yellow with the ripening wheat, formed a fitting setting to the dwelling of a prosperous farmer.

The green slopes were dotted every here and there with dark clumps of gorse bushes, all alight with the flaming yellow blossoms. To the left lay the broad Portsmouth Road curving over the hill, with a line of gaunt telegraph posts marking its course. Beyond a huge white chasm opened in the grass, where the great Butser chalk quarry had been sunk. From its depths rose the distant murmur of voices, and the clinking of hammers. Just above it, between two curves of green hill, might be seen a little triangle of leaden-coloured sea, flecked with a single white sail.

Down the Portsmouth Road two women were walking, one elderly, florid and stout, with a yellow-brown Paisley shawl and a coarse serge dress, the other young and fair, with large grey eyes, and a face which was freckled like a plover's egg. Her neat white blouse with its trim black belt, and plain, close-cut skirt, gave her an air of refinement which was wanting in her companion, but there was sufficient resemblance between them to show that they were mother and daughter. The one was gnarled and hardened and wrinkled by rough country work, the other fresh and pliant from the benign influence of the Board School; but their step, their slope of the shoulders, and the movement of their hips as they walked, all marked them as of one blood.

"Mother, I can see father in the five-acre field," cried the younger, pointing down in the direction of the farm.

The older woman screwed up her eyes, and shaded them with her hand.

"Who's that with him?" she asked.

"There's Bill."

"Oh, he's nobody. He's a-talkin' to some one."

"I don't know, mother. It's some one in a straw hat. Adam Wilson of the Quarry wears a straw hat."

"Aye, of course, it's Adam sure enough. Well, I'm glad we're back home time enough to see him. He'd have been disappointed if he had come over and you'd been away. Drat this dust! It makes one not fit to be seen."

The same idea seemed to have occurred to her daughter, for she had taken out her handkerchief, and was flicking her sleeves and the front of her dress.

"That's right, Dolly. There's some on your flounces. But, Lor' bless you, Dolly, it don't matter to him. It's not your dress he looks at, but your face. Now I shouldn't be very surprised if he hadn't come over to ask you from father."

"I think he'd best begin by asking me from myself," remarked the girl.

"Ah, but you'll have him, Dolly, when he does."

"I'm not so sure of that, mother." The older woman threw up her hands. "There! I don't know what the gals are coming to. I don't indeed. It's the Board Schools as does it. When I was a gal, if a decent young man came a-courtin', we gave him a 'Yes' or a 'No.' We didn't keep him hanging on like a half-clipped sheep. Now, here are you with two of them at your beck, and you can't give an answer to either of them."

"Why, mother, that's it," cried the daughter, with something between a laugh and a sob. "May be if they came one at a time I'd know what to say."

"What have you agin Adam Wilson?"

"Nothing. But I have nothing against Elias Mason."

"Nor I, either. But I know which is the most proper-looking young man."

"Looks isn't everything, mother. You should hear Elias Mason talk. You should hear him repeat poetry."

"Well, then, have Elias."

"Ah, but I haven't the heart to turn against Adam."

"There, now! I never saw such a gal. You're like a calf betwixt two hayricks; you have a nibble at the one and a nibble at the other. There's not one in a hundred as lucky as you. Here's Adam with three pound ten a week, foreman already at the Chalk Works, and likely enough to be manager if he's spared. And there's Elias, head telegraph clerk at the Post Office, and earning good money too. You can't keep 'em both on. You've got to take one or t'other, and it's my belief you'll get neither if you don't stop this shilly-shally."

"I don't care. I don't want them. What do they want to come bothering for?"

"It's human natur', gal. They must do it. If they didn't, you'd be the first to cry out maybe. It's in the Scriptures. 'Man is born for woman, as the sparks fly upwards.'" She looked up out of the corner of her eyes as if not very sure of her quotation. "Why, here be that dratted Bill. The good book says as we are all made of clay, but Bill does show it more than any lad I ever saw."

They had turned from the road into a narrow, deeply rutted lane, which led towards the farm. A youth was running towards them, loose-jointed and long-limbed, with a boyish, lumbering haste, clumping fearlessly with his great yellow clogs through pool and mire. He wore brown corduroys, a dingy shirt, and a red handkerchief tied loosely round his neck. A tattered old straw hat was tilted back upon his shock of coarse, matted, brown hair. His sleeves were turned up to the elbows, and his arms and face were both tanned and roughened until his skin looked like the bark of some young sapling. As he looked up at the sound of the steps, his face with its blue eyes, brown skin, and first slight down of a tawny moustache, was not an uncomely one, were it not marred by the heavy, stolid, somewhat sulky expression of the country yokel.

"Please, mum," said he, touching the brim of his wreck of a hat, "measter seed ye coming. He sent to say as 'ow 'e were in the five-acre lot."

"Run back, Bill, and say that we are coming," answered the farmer's wife, and the awkward figure sped away upon its return journey.

"I say, mother, what is Bill's other name?" asked the girl, with languid curiosity.

"He's not got one."

"No name?"

"No, Dolly, he's a found child, and never had no father or mother that ever was heard of. We had him from the work'us when he was seven, to chop mangel wurzel, and here he's been ever since, nigh twelve year. He was Bill there, and he's Bill here."

"What fun! Fancy having only one name. I wonder what they'll call his wife?"

"I don't know. Time to talk of that when he can keep one. But now, Dolly dear, here's your father and Adam Wilson comin' across the field. I want to see you settled, Dolly. He's a steady young man. He's blue ribbon, and has money in the Post Office."

"I wish I knew which liked me best," said her daughter glancing from under her hat-brim at the approaching figures. "That's the one I should like. But it's all right, mother, and I know how to find out, so don't you fret yourself any more."

The suitor was a well-grown young fellow in a grey suit, with a straw hat jauntily ribboned in red and black. He was smoking, but as he approached he thrust his pipe into his breast-pocket, and came forward with one hand outstretched, and the other gripping nervously at his watch-chain.

"Your servant, Mrs. Foster. And how are you, Miss Dolly? Another fortnight of this and you will be starting on your harvest, I suppose."

"It's bad to say beforehand what you will do in this country," said Farmer Foster, with an apprehensive glance round the heavens.

"It's all God's doing," remarked his wife piously.

"And He does the best for us, of course. Yet He does seem these last seasons to have kind of lost His grip over the weather. Well, maybe it will be made up to us this year. And what did you do at Horndean, mother?"

The old couple walked in front, and the other dropped behind, the young man lingering, and taking short steps to increase the distance.

"I say, Dolly," he murmured at last, flushing slightly as he glanced at her, "I've been speaking to your father about—you know what."

But Dolly didn't know what. She hadn't the slightest idea of what. She turned her pretty little freckled face up to him and was full of curiosity upon the point.

Adam Wilson's face flushed to a deeper red. "You know very well," said he, impatiently, "I spoke to him about marriage."

"Oh, then it's him you want."

"There, that's the way you always go on. It's easy to make fun, but I tell you that I am in earnest, Dolly. Your father says that he would have no objection to me in the family. You know that I love you true."

"How do I know that then?"

"I tell you so. What more can I do?"

"Did you ever do anything to prove it?"

"Set me something and see if I don't do it."

"Then you haven't done anything yet?"

"I don't know. I've done what I could."

"How about this?" She pulled a little crumpled sprig of dog-rose, such as grows wild in the wayside hedges, out of her bosom. "Do you know anything of that?"

He smiled, and was about to answer, when his brows suddenly contracted, his mouth set, and his eyes flashed angrily as they focussed some distant object. Following his gaze, she saw a slim, dark figure, some three fields off, walking swiftly in their direction. "It's my friend, Mr. Elias Mason," said she.

"Your friend!" He had lost his diffidence in his anger. "I know all about that. What does he want here every second evening?"

"Perhaps he wonders what you want."

"Does he? I wish he'd come and ask me. I'd let him see what I wanted. Quick too."

"He can see it now. He has taken off his hat to me," Dolly said, laughing.

Her laughter was the finishing touch. He had meant to be impressive, and it seemed that he had only been ridiculous. He swung round upon his heel.

"Very well, Miss Foster," said he, in a choking voice, "that's all right. We know where we are now. I didn't come here to be made a fool of, so good day to you." He plucked at his hat, and walked furiously off in the direction from which they had come. She looked after him, half frightened, in the hope of seeing some sign that he had relented, but he strode onwards with a rigid neck, and vanished at a turn of the lane.

When she turned again her other visitor was close upon her—a thin, wiry, sharp-featured man with a sallow face, and a quick, nervous manner.

"Good evening, Miss Foster. I thought that I would walk over as the weather was so beautiful, but I did not expect to have the good fortune to meet you in the fields."

"I am sure that father will be very glad to see you, Mr. Mason. You must come in and have a glass of milk."

"No, thank you, Miss Foster, I should very much prefer to stay out here with you. But I am afraid that I have interrupted you in a chat. Was not that Mr. Adam Wilson who left you this moment?" His manner was subdued, but his questioning eyes and compressed lips told of a deeper and more furious jealousy than that of his rival.

"Yes. It was Mr. Adam Wilson." There was something about Mason, a certain concentration of manner, which made it impossible for the girl to treat him lightly as she had done the other.

"I have noticed him here several times lately."

"Yes. He is head foreman, you know, at the big quarry."

"Oh, indeed. He is fond of your society, Miss Foster. I can't blame him for that, can I, since I am equally so myself. But I should like to come to some understanding with you. You cannot have misunderstood what my

137

feelings are to you? I am in a position to offer you a comfortable home. Will you be my wife, Miss Foster?"

Dolly would have liked to make some jesting reply, but it was hard to be funny with those two eager, fiery eyes fixed so intently upon her own. She began to walk slowly towards the house, while he paced along beside her, still waiting for his answer.

"You must give me a little time, Mr. Mason," she said at last. "'Marry in haste,' they say, 'and repent at leisure.'"

"But you shall never have cause to repent."

"I don't know. One hears such things."

"You shall be the happiest woman in England."

"That sounds very nice. You are a poet, Mr. Mason, are you not?"

"I am a lover of poetry."

"And poets are fond of flowers?"

"I am very fond of flowers."

"Then perhaps you know something of these?" She took out the humble little sprig, and held it out to him with an arch questioning glance. He took it and pressed it to his lips.

"I know that it has been near you, where I should wish to be," said he.

"Good evening, Mr. Mason!" It was Mrs. Foster who had come out to meet them. "Where's Mr.—? Oh—ah! Yes, of course. The teapot's on the table, and you'd best come in afore it's over-drawn."

When Elias Mason left the farmhouse that evening, he drew Dolly aside at the door.

"I won't be able to come before Saturday," said he.

"We shall be glad to see you, Mr. Mason."

"I shall want my answer then."

"Oh, I cannot give any promise, you know."

"But I shall live in hope."

"Well, no one can prevent you from doing that." As she came to realize her power over him she had lost something of her fear, and could answer him now nearly as freely as if he were simple Adam Wilson.

She stood at the door, leaning against the wooden porch, with the long trailers of the honeysuckle framing her tall, slight figure. The great red sun was low in the west, its upper rim peeping over the low hills, shooting long, dark shadows from the beech-tree in the field, from the little group of tawny cows, and from the man who walked away from her. She smiled to see how immense the legs were, and how tiny the body in the great flat giant which kept pace beside him. In front of her in the little garden the bees droned, a belated butterfly or an early moth fluttered slowly over the flower-beds, a thousand little creatures buzzed and hummed, all busy working out their tiny destinies, as she, too, was working out hers, and each doubtless looking upon their own as the central point of the universe. A few months for the gnat, a few years for the girl, but each was happy now in the heavy summer air. A beetle scuttled out upon the gravel path and bored onwards, its six legs all working hard, butting up against stones, upsetting itself on ridges, but still gathering itself up and rushing onwards to some all-important appointment somewhere in the grass plot. A bat fluttered up from behind the beech-tree. A breath of night air sighed softly over the hillside with a little tinge of the chill sea spray in its coolness. Dolly Foster shivered, and had turned to go in when her mother came out from the passage.

"Whatever is that Bill doing there?" she cried.

Dolly looked, and saw for the first time that the nameless farm-labourer was crouching under the beech, his browns and yellows blending with the bark behind him.

"You go out o' that, Bill!" screamed the farmer's wife.

"What be I to do?" he asked humbly, slouching forward.

"Go, cut chaff in the barn." He nodded and strolled away, a comical figure in his mud-crusted boots, his strap-tied corduroys and his almond-coloured skin.

"Well, then, you've taken Elias," said the mother, passing her hand round her daughter's waist. "I seed him a-kissing your flower. Well, I'm sorry for Adam, for he is a well-grown young man, a proper young man, blue ribbon, with money in the Post Office. Still some one must suffer, else how could we be purified. If the milk's left alone it won't ever turn into butter. It wants troubling and stirring and churning. That's what we want, too, before we can turn angels. It's just the same as butter."

Dolly laughed. "I have not taken Elias yet," said she.

"No? What about Adam then?"

"Nor him either."

"Oh, Dolly girl, can you not take advice from them that is older. I tell you again that you'll lose them both."

"No, no, mother. Don't you fret yourself. It's all right. But you can see how hard it is. I like Elias, for he can speak so well, and is so sure and masterful. And I like Adam because—well, because I know very well that Adam loves me."

"Well, bless my heart, you can't marry them both. You'd like all the pears in the basket."

"No, mother, but I know how to choose. You see this bit of a flower, dear."

"It's a common dog-rose."

"Well, where d'you think I found it?"

"In the hedge likely."

"No, but on my window-ledge."

"Oh, but when?"

"This morning. It was six when I got up, and there it lay fresh and sweet, and new-plucked. 'Twas the same yesterday and the day before. Every morning there it lies. It's a common flower, as you say, mother, but it is not so common to find a man who'll break short his sleep day after day just to show a girl that the thought of her is in his heart."

"And which was it?"

"Ah, if I knew! I think it's Elias. He's a poet, you know, and poets do nice things like that."

"And how will you be sure?"

"I'll know before morning. He will come again, whichever it is. And whichever it is he's the man for me. Did father ever do that for you before you married?"

"I can't say he did, dear. But father was always a powerful heavy sleeper."

"Well then, mother, you needn't fret any more about me, for as sure as I stand here, I'll tell you to-morrow which of them it is to be."

That evening the farmer's daughter set herself to clearing off all those odd jobs which accumulate in a large household. She polished the dark, old-fashioned furniture in the sitting-room. She cleared out the cellar, re-arranged the bins, counted up the cider, made a great cauldron full of raspberry jam, potted, papered, and labelled it. Long after the whole household was in bed she pushed on with her self-imposed tasks until the night was far gone and she very spent and weary. Then she stirred up the smouldering kitchen fire and made herself a cup of tea, and, carrying it up to her own room, she sat sipping it and glancing over an old bound volume of the *Leisure Hour*. Her seat was behind the little dimity window curtains, whence she could see without being seen.

The morning had broken, and a brisk wind had sprung up with the dawn. The sky was of the lightest, palest blue, with a scud of flying white clouds shredded out over the face of it, dividing, coalescing, overtaking one another, but sweeping ever from the pink of the east to the still shadowy west. The high, eager voice of the wind whistled and sang outside, rising from moan to shriek, and then sinking again to a dull mutter and grumble. Dolly rose to wrap her shawl around her, and as she sat down again in an instant her doubts were resolved, and she had seen that for which she had waited.

Her window faced the inner yard, and was some eight feet from the ground. A man standing beneath it could not be seen from above. But she saw enough to tell her all that she wished to know. Silently, suddenly, a hand had appeared from below, had laid a sprig of flower upon her ledge, and had disappeared. It did not take two seconds; she saw no face, she heard no sound, but she had seen the hand and she wanted nothing more. With a smile she threw herself upon the bed, drew a rug over her, and dropped into a heavy slumber.

She was awakened by her mother plucking at her shoulder.

"It's breakfast time, Dolly, but I thought you would be weary, so I brought you lip some bread and coffee. Sit up, like a dearie, and take it."

"All right, mother. Thank you. I'm all dressed, so I'll be ready to come down soon."

"Bless the gal, she's never had her things off! And, dearie me, here's the flower outside the window, sure enough! Well, and did you see who put it there?"

"Yes, I did."

"Who was it then?"

"It was Adam."

"Was it now? Well, I shouldn't have thought that he had it in him. Then Adam it's to be. Well, he's steady, and that's better than being clever, yea, seven-and-seventy fold. Did he come across the yard?"

"No, along by the wall."

"How did you see him then?"

"I didn't see him."

"Then how can you tell?"

"I saw his hand."

"But d'you tell me you know Adam's hand?"

"It would be a blind man that couldn't tell it from Elias' hand. Why, the one is as brown as that coffee, and the other as white as the cup, with great blue veins all over it."

"Well, now I shouldn't have thought of it, but so it is. Well, it'll be a busy day, Dolly. Just hark to the wind!"

It had, indeed, increased during the few hours since dawn to a very violent tempest. The panes of the window rattled and shook. Glancing out, Dolly saw cabbage leaves and straw whirling up past the casement.

"The great hayrick is giving. They're all out trying to prop it up. My, but it do blow!"

It did indeed! When Dolly came downstairs it was all that she could do to push her way through the porch. All along the horizon the sky was brassy-yellow, but above the wind screamed and stormed, and the torn, hurrying clouds were now huddled together, and now frayed off into countless tattered streamers. In the field near the house her father and three or four labourers were working with poles and ropes, hatless, their hair and beards flying, staving up a great bulging hayrick. Dolly watched them for a moment, and then, stooping her head and rounding her shoulders, with one hand up to her little black straw hat, she staggered off across the fields.

Adam Wilson was at work always on a particular part of the hillside, and hither it was that she bent her steps. He saw the trim, dapper figure, with its flying skirts and hat-ribbons, and he came forward to meet her with a great white crowbar in his hand. He walked slowly, however, and his eyes were downcast, with the air of a man who still treasures a grievance.

"Good mornin', Miss Foster."

"Good morning, Mr. Wilson. Oh, if you are going to be cross with me, I'd best go home again."

"I'm not cross, Miss Foster. I take it very kindly that you should come out this way on such a day."

"I wanted to say to you—I wanted to say that I was sorry if I made you angry yesterday. I didn't mean to make fun. I didn't, indeed. It is only my way of talking. It was so good of you, so noble of you, to let it make no difference."

"None at all, Dolly." He was quite radiant again. "If I didn't love you so, I wouldn't mind what that other chap said or did. And if I could only think that you cared more for me than for him—"

"I do, Adam."

"God bless you for saying so! You've lightened my heart, Dolly. I have to go to Portsmouth for the firm today. To-morrow night I'll come and see you."

"Very well, Adam, I—Oh, my God, what's that!"

A rending breaking noise in the distance, a dull rumble, and a burst of shouts and cries.

"The rick's down! There's been an accident!" They both started running down the hill.

"Father!" panted the girl, "father!"

"He's all right!" shouted her companion, "I can see him. But there's some one down. They're lifting him now. And here's one running like mad for the doctor."

A farm-labourer came rushing wildly up the lane. "Don't you go, Missey," he cried. "A man's hurt."

"Who?"

"It's Bill. The rick came down and the ridge-pole caught him across the back. He's dead, I think. Leastwise, there's not much life in him. I'm off for Doctor Strong!" He bent his shoulder to the wind, and lumbered off down the road.

"Poor Bill! Thank God it wasn't father!" They were at the edge of the field now in which the accident had taken place. The rick lay, a shapeless mound upon the earth, with a long thick pole protruding from it, which had formerly supported the tarpaulin drawn across it in case of rain. Four men were walking slowly away, one shoulder humped, one hanging, and betwixt them they bore a formless clay-coloured bundle. He might have been a clod of the earth that he tilled, so passive, so silent, still brown, for death itself could not have taken the burn from his skin, but with patient, bovine eyes looking out heavily from under half-closed lids. He breathed jerkily, but he neither cried out nor groaned. There was something almost brutal and inhuman in his absolute stolidity. He asked no sympathy, for his life had been without it. It was a broken tool rather than an injured man.

"Can I do anything, father?"

"No, lass, no. This is no place for you. I've sent for the doctor. He'll be here soon."

"But where are they taking him?"

"To the loft where he sleeps."

"I'm sure he's welcome to my room, father."

"No, no, lass. Better leave it alone."

But the little group were passing as they spoke, and the injured lad had heard the girl's words.

"Thank ye kindly, Missey," he murmured, with a little flicker of life, and then sank back again into his stolidity and his silence.

Well, a farm hand is a useful thing, but what is a man to do with one who has an injured spine and half his ribs smashed. Farmer Foster shook his head and scratched his chin as he listened to the doctor's report.

"He can't get better?"

"No."

"Then we had better move him."

"Where to?"

"To the work'us hospital. He came from there just this time eleven years. It'll be like going home to him."

"I fear that he is going home," said the doctor gravely. "But it's out of the question to move him now. He must lie where he is for better or for worse."

And it certainly looked for worse rather than for better. In a little loft above the stable he was stretched upon a tiny blue pallet which lay upon the planks. Above were the gaunt rafters, hung with saddles, harness, old scythe blades—the hundred things which droop, like bats, from inside such buildings. Beneath them upon two pegs hung his own pitiable wardrobe, the blue shirt and the grey, the stained trousers, and the muddy coat. A gaunt chaff-cutting machine stood at his head, and a great bin of the chaff behind it. He lay very quiet, still dumb, still uncomplaining, his eyes fixed upon the small square window looking out at the drifting sky, and at this strange world which God has made so queerly—so very queerly.

An old woman, the wife of a labourer, had been set to nurse him, for the doctor had said that he was not to be left. She moved about the room, arranging and ordering, grumbling to herself from time to time at this lonely task which had been assigned to her. There were some flowers in broken jars upon a cross-beam, and these, with a touch of tenderness, she carried over and arranged upon a deal packing-case beside the patient's head. He lay motionless, and as he breathed there came a gritty rubbing sound from somewhere in his side, but he followed his companion about with his eyes and even smiled once as she grouped the flowers round him.

He smiled again when he heard that Mrs. Foster and her daughter had been to ask after him that evening. They had been down to the Post Office together, where Dolly had sent off a letter which she had very carefully drawn up, addressed to Elias Mason, Esq., and explaining to that gentleman that she had formed her plans for life, and that he need spare himself the pain of coming for his answer on the Saturday. As they came back they stopped in the stable and inquired through the loft door as to the sufferer. From where they stood they could hear that horrible grating sound in his breathing. Dolly hurried away with her face quite pale under her freckles. She was too young to face the horrid details of suffering, and yet she was a year older than this poor waif, who lay in silence, facing death itself.

All night he lay very quiet—so quiet that were it not for that one sinister sound his nurse might have doubted whether life was still in him. She had watched him and tended him as well as she might, but she was herself feeble and old, and just as the morning light began to steal palely through the small loft window, she sank back in her chair in a dreamless sleep. Two hours passed, and the first voices of the men as they gathered for their work aroused her. She sprang to her feet. Great heaven! the pallet was empty. She rushed down into the stables, distracted, wringing her hands. There was no sign of him. But the stable door was open. He must have walked-but how could he walk?—he must have crawled—have writhed that way. Out she rushed, and as they heard her tale, the newly risen labourers ran with her, until the farmer with his wife and daughter were called from their breakfast by the bustle, and joined also in this strange chase. A whoop, a cry, and they were drawn round to the corner of the yard on which Miss Dolly's window opened. There he lay within a few yards of the window, his face upon the stones, his feet thrusting out from his tattered night-gown, and his track marked by the blood from his wounded knees. One hand was thrown out before him, and in it he held a little sprig of the pink dog-rose.

They carried him back, cold and stiff, to the pallet in the loft, and the old nurse drew the sheet over him and left him, for there was no need to watch him now. The girl had gone to her room, and her mother followed her thither, all unnerved by this glimpse of death.

"And to think," said she, "that it was only *him*, after all."

But Dolly sat at the side of her bed, and sobbed bitterly in her apron.

"De Profundis"

SO LONG AS THE OCEANS are the ligaments which bind together the great broad-cast British Empire, so long will there be a dash of romance in our minds. For the soul is swayed by the waters, as the waters are by the moon, and when the great highways of an empire are along such roads as these, so full of strange sights and sounds, with danger ever running like a hedge on either side of the course, it is a dull mind indeed which does not bear away with it some trace of such a passage. And now, Britain lies far beyond herself, for the three-mile limit of every seaboard is her frontier, which has been won by hammer and loom and pick rather than by arts of war. For it is written in history that neither king nor army can bar the path to the man who having twopence in his strong box, and knowing well where he can turn it to threepence, sets his mind to that one end. And as the frontier has broadened, the mind of Britain has broadened too, spreading out until all men can see that the ways of the island are continental, even as those of the Continent are insular.

But for this a price must be paid, and the price is a grievous one. As the beast of old must have one young human life as a tribute every year, so to our Empire we throw from day to day the pick and flower of our youth. The engine is world-wide and strong, but the only fuel that will drive it is the lives of British men. Thus it is that in the grey old cathedrals, as we look round upon the brasses on the walls, we see strange names, such names as they who reared those walls had never heard, for it is in Peshawar, and Umballah, and Korti and Fort Pearson that the youngsters die, leaving only a precedent and a brass behind them. But if every man had his obelisk, even where he lay, then no frontier line need be drawn, for a cordon of British graves would ever show how high the Anglo-Celtic tide had lapped.

This, then, as well as the waters which join us to the world, has done something to tinge us with romance. For when so many have their loved ones over the seas, walking amid hillmen's bullets, or swamp malaria, where death is sudden and distance great, then mind communes with mind, and strange stories arise of dream, presentiment or vision, where the mother sees her dying son, and is past the first bitterness of her grief ere the message comes which should have broken the news. The learned have of late looked into the matter and have even labelled it with a name; but what can we know more of it save that a poor stricken soul, when hard-pressed and driven, can shoot across the earth some ten-thousand-mile-distant picture of its trouble to the mind which is most akin to it. Far be it from me to say that there lies no such power within us, for of all things which the brain will grasp the last will be itself; but yet it is well to be very cautious over such matters, for once at least I have known that which was within the laws of nature seem to be far upon the further side of them.

John Vansittart was the younger partner of the firm of Hudson and Vansittart, coffee exporters of the Island of Ceylon, three-quarters Dutchman by descent, but wholly English in his sympathies. For years I had been his agent in London, and when in '72 he came over to England for a three months' holiday, he turned to me for the introductions which would enable him to see something of town and country life. Armed with seven letters he left my offices, and for many weeks scrappy notes from different parts of the country let me know that he had found favour in the eyes of my friends. Then came word of his engagement to Emily Lawson, of a cadet branch of the Hereford Lawsons, and at the very tail of the first flying rumour the news of his absolute marriage, for the wooing of a wanderer must be short, and the days were already crowding on towards the date when he must be upon his homeward journey. They were to return together to Colombo in one of the firm's own thousand-ton barque-rigged sailing ships, and this was to be their princely honeymoon, at once a necessity and a delight.

Those were the royal days of coffee-planting in Ceylon, before a single season and a rotten fungus drove a whole community through years of despair to one of the greatest commercial victories which pluck and ingenuity ever won. Not often is it that men have the heart when their one great industry is withered to rear up in a few years another as rich to take its place, and the tea-fields of Ceylon are as true a monument to courage as is the lion at Waterloo. But in '72 there was no cloud yet above the skyline, and the hopes of the planters were as high and as bright as the hillsides on which they reared their crops. Vansittart came down to London with his young and beautiful wife. I was introduced, dined with them, and it was finally arranged that I, since business called me also to Ceylon, should be a fellow-passenger with them on the *Eastern Star*, which was timed to sail on the following Monday.

It was on the Sunday evening that I saw him again. He was shown up into my rooms about nine o'clock at night, with the air of a man who is bothered and out of sorts. His hand, as I shook it, was hot and dry.

"I wish, Atkinson," said he, "that you could give me a little lime juice and water. I have a beastly thirst upon me, and the more I take the more I seem to want."

I rang and ordered a carafe and glasses. "You are flushed," said I. "You don't look the thing."

"No, I'm clean off colour. Got a touch of rheumatism in my back, and don't seem to taste my food. It is this vile London that is choking me. I'm not used to breathing air which has been used up by four million lungs all sucking away on every side of you." He flapped his crooked hands before his face, like a man who really struggles for his breath.

"A touch of the sea will soon set you right."

"Yes, I'm of one mind with you there. That's the thing for me. I want no other doctor. If I don't get to sea to-morrow I'll have an illness. There are no two ways about it." He drank off a tumbler of lime juice, and clapped his two hands with his knuckles doubled up into the small of his back.

"That seems to ease me," said he, looking at me with a filmy eye. "Now I want your help, Atkinson, for I am rather awkwardly placed."

"As how?"

"This way. My wife's mother got ill and wired for her. I couldn't go—you know best yourself how tied I have been—so she had to go alone. Now I've had another wire to say that she can't come to-morrow, but that she will pick up the ship at Falmouth on Wednesday. We put in there, you know, and in, though I count it hard, Atkinson, that a man should be asked to believe in a mystery, and cursed if he can't do it. Cursed, mind you, no less." He leaned forward and began to draw a catchy breath like a man who is poised on the very edge of a sob.

Then first it came to my mind that I had heard much of the hard-drinking life of the island, and that from brandy came those wild words and fevered hands. The flushed cheek and the glazing eye were those of one whose drink is strong upon him. Sad it was to see so noble a young man in the grip of that most bestial of all the devils.

"You should lie down," I said, with some severity.

He screwed up his eyes like a man who is striving to wake himself, and looked up with an air of surprise.

"So I shall presently," said he, quite rationally. "I felt quite swimmy just now, but I am my own man again now. Let me see, what was I talking about? Oh ah, of course, about the wife. She joins the ship at Falmouth. Now I want to go round by water. I believe my health depends upon it. I just want a little clean first-lung air to set me on my feet again. I ask you, like a good fellow, to go to Falmouth by rail, so that in case we should be late you may be there to look after the wife. Put up at the Royal Hotel, and I will wire her that you are there. Her sister will bring her down, so that it will be all plain sailing."

"I'll do it with pleasure," said I. "In fact, I would rather go by rail, for we shall have enough and to spare of the sea before we reach Colombo. I believe too that you badly need a change. Now, I should go and turn in, if I were you."

"Yes, I will. I sleep aboard tonight. You know," he continued, as the film settled down again over his eyes, "I've not slept well the last few nights. I've been troubled with theolololog—that is to say, theologological—hang it," with a desperate effort, "with the doubts of theolologicians. Wondering why the Almighty made us, you know, and why He made our heads swimmy, and fixed little pains into the small of our backs. Maybe I'll do better tonight." He rose and steadied himself with an effort against the corner of the chair back.

"Look here, Vansittart," said I, gravely, stepping up to him, and laying my hand upon his sleeve, "I can give you a shakedown here. You are not fit to go out. You are all over the place. You've been mixing your drinks."

"Drinks!" He stared at me stupidly.

"You used to carry your liquor better than this."

"I give you my word, Atkinson, that I have not had a drain for two days. It's not drink. I don't know what it is. I suppose you think this is drink." He took up my hand in his burning grasp, and passed it over his own forehead.

"Great Lord!" said I.

His skin felt like a thin sheet of velvet beneath which lies a close-packed layer of small shot. It was smooth to the touch at any one place, but to a finger passed along it, rough as a nutmeg grater.

"It's all right," said he, smiling at my startled face. "I've had the prickly heat nearly as bad."

"But this is never prickly heat."

"No, it's London. It's breathing bad air. But tomorrow it'll be all right. There's a surgeon aboard, so I shall be in safe hands. I must be off now."

"Not you," said I, pushing him back into a chair. "This is past a joke. You don't move from here until a doctor sees you. Just stay where you are."

149

I caught up my hat, and rushing round to the house of a neighbouring physician, I brought him back with me. The room was empty and Vansittart gone. I rang the bell. The servant said that the gentleman had ordered a cab the instant that I had left, and had gone off in it. He had told the cabman to drive to the docks.

"Did the gentleman seem ill?" I asked.

"Ill!" The man smiled. "No, sir, he was singin' his 'ardest all the time."

The information was not as reassuring as my servant seemed to think, but I reflected that he was going straight back to the *Eastern Star*, and that there was a doctor aboard of her, so that there was nothing which I could do in the matter. None the less, when I thought of his thirst, his burning hands, his heavy eye, his tripping speech, and lastly, of that leprous forehead, I carried with me to bed an unpleasant memory of my visitor and his visit.

At eleven o'clock next day I was at the docks, but the *Eastern Star* had already moved down the river, and was nearly at Gravesend. To Gravesend I went by train, but only to see her topmasts far off, with a plume of smoke from a tug in front of her. I would hear no more of my friend until I rejoined him at Falmouth. When I got back to my offices, a telegram was awaiting me from Mrs. Vansittart, asking me to meet her; and next evening found us both at the Royal Hotel, Falmouth, where we were to wait for the *Eastern Star*. Ten days passed, and there came no news of her.

They were ten days which I am not likely to forget. On the very day that the *Eastern Star* had cleared from the Thames, a furious easterly gale had sprung up, and blew on from day to day for the greater part of a week without the sign of a lull. Such a screaming, raving, long-drawn storm has never been known on the southern coast. From our hotel windows the sea view was all banked in haze, with a little rain-swept half-circle under our very eyes, churned and lashed into one tossing stretch of foam. So heavy was the wind upon the waves that little sea could rise, for the crest of each billow was torn shrieking from it, and lashed broadcast over the bay. Clouds, wind, sea, all were rushing to the west, and there, looking down at this mad jumble of elements, I waited on day after day, my sole companion a white, silent woman, with terror in her eyes, her forehead pressed ever against the window, her gaze from early morning to the fall of night fixed upon that wall of grey haze through which the loom of a vessel might come. She said nothing, but that face of hers was one long wail of fear.

On the fifth day I took counsel with an old seaman. I should have preferred to have done so alone, but she saw me speak with him, and was at our side in an instant, with parted lips and a prayer in her eyes.

150

"Seven days out from London," said he, "and five in the gale. Well, the Channel's swept clear by this wind. There's three things for it. She may have popped into port on the French side. That's like enough."

"No, no; he knew we were here. He would have telegraphed."

"Ah, yes, so he would. Well, then, he might have run for it, and if he did that he won't be very far from Madeira by now. That'll be it, marm, you may depend."

"Or else? You said there was a third chance."

"Did I, marm? No, only two, I think. I don't think I said anything of a third. Your ship's out there, depend upon it, away out in the Atlantic, and you'll hear of it time enough, for the weather is breaking. Now don't you fret, marm, and wait quiet, and you'll find a real blue Cornish sky tomorrow."

The old seaman was right in his surmise, for the next day broke calm and bright, with only a low dwindling cloud in the west to mark the last trailing wreaths of the storm-wrack. But still there came no word from the sea, and no sign of the ship. Three more weary days had passed, the weariest that I have ever spent, when there came a seafaring man to the hotel with a letter. I gave a shout of joy. It was from the captain of the *Eastern Star*. As I read the first lines of it I whisked my hand over it, but she laid her own upon it and drew it away. "I have seen it," said she, in a cold, quiet voice. "I may as well see the rest, too."

"Dear Sir," *said the letter,*

"Mr. Vansittart is down with the small-pox, and we are blown so far on our course that we don't know what to do, he being off his head and unfit to tell us. By dead reckoning we are but three hundred miles from Funchal, so I take it that it is best that we should push on there, get Mr. V. into hospital, and wait in the Bay until you come. There's a sailing-ship due from Falmouth to Funchal in a few days' time, as I understand. This goes by the brig *Marian* of Falmouth, and five pounds is due to the master, Yours respectfully,

"Jno. Hines."

She was a wonderful woman that, only a chit of a girl fresh from school, but as quiet and strong as a man. She said nothing—only pressed her lips together tight, and put on her bonnet.

"You are going out?" I asked.

"Yes."

"Can I be of use?"

"No; I am going to the doctor's."

"To the doctor's?"

"Yes. To learn how to nurse a small-pox case."

She was busy at that all the evening, and next morning we were off with a fine ten-knot breeze in the barque *Rose of Sharon* for Madeira. For five days we made good time, and were no great way from the island; but on the sixth there fell a calm, and we lay without motion on a sea of oil, heaving slowly, but making not a foot of way.

At ten o'clock that night Emily Vansittart and I stood leaning on the starboard railing of the poop, with a full moon shining at our backs, and casting a black shadow of the barque, and of our own two heads upon the shining water. From the shadow a broadening path of moonshine stretched away to the lonely sky-line, flickering and shimmering in the gentle heave of the swell. We were talking with bent heads, chatting of the calm, of the chances of wind, of the look of the sky, when there came a sudden plop, like a rising salmon, and there, in the clear light, John Vansittart sprang out of the water and looked up at us.

I never saw anything clearer in my life than I saw that man. The moon shone full upon him, and he was but three oars' lengths away. His face was more puffed than when I had seen him last, mottled here and there with dark scabs, his mouth and eyes open as one who is struck with some overpowering surprise. He had some white stuff streaming from his shoulders, and one hand was raised to his ear, the other crooked across his breast. I saw him leap from the water into the air, and in the dead calm the waves of his coming lapped up against the sides of the vessel. Then his figure sank back into the water again, and I heard a rending, crackling sound like a bundle of brushwood snapping in the fire on a frosty night. There were no signs of him when I looked again, but a swift swirl and eddy on the still sea still marked the spot where he had been. How long I stood there, tingling to my finger-tips, holding up an unconscious woman with one hand, clutching at the rail of the vessel with the other, was more than I could afterwards tell. I had been noted as a man of slow and unresponsive emotions, but this time at least I was shaken to the core. Once and twice I struck my foot upon the deck to be certain that I was indeed the master of my own senses, and that this was not some mad prank of an unruly brain. As I stood, still marvelling, the woman shivered, opened her eyes, gasped, and then standing erect with her hands upon the rail, looked out over the moonlit sea with a face which had aged ten years in a summer night.

"You saw his vision?" she murmured.

"I saw something."

"It was he! It was John! He is dead!"

I muttered some lame words of doubt.

"Doubtless he died at this hour," she whispered. "In hospital at Madeira. I have read of such things. His thoughts were with me. His vision came to me. Oh, my John, my dear, dear, lost John!"

She broke out suddenly into a storm of weeping, and I led her down into her cabin, where I left her with her sorrow. That night a brisk breeze blew up from the east, and in the evening of the next day we passed the two islets of Los Desertos, and dropped anchor at sundown in the Bay of Funchal. The *Eastern Star* lay no great distance from us, with the quarantine flag flying from her main, and her Jack half-way up her peak.

"You see," said Mrs. Vansittart, quickly. She was dry-eyed now, for she had known how it would be.

That night we received permission from the authorities to move on board the *Eastern Star*. The captain, Hines, was waiting upon deck with confusion and grief contending upon his bluff face as he sought for words with which to break this heavy tidings, but she took the story from his lips.

"I know that my husband is dead," she said. "He died yesterday night, about ten o'clock, in hospital at Madeira, did he not?"

The seaman stared aghast. "No, marm, he died eight days ago at sea, and we had to bury him out there, for we lay in a belt of calm, and could not say when we might make the land."

Well, those are the main facts about the death of John Vansittart, and his appearance to his wife somewhere about lat. 35 N. and long. 15 W. A clearer case of a wraith has seldom been made out, and since then it has been told as such, and put into print as such, and endorsed by a learned society as such, and so floated off with many others to support the recent theory of telepathy. For myself, I hold telepathy to be proved, but I would snatch this one case from amid the evidence, and say that I do not think that it was the wraith of John Vansittart, but John Vansittart himself whom we saw that night leaping into the moonlight out of the depths of the Atlantic. It has ever been my belief that some strange chance—one of those chances which seem so improbable and yet so constantly occur—had becalmed us over the very spot where the man had been buried a week before. For the rest, the surgeon tells me that the leaden weight was not too firmly fixed, and that seven days bring about changes which fetch a body to the surface. Coming from the depth to which the weight would have sunk it, he explains that it might well attain such a velocity as to carry it clear of the water. Such is my own explanation of the matter, and if you ask me what then became of the body, I must recall to you that snapping, crackling sound, with the swirl in the water. The shark is a surface feeder and is plentiful in those parts.

The Great Brown-Pericord Motor

IT WAS A COLD, foggy, dreary evening in May. Along the Strand blurred patches of light marked the position of the lamps. The flaring shop windows flickered vaguely with steamy brightness through the thick and heavy atmosphere.

The high lines of houses which lead down to the Embankment were all dark and deserted, or illuminated only by the glimmering lamp of the caretaker. At one point, however, there shone out from three windows upon the second floor a rich flood of light, which broke the sombre monotony of the terrace. Passers-by glanced up curiously, and drew each other's attention to the ruddy glare, for it marked the chambers of Francis Pericord, the inventor and electrical engineer. Long into the watches of the night the gleam of his lamps bore witness to the untiring energy and restless industry which was rapidly carrying him to the first rank in his profession.

Within the chamber sat two men. The one was Pericord himself—hawk-faced and angular, with the black hair and brisk bearing which spoke of his Celtic origin. The other—thick, sturdy, and blue-eyed—was Jeremy Brown, the well-known mechanician. They had been partners in many an invention, in which the creative genius of the one had been aided by the practical abilities of the other. It was a question among their friends as to which was the better man.

It was no chance visit which had brought Brown into Pericord's workshop at so late an hour. Business was to be done—business which was to decide the failure or success of months of work, and which might affect their whole careers. Between them lay a long brown table, stained and corroded by strong acids, and littered with giant carboys, Faure's accumulators, voltaic piles, coils of wire, and great blocks of non-conducting

154

porcelain. In the midst of all this lumber there stood a singular whizzing, whirring machine, upon which the eyes of both partners were riveted.

A small square metal receptacle was connected by numerous wires to a broad steel girdle, furnished on either side with two powerful projecting joints. The girdle was motionless, but the joints with the short arms attached to them flashed round every few seconds, with a pause between each rhythmic turn. The power which moved them came evidently from the metal box. A subtle odour of ozone was in the air.

"How about the flanges, Brown?" asked the inventor.

"They were too large to bring. They are seven foot by three. There is power enough there to work them, however. I will answer for that."

"Aluminium with an alloy of copper?"

"Yes."

"See how beautifully it works." Pericord stretched out a thin, nervous hand, and pressed a button upon the machine. The joints revolved more slowly, and came presently to a dead stop. Again he touched a spring and the arms shivered and woke up again into their crisp metallic life. "The experimenter need not exert his muscular powers," he remarked. "He has only to be passive, and use his intelligence."

"Thanks to my motor," said Brown.

"*Our* motor," the other broke in sharply.

"Oh, of course," said his colleague impatiently.

"The motor which you thought of, and which I reduced to practice— call it what you like."

"I call it the Brown-Pericord Motor," cried the inventor with an angry flash of his dark eyes. "You worked out the details, but the abstract thought is mine, and mine alone."

"An abstract thought won't turn an engine," said Brown, doggedly.

"That was why I took you into partnership," the other retorted, drumming nervously with his fingers upon the table. "I invent, you build. It is a fair division of labour."

Brown pursed up his lips, as though by no means satisfied upon the point. Seeing, however, that further argument was useless, he turned his attention to the machine, which was shivering and rocking with each swing of its arms, as though a very little more would send it skimming from the table.

"Is it not splendid?" cried Pericord.

"It is satisfactory," said the more phlegmatic Anglo-Saxon.

"There's immortality in it!"

"There's money in it!"

"Our names will go down with Montgolfier's."

"With Rothschild's, I hope."

"No, no, Brown; you take too material a view," cried the inventor, raising his gleaming eyes from the machine to his companion. "Our fortunes are a mere detail. Money is a thing which every heavy-witted plutocrat in the country shares with us. My hopes rise to something higher than that. Our true reward will come in the gratitude and goodwill of the human race."

Brown shrugged his shoulders. "You may have my share of that," he said. "I am a practical man. We must test our invention."

"Where can we do it?"

"That is what I wanted to speak about. It must be absolutely secret. If we had private grounds of our own it would be an easy matter, but there is no privacy in London."

"We must take it into the country."

"I have a suggestion to offer," said Brown. "My brother has a place in Sussex on the high land near Beachy Head. There is, I remember, a large and lofty barn near the house. Will is in Scotland, but the key is always at my disposal. Why not take the machine down tomorrow and test it in the barn?"

"Nothing could be better."

"There is a train to Eastbourne at one."

"I shall be at the station."

"Bring the gear with you, and I will bring the flanges," said the mechanician, rising. "Tomorrow will prove whether we have been following a shadow, or whether fortune is at our feet. One o'clock at Victoria." He walked swiftly down the stair and was quickly reabsorbed into the flood of comfortless clammy humanity which ebbed and flowed along the Strand.

The morning was bright and spring-like. A pale blue sky arched over London, with a few gauzy white clouds drifting lazily across it. At eleven o'clock Brown might have been seen entering the Patent Office with a great roll of parchment, diagrams, and plans under his arm. At twelve he emerged again smiling, and, opening his pocket-book, he packed away very carefully a small slip of official blue paper. At five minutes to one his cab rolled into Victoria Station. Two giant canvas-covered parcels, like enormous kites, were handed down by the cabman from the top, and consigned to the care of a guard. On the platform Pericord was pacing up and down, with long eager step and swinging arms, a tinge of pink upon his sunken and sallow cheeks.

"All right?" he asked.

Brown pointed in answer to his baggage.

"I have the motor and the girdle already packed away in the guard's van. Be careful, guard, for it is delicate machinery of great value. So! Now we can start with an easy conscience."

At Eastbourne the precious motor was carried to a four-wheeler, and the great flanges hoisted on the top. A long drive took them to the house where the keys were kept, whence they set off across the barren Downs. The building which was their destination was a commonplace white-washed structure, with straggling stables and out-houses, standing in a grassy hollow which sloped down from the edge of the chalk cliffs. It was a cheerless house even when in use, but now with its smokeless chimneys and shuttered windows it looked doubly dreary. The owner had planted a grove of young larches and firs around it, but the sweeping spray had blighted them, and they hung their withered heads in melancholy groups. It was a gloomy and forbidding spot.

But the inventors were in no mood to be moved by such trifles. The lonelier the place, the more fitted for their purpose. With the help of the cabman they carried their packages down the footpath, and laid them in the darkened dining-room. The sun was setting as the distant murmur of wheels told them that they were finally alone.

Pericord had thrown open the shutters and the mellow evening light streamed in through the discoloured windows. Brown drew a knife from his pocket and cut the pack-thread with which the canvas was secured. As the brown covering fell away it disclosed two great yellow metal fans. These he leaned carefully against the wall. The girdle, the connecting-bands, and the motor were then in turn unpacked. It was dark before all was set out in order. A lamp was lit, and by its light the two men con-tinued to tighten screws, clinch rivets, and make the last preparations for their experiment.

"That finishes it," said Brown at last, stepping back and surveying the machine.

Pericord said nothing, but his face glowed with pride and expectation.

"We must have something to eat," Brown remarked, laying out some provisions which he had brought with him.

"Afterwards."

"No, now," said the stolid mechanician. "I am half starved." He pulled up to the table and made a hearty meal, while his Celtic companion strode impatiently up and down, with twitching fingers and restless eyes.

"Now then," said Brown, facing round, and brushing the crumbs from his lap, "who is to put it on?"

"I shall," cried his companion eagerly. "What we do to-night is likely to be historic."

"But there is some danger," suggested Brown. "We cannot quite tell how it may act."

"That is nothing," said Pericord, with a wave of his hand.

"But there is no use our going out of our way to incur danger."

"What then? One of us must do it."

"Not at all. The motor would act equally well if attached to any inanimate object."

"That is true," said Pericord, thoughtfully.

"There are bricks by the barn. I have a sack here. Why should not a bagful of them take your place?"

"It is a good idea. I see no objection."

"Come on then," and the two sallied out, bearing with them the various sections of their machine. The moon was shining cold and clear though an occasional ragged cloud drifted across her face. All was still and silent upon the Downs. They stood and listened before they entered the barn, but not a sound came to their ears, save the dull murmur of the sea and the distant barking of a dog. Pericord journeyed backwards and forwards with all that they might need, while Brown filled a long narrow sack with bricks.

When all was ready, the door of the barn was closed, and the lamp balanced upon an empty packing-case. The bag of bricks was laid upon two trestles, and the broad steel girdle was buckled round it. Then the great flanges, the wires, and the metal box containing the motor were in turn attached to the girdle. Last of all a flat steel rudder, shaped like a fish's tail, was secured to the bottom of the sack.

"We must make it travel in a small circle," said Pericord, glancing round at the bare high walls.

"Tie the rudder down at one side," suggested Brown. "Now it is ready. Press the connection and off she goes!"

Pericord leaned forward, his long sallow face quivering with excitement. His white nervous hands darted here and there among the wires. Brown stood impassive with critical eyes. There was a sharp burr from the machine. The huge yellow wings gave a convulsive flap. Then another. Then a third, slower and stronger, with a fuller sweep. Then a fourth which filled the barn with a blast of driven air. At the fifth the bag of bricks began to dance upon the trestles. At the sixth it sprang into the air, and would have fallen to the ground, but the seventh came to save it, and fluttered it forward through the air. Slowly rising, it flapped heavily round in a circle, like some great clumsy bird, filling the barn with its buzzing and whirring. In the uncertain yellow light of the single lamp it was strange to see the loom of the ungainly thing, flapping off into the shadows, and then circling back into the narrow zone of light.

The two men stood for a while in silence. Then Pericord threw his long arms up into the air.

"It acts!" he cried. "The Brown-Pericord Motor acts!" He danced about like a madman in his delight. Brown's eyes twinkled, and he began to whistle.

"See how smoothly it goes, Brown!" cried the inventor. "And the rudder—how well it acts! We must register it tomorrow."

His comrade's face darkened and set. "It *is* registered," he said, with a forced laugh.

"Registered?" said Pericord. "Registered?" He repeated the word first in a whisper, and then in a kind of scream. "Who has dared to register my invention?"

"I did it this morning. There is nothing to be excited about. It is all right."

"You registered the motor! Under whose name?"

"Under my own," said Brown, sullenly. "I consider that I have the best right to it."

"And my name does not appear?"

"No, but—"

"You villain!" screamed Pericord. "You thief and villain! You would steal my work! You would filch my credit! I will have that patent back if I have to tear your throat out!" A sombre fire burned in his black eyes, and his hands writhed themselves together with passion. Brown was no coward, but he shrank back as the other advanced upon him.

"Keep your hands off!" he said, drawing a knife from his pocket. "I will defend myself if you attack me."

"You threaten me?" cried Pericord, whose face was livid with anger. "You are a bully as well as a cheat. Will you give up the patent?"

"No, I will not."

"Brown, I say, give it up!"

"I will not. I did the work."

Pericord sprang madly forward with blazing eyes and clutching fingers. His companion writhed out of his grasp, but was dashed against the packing-case, over which he fell. The lamp was extinguished, and the whole barn plunged into darkness. A single ray of moonlight shining through a narrow chink flickered over the great waving fans as they came and went.

"Will you give up the patent, Brown?"

There was no answer.

"Will you give it up?"

Again no answer. Not a sound save the humming and creaking over-head. A cold pang of fear and doubt struck through Pericord's heart. He felt aimlessly about in the dark and his fingers closed upon a hand. It was cold and unresponsive. With all his anger turned to icy horror he struck a match, set the lamp up, and lit it.

Brown lay huddled up on the other side of the packing-case. Pericord seized him in his arms, and with convulsive strength lifted him across. Then the mystery of his silence was explained. He had fallen with his right arms doubled up under him, and his own weight had driven the knife deeply into his body. He had died without a groan. The tragedy had been sudden, horrible, and complete.

Pericord sat silently on the edge of the case, staring blankly down, and shivering like one with the ague, while the great Brown-Pericord Motor boomed and hurtled above him. How long he sat there can never be known. It might have been minutes or it might have been hours. A thousand mad schemes flashed through his dazed brain. It was true that he had been only the indirect cause. But who would believe that? He glanced down at his blood-spattered clothing. Everything was against him. It would be better to fly than to give himself up, relying upon his innocence. No one in London knew where they were. If he could dispose of the body he might have a few days clear before any suspicion would be aroused.

Suddenly a loud crash recalled him to himself. The flying sack had gradually risen with each successive circle until it had struck against the rafters. The blow displaced the connecting-gear, and the machine fell heavily to the ground. Pericord undid the girdle. The motor was unin-jured. A sudden strange thought flashed upon him as he looked at it. The machine had become hateful to him. He might dispose both of it and the body in a way that would baffle all human search.

He threw open the barn door, and carried his companion out into the moonlight. There was a hillock outside, and on the summit of this he laid him reverently down. Then he brought from the barn the motor, the girdle and the flanges. With trembling fingers he fastened the broad steel belt round the dead man's waist. Then he screwed the wings into the sockets. Beneath he slung the motor-box, fastened the wires, and switched on the connection. For a minute or two the huge yellow fans flapped and flickered. Then the body began to move in little jumps down the side of the hillock, gathering a gradual momentum, until at last it heaved up into the air and soared off in the moonlight. He had not used the rudder, but had turned the head for the south. Gradually the weird thing rose higher, and sped faster, until it had passed over the line of cliff, and was sweep-ing over the silent sea. Pericord watched it with a white drawn face, until it looked like a black bird with golden wings half shrouded in the mist which lay over the waters.

In the New York State Lunatic Asylum there is a wild-eyed man whose name and birth-place are alike unknown. His reason has been unseated by some sudden shock, the doctors say, though of what nature they are unable to determine. "It is the most delicate machine which is most readily put out of gear," they remark, and point, in proof of their axiom, to the complicated electric engines, and remarkable aeronautic machines which the patient is fond of devising in his more lucid moments.

The Terror of Blue John Gap

THE FOLLOWING NARRATIVE was found among the papers of Dr. James Hardcastle, who died of phthisis on February 4th, 1908, at 36, Upper Coventry Flats, South Kensington. Those who knew him best, while refusing to express an opinion upon this particular statement, are unanimous in asserting that he was a man of a sober and scientific turn of mind, absolutely devoid of imagination, and most unlikely to invent any abnormal series of events. The paper was contained in an envelope, which was docketed, "A Short Account of the Circumstances which occurred near Miss Allerton's Farm in North-West Derbyshire in the Spring of Last Year." The envelope was sealed, and on the other side was written in pencil—

"Dear Seaton,

"It may interest, and perhaps pain you, to know that the incredulity with which you met my story has prevented me from ever opening my mouth upon the subject again. I leave this record after my death, and perhaps strangers may be found to have more confidence in me than my friend."

Inquiry has failed to elicit who this Seaton may have been. I may add that the visit of the deceased to Allerton's Farm, and the general nature of the alarm there, apart from his particular explanation, have been absolutely established. With this foreword I append his account exactly as he left it. It is in the form of a diary, some entries in which have been expanded, while a few have been erased.

APRIL 17.—Already I feel the benefit of this wonderful upland air. The farm of the Allertons lies fourteen hundred and twenty feet above sea-level, so it may well be a bracing climate. Beyond the usual morning cough

I have very little discomfort, and, what with the fresh milk and the home-grown mutton, I have every chance of putting on weight. I think Saunderson will be pleased.

The two Miss Allertons are charmingly quaint and kind, two dear little hard-working old maids, who are ready to lavish all the heart which might have gone out to husband and to children upon an invalid stranger. Truly, the old maid is a most useful person, one of the reserve forces of the community. They talk of the superfluous woman, but what would the poor superfluous man do without her kindly presence? By the way, in their simplicity they very quickly let out the reason why Saunderson recommended their farm. The Professor rose from the ranks himself, and I believe that in his youth he was not above scaring crows in these very fields.

It is a most lonely spot, and the walks are picturesque in the extreme. The farm consists of grazing land lying at the bottom of an irregular valley. On each side are the fantastic limestone hills, formed of rock so soft that you can break it away with your hands. All this country is hollow. Could you strike it with some gigantic hammer it would boom like a drum, or possibly cave in altogether and expose some huge subterranean sea. A great sea there must surely be, for on all sides the streams run into the mountain itself, never to reappear. There are gaps everywhere amid the rocks, and when you pass through them you find yourself in great caverns, which wind down into the bowels of the earth. I have a small bicycle lamp, and it is a perpetual joy to me to carry it into these weird solitudes, and to see the wonderful silver and black effect when I throw its light upon the stalactites which drape the lofty roofs. Shut off the lamp, and you are in the blackest darkness. Turn it on, and it is a scene from the Arabian Nights.

But there is one of these strange openings in the earth which has a special interest, for it is the handiwork, not of nature, but of man. I had never heard of Blue John when I came to these parts. It is the name given to a peculiar mineral of a beautiful purple shade, which is only found at one or two places in the world. It is so rare that an ordinary vase of Blue John would be valued at a great price. The Romans, with that extraordinary instinct of theirs, discovered that it was to be found in this valley, and sank a horizontal shaft deep into the mountain side. The opening of their mine has been called Blue John Gap, a clean-cut arch in the rock, the mouth all overgrown with bushes. It is a goodly passage which the Roman miners have cut, and it intersects some of the great water-worn caves, so that if you enter Blue John Gap you would do well to mark your steps and to have a good store of candles, or you may never make your way back to the daylight again. I have not yet gone deeply into it, but this very day I stood at the mouth of the arched tunnel, and peering down into the black recesses beyond, I vowed that when my health returned I would devote some holiday to exploring those mysterious depths and finding out for myself how far the Roman had penetrated into the Derbyshire hills.

Strange how superstitious these countrymen are! I should have thought better of young Armitage, for he is a man of some education and character, and a very fine fellow for his station in life. I was standing at the Blue John Gap when he came across the field to me.

"Well, doctor," said he, "you're not afraid, anyhow."

"Afraid!" I answered. "Afraid of what?"

"Of it," said he, with a jerk of his thumb towards the black vault, "of the Terror that lives in the Blue John Cave."

How absurdly easy it is for a legend to arise in a lonely countryside! I examined him as to the reasons for his weird belief. It seems that from time to time sheep have been missing from the fields, carried bodily away, according to Armitage. That they could have wandered away of their own accord and disappeared among the mountains was an explanation to which he would not listen. On one occasion a pool of blood had been found, and some tufts of wool. That also, I pointed out, could be explained in a perfectly natural way. Further, the nights upon which sheep disappeared were invariably very dark, cloudy nights with no moon. This I met with the obvious retort that those were the nights which a commonplace sheep-stealer would naturally choose for his work. On one occasion a gap had been made in a wall, and some of the stones scattered for a considerable distance. Human agency again, in my opinion. Finally, Armitage clinched all his arguments by telling me that he had actually heard the Creature—indeed, that anyone could hear it who remained long enough at the Gap. It was a distant roaring of an immense volume. I could not but smile at this, knowing, as I do, the strange reverberations which come out of an underground water system running amid the chasms of a limestone formation. My incredulity annoyed Armitage, so that he turned and left me with some abruptness.

And now comes the queer point about the whole business. I was still standing near the mouth of the cave turning over in my mind the various statements of Armitage, and reflecting how readily they could be explained away, when suddenly, from the depth of the tunnel beside me, there issued a most extraordinary sound. How shall I describe it? First of all it seemed to be a great distance away, far down in the bowels of the earth. Secondly, in spite of this suggestion of distance, it was very loud. Lastly, it was not a boom, nor a crash, such as one would associate with falling water or tumbling rock, but it was a high whine, tremulous and vibrating, almost like the whinnying of a horse. It was certainly a most remarkable experience, and one which for a moment, I must admit, gave a new significance to Armitage's words. I waited by the Blue John Gap for half an hour or more, but there was no return of the sound, so at last I wandered back to the farmhouse, rather mystified by what had occurred. Decidedly I shall explore that cavern when my strength is restored. Of course, Armitage's explanation is too absurd for discussion, and yet that sound was certainly very strange. It still rings in my ears as I write.

APRIL 20.—In the last three days I have made several expeditions to the Blue John Gap, and have even penetrated some short distance, but my bicycle lantern is so small and weak that I dare not trust myself very far. I shall do the thing more systematically. I have heard no sound at all, and could almost believe that I had been the victim of some hallucination, suggested, perhaps, by Armitage's conversation. Of course, the whole idea is absurd, and yet I must confess that those bushes at the entrance of the cave do present an appearance as if some heavy creature had forced its way through them. I begin to be keenly interested. I have said nothing to the Miss Allertons, for they are quite superstitious enough already, but I have bought some candles, and mean to investigate for myself.

I observed this morning that among the numerous tufts of sheep's wool which lay among the bushes near the cavern there was one which was smeared with blood. Of course, my reason tells me that if sheep wander into such rocky places they are likely to injure themselves, and yet somehow that splash of crimson gave me a sudden shock, and for a moment I found myself shrinking back in horror from the old Roman arch. A fetid breath seemed to ooze from the black depths into which I peered. Could it indeed be possible that some nameless thing, some dreadful presence, was lurking down yonder? I should have been incapable of such feelings in the days of my strength, but one grows more nervous and fanciful when one's health is shaken.

For the moment I weakened in my resolution, and was ready to leave the secret of the old mine, if one exists, for ever unsolved. But tonight my interest has returned and my nerves grown more steady. Tomorrow I trust that I shall have gone more deeply into this matter.

APRIL 22.—Let me try and set down as accurately as I can my extraordinary experience of yesterday. I started in the afternoon, and made my way to the Blue John Gap. I confess that my misgivings returned as I gazed into its depths, and I wished that I had brought a companion to share my exploration. Finally, with a return of resolution, I lit my candle, pushed my way through the briars, and descended into the rocky shaft.

It went down at an acute angle for some fifty feet, the floor being covered with broken stone. Thence there extended a long, straight passage cut in the solid rock. I am no geologist, but the lining of this corridor was certainly of some harder material than limestone, for there were points where I could actually see the tool-marks which the old miners had left in their excavation, as fresh as if they had been done yesterday. Down this strange, old-world corridor I stumbled, my feeble flame throwing a dim circle of light around me, which made the shadows beyond the more threatening and obscure. Finally, I came to a spot where the Roman tunnel opened into a water-worn cavern—a huge hall, hung with long white icicles of lime deposit. From this central chamber I could dimly perceive that a number of passages worn by the subterranean streams wound away into the depths of the earth. I was standing there wondering whether I had better return, or whether I dare venture farther into this dangerous labyrinth, when my eyes fell upon something at my feet which strongly arrested my attention.

The greater part of the floor of the cavern was covered with boulders of rock or with hard incrustations of lime, but at this particular point there had been a drip from the distant roof, which had left a patch of soft mud. In the very centre of this there was a huge mark—an ill-defined blotch, deep, broad and irregular, as if a great boulder had fallen upon it. No loose stone lay near, however, nor was there anything to account for the impression. It was far too large to be caused by any possible animal, and besides, there was only the one, and the patch of mud was of such a size that no reasonable stride could have covered it. As I rose from the examination of that singular mark and then looked round into the black shadows which hemmed me in, I must confess that I felt for a moment a most unpleasant sinking of my heart, and that, do what I could, the candle trembled in my outstretched hand.

I soon recovered my nerve, however, when I reflected how absurd it was to associate so huge and shapeless a mark with the track of any known animal. Even an elephant could not have produced it. I determined, therefore, that I would not be scared by vague and senseless fears from carrying out my exploration. Before proceeding, I took good note of a curious rock formation in the wall by which I could recognize the entrance of the Roman tunnel. The precaution was very necessary, for the great cave, so far as I could see it, was intersected by passages. Having made sure of my position, and reassured myself by examining my spare candles and my matches, I advanced slowly over the rocky and uneven surface of the cavern.

And now I come to the point where I met with such sudden and desperate disaster. A stream, some twenty feet broad, ran across my path, and

I walked for some little distance along the bank to find a spot where I could cross dry-shod. Finally, I came to a place where a single flat boulder lay near the centre, which I could reach in a stride. As it chanced, however, the rock had been cut away and made top-heavy by the rush of the stream, so that it tilted over as I landed on it and shot me into the ice-cold water. My candle went out, and I found myself floundering about in utter and absolute darkness.

I staggered to my feet again, more amused than alarmed by my adventure. The candle had fallen from my hand, and was lost in the stream, but I had two others in my pocket, so that it was of no importance. I got one of them ready, and drew out my box of matches to light it. Only then did I realize my position. The box had been soaked in my fall into the river. It was impossible to strike the matches.

A cold hand seemed to close round my heart as I realized my position. The darkness was opaque and horrible. It was so utter that one put one's hand up to one's face as if to press off something solid. I stood still, and by an effort I steadied myself. I tried to reconstruct in my mind a map of the floor of the cavern as I had last seen it. Alas! the bearings which had impressed themselves upon my mind were high on the wall, and not to be found by touch. Still, I remembered in a general way how the sides were situated, and I hoped that by groping my way along them I should at last come to the opening of the Roman tunnel. Moving very slowly, and continually striking against the rocks, I set out on this desperate quest.

But I very soon realized how impossible it was. In that black, velvety darkness one lost all one's bearings in an instant. Before I had made a dozen paces, I was utterly bewildered as to my whereabouts. The rippling of the stream, which was the one sound audible, showed me where it lay, but the moment that I left its bank I was utterly lost. The idea of finding my way back in absolute darkness through that limestone labyrinth was clearly an impossible one.

I sat down upon a boulder and reflected upon my unfortunate plight. I had not told anyone that I proposed to come to the Blue John mine, and it was unlikely that a search party would come after me. Therefore I must trust to my own resources to get clear of the danger. There was only one hope, and that was that the matches might dry. When I fell into the river, only half of me had got thoroughly wet. My left shoulder had remained above the water. I took the box of matches, therefore, and put it into my left armpit. The moist air of the cavern might possibly be counteracted by the heat of my body, but even so, I knew that I could not hope to get a light for many hours. Meanwhile there was nothing for it but to wait.

By good luck I had slipped several biscuits into my pocket before I left the farm-house. These I now devoured, and washed them down with a draught from that wretched stream which had been the cause of all my misfortunes. Then I felt about for a comfortable seat among the rocks, and, having discovered a place where I could get a support for my back, I stretched out my legs and settled myself down to wait. I was wretchedly damp and cold, but I tried to cheer myself with the reflection that modern science prescribed open windows and walks in all weather for my disease. Gradually, lulled by the monotonous gurgle of the stream, and by the absolute darkness, I sank into an uneasy slumber.

How long this lasted I cannot say. It may have been for an hour, it may have been for several. Suddenly I sat up on my rock couch, with every nerve thrilling and every sense acutely on the alert. Beyond all doubt I had heard a sound—some sound very distinct from the gurgling of the waters. It had passed, but the reverberation of it still lingered in my ear. Was it a search party? They would most certainly have shouted, and vague as this sound was which had wakened me, it was very distinct from the human voice. I sat palpitating and hardly daring to breathe. There it was again! And again! Now it had become continuous. It was a tread—yes, surely it was the tread of some living creature. But what a tread it was! It gave one the impression of enormous weight carried upon sponge-like feet, which gave forth a muffled but ear-filling sound. The darkness was as complete as ever, but the tread was regular and decisive. And it was coming beyond all question in my direction.

My skin grew cold, and my hair stood on end as I listened to that steady and ponderous footfall. There was some creature there, and surely by the speed of its advance, it was one which could see in the dark. I crouched low on my rock and tried to blend myself into it. The steps grew nearer still, then stopped, and presently I was aware of a loud lapping and gurgling. The creature was drinking at the stream. Then again there was silence, broken by a succession of long sniffs and snorts of tremendous volume and energy. Had it caught the scent of me? My own nostrils were filled by a low fetid odour, mephitic and abominable. Then I heard the steps again. They were on my side of the stream now. The stones rattled within a few yards of where I lay. Hardly daring to breathe, I crouched upon my rock. Then the steps drew away. I heard the splash as it returned across the river, and the sound died away into the distance in the direction from which it had come.

For a long time I lay upon the rock, too much horrified to move. I thought of the sound which I had heard coming from the depths of the cave, of Armitage's fears, of the strange impression in the mud, and now came this final and absolute proof that there was indeed some inconceivable monster, something utterly unearthly and dreadful, which lurked in the hollow of the mountain. Of its nature or form I could frame no conception, save that it was both light-footed and gigantic. The combat between my reason, which told me that such things could not be, and my senses, which told me that they were, raged within me as I lay. Finally, I was almost ready to persuade myself that this experience had been part of some evil dream, and that my abnormal condition might have conjured up an hallucination. But there remained one final experience which removed the last possibility of doubt from my mind.

I had taken my matches from my armpit and felt them. They seemed perfectly hard and dry. Stooping down into a crevice of the rocks, I tried one of them. To my delight it took fire at once. I lit the candle, and, with a terrified backward glance into the obscure depths of the cavern, I hurried in the direction of the Roman passage. As I did so I passed the patch of mud on which I had seen the huge imprint. Now I stood astonished before it, for there were three similar imprints upon its surface, enormous in size, irregular in outline, of a depth which indicated the ponderous weight which had left them. Then a great terror surged over me. Stooping and shading my candle with my hand, I ran in a frenzy of fear to the rocky archway, hastened up it, and never stopped until, with weary feet and panting lungs, I rushed up the final slope of stones, broke through the tangle of briars, and flung myself exhausted upon the soft grass under the peaceful light of the stars. It was three in the morning when I reached the farm-house, and today I am all unstrung and quivering after my terrific adventure. As yet I have told no one. I must move warily in the matter. What would the poor lonely women, or the uneducated yokels here think of it if I were to tell them my experience? Let me go to someone who can understand and advise.

APRIL 25.—I was laid up in bed for two days after my incredible adventure in the cavern. I use the adjective with a very definite meaning, for I have had an experience since which has shocked me almost as much as the other. I have said that I was looking round for someone who could advise me. There is a Dr. Mark Johnson who practices some few miles away, to whom I had a note of recommendation from Professor Saunderson. To him I drove, when I was strong enough to get about, and I recounted to him my whole strange experience. He listened intently, and then carefully examined me, paying special attention to my reflexes and to the pupils of my eyes. When he had finished, he refused to discuss my adventure, saying that it was entirely beyond him, but he gave me the card of a Mr.

Picton at Castleton, with the advice that I should instantly go to him and tell him the story exactly as I had done to himself. He was, according to my adviser, the very man who was pre-eminently suited to help me. I went on to the station, therefore, and made my way to the little town, which is some ten miles away. Mr. Picton appeared to be a man of importance, as his brass plate was displayed upon the door of a considerable building on the outskirts of the town. I was about to ring his bell, when some misgiving came into my mind, and, crossing to a neighbouring shop, I asked the man behind the counter if he could tell me anything of Mr. Picton. "Why," said he, "he is the best mad doctor in Derbyshire, and yonder is his asylum." You can imagine that it was not long before I had shaken the dust of Castleton from my feet and returned to the farm, cursing all unimaginative pedants who cannot conceive that there may be things in creation which have never yet chanced to come across their mole's vision. After all, now that I am cooler, I can afford to admit that I have been no more sympathetic to Armitage than Dr. Johnson has been to me.

APRIL 27.—When I was a student I had the reputation of being a man of courage and enterprise. I remember that when there was a ghost-hunt at Coltbridge it was I who sat up in the haunted house. Is it advancing years (after all, I am only thirty-five), or is it this physical malady which has caused degeneration? Certainly my heart quails when I think of that horrible cavern in the hill, and the certainty that it has some monstrous occupant. What shall I do? There is not an hour in the day that I do not debate the question. If I say nothing, then the mystery remains unsolved. If I do say anything, then I have the alternative of mad alarm over the whole countryside, or of absolute incredulity which may end in consigning me to an asylum. On the whole, I think that my best course is to wait, and to prepare for some expedition which shall be more deliberate and better thought out than the last. As a first step I have been to Castleton and obtained a few essentials—a large acetylene lantern for one thing, and a good double-barrelled sporting rifle for another. The latter I have hired, but I have bought a dozen heavy game cartridges, which would bring down a rhinoceros. Now I am ready for my troglodyte friend. Give me better health and a little spate of energy, and I shall try conclusions with him yet. But who and what is he? Ah! there is the question which stands between me and my sleep. How many theories do I form, only to discard each in turn! It is all so utterly unthinkable. And yet the cry, the footmark, the tread in the cavern—no reasoning can get past these. I think of the old-world legends of dragons and of other monsters. Were they, perhaps, not such fairy-tales as we have thought? Can it be that there is some fact which underlies them, and am I, of all mortals, the one who is chosen to expose it?

MAY 3.—For several days I have been laid up by the vagaries of an English spring, and during those days there have been developments, the true and sinister meaning of which no one can appreciate save myself. I may say that we have had cloudy and moonless nights of late, which according to my information were the seasons upon which sheep disappeared. Well, sheep *have* disappeared. Two of Miss Allerton's, one of old Pearson's of the Cat Walk, and one of Mrs. Moulton's. Four in all during three nights. No trace is left of them at all, and the countryside is buzzing with rumours of gipsies and of sheep-stealers.

But there is something more serious than that. Young Armitage has disappeared also. He left his moorland cottage early on Wednesday night and has never been heard of since. He was an unattached man, so there is less sensation than would otherwise be the case. The popular explanation is that he owes money, and has found a situation in some other part of the country, whence he will presently write for his belongings. But I have grave misgivings. Is it not much more likely that the recent tragedy of the sheep has caused him to take some steps which may have ended in his own destruction? He may, for example, have lain in wait for the creature and been carried off by it into the recesses of the mountains. What an inconceivable fate for a civilized Englishman of the twentieth century! And yet I feel that it is possible and even probable. But in that case, how far am I answerable both for his death and for any other mishap which may occur? Surely with the knowledge I already possess it must be my duty to see that something is done, or if necessary to do it myself. It must be the latter, for this morning I went down to the local police-station and told my story. The inspector entered it all in a large book and bowed me out with commendable gravity, but I heard a burst of laughter before I had got down his garden path. No doubt he was recounting my adventure to his family.

JUNE 10.—I am writing this, propped up in bed, six weeks after my last entry in this journal. I have gone through a terrible shock both to mind and body, arising from such an experience as has seldom befallen a human being before. But I have attained my end. The danger from the Terror which dwells in the Blue John Gap has passed never to return. Thus much at least I, a broken invalid, have done for the common good. Let me now recount what occurred as clearly as I may.

The night of Friday, May 3rd, was dark and cloudy—the very night for the monster to walk. About eleven o'clock I went from the farm-house with my lantern and my rifle, having first left a note upon the table of my bedroom in which I said that, if I were missing, search should be made for me in the direction of the Gap. I made my way to the mouth of the Roman shaft, and, having perched myself among the rocks close to the opening, I shut off my lantern and waited patiently with my loaded rifle ready to my hand.

It was a melancholy vigil. All down the winding valley I could see the scattered lights of the farm-houses, and the church clock of Chapel-le-Dale tolling the hours came faintly to my ears. These tokens of my fellow-men served only to make my own position seem the more lonely, and to call for a greater effort to overcome the terror which tempted me continually to get back to the farm, and abandon for ever this dangerous quest. And yet there lies deep in every man a rooted self-respect which makes it hard for him to turn back from that which he has once undertaken. This feeling of personal pride was my salvation now, and it was that alone which held me fast when every instinct of my nature was dragging me away. I am glad now that I had the strength. In spite of all that is has cost me, my manhood is at least above reproach.

Twelve o'clock struck in the distant church, then one, then two. It was the darkest hour of the night. The clouds were drifting low, and there was not a star in the sky. An owl was hooting somewhere among the rocks, but no other sound, save the gentle sough of the wind, came to my ears. And then suddenly I heard it! From far away down the tunnel came those muffled steps, so soft and yet so ponderous. I heard also the rattle of stones as they gave way under that giant tread. They drew nearer. They were close upon me. I heard the crashing of the bushes round the entrance, and then dimly through the darkness I was conscious of the loom of some enormous shape, some monstrous inchoate creature, passing swiftly and very silently out from the tunnel. I was paralysed with fear and amazement. Long as I had waited, now that it had actually come I was unprepared for the shock. I lay motionless and breathless, whilst the great dark mass whisked by me and was swallowed up in the night.

But now I nerved myself for its return. No sound came from the sleeping countryside to tell of the horror which was loose. In no way could I judge how far off it was, what it was doing, or when it might be back. But not a second time should my nerve fail me, not a second time should it pass unchallenged. I swore it between my clenched teeth as I laid my cocked rifle across the rock.

And yet it nearly happened. There was no warning of approach now as the creature passed over the grass. Suddenly, like a dark, drifting shadow, the huge bulk loomed up once more before me, making for the entrance of the cave. Again came that paralysis of volition which held my crooked forefinger impotent upon the trigger. But with a desperate effort I shook it off. Even as the brushwood rustled, and the monstrous beast blended with the shadow of the Gap, I fired at the retreating form. In the blaze of the gun I caught a glimpse of a great shaggy mass, something with rough and bristling hair of a withered grey colour, fading away to white in its lower parts, the huge body supported upon short, thick, curving legs. I had just that glance, and then I heard the rattle of the stones as the creature tore down into its burrow. In an instant, with a triumphant revulsion of feeling, I had cast my fears to the wind, and uncovering my powerful lantern, with my rifle in my hand, I sprang down from my rock and rushed after the monster down the old Roman shaft.

My splendid lamp cast a brilliant flood of vivid light in front of me, very different from the yellow glimmer which had aided me down the same passage only twelve days before. As I ran, I saw the great beast lurching along before me, its huge bulk filling up the whole space from wall to wall. Its hair looked like coarse faded oakum, and hung down in long, dense masses which swayed as it moved. It was like an enormous un-clipped sheep in its fleece, but in size it was far larger than the largest elephant, and its breadth seemed to be nearly as great as its height. It fills me with amazement now to think that I should have dared to follow such a horror into the bowels of the earth, but when one's blood is up, and when one's quarry seems to be flying, the old primeval hunting-spirit awakes and prudence is cast to the wind. Rifle in hand, I ran at the top of my speed upon the trail of the monster.

I had seen that the creature was swift. Now I was to find out to my cost that it was also very cunning. I had imagined that it was in panic flight, and that I had only to pursue it. The idea that it might turn upon me never entered my excited brain. I have already explained that the passage down which I was racing opened into a great central cave. Into this I rushed, fearful lest I should lose all trace of the beast. But he had turned upon his own traces, and in a moment we were face to face.

That picture, seen in the brilliant white light of the lantern, is etched for ever upon my brain. He had reared up on his hind legs as a bear would do, and stood above me, enormous, menacing—such a creature as no nightmare had ever brought to my imagination. I have said that he reared like a bear, and there was something bear-like—if one could conceive a bear which was ten-fold the bulk of any bear seen upon earth—in his whole pose and attitude, in his great crooked forelegs with their ivory-white claws, in his rugged skin, and in his red, gaping mouth, fringed with monstrous fangs. Only in one point did he differ from the bear, or from any other creature which walks the earth, and even at that supreme moment a shudder of horror passed over me as I observed that the eyes which glistened in the glow of my lantern were huge, projecting bulbs, white and sightless. For a moment his great paws swung over my head. The next he fell forward upon me, I and my broken lantern crashed to the earth, and I remember no more.

When I came to myself I was back in the farm-house of the Allertons. Two days had passed since my terrible adventure in the Blue John Gap. It seems that I had lain all night in the cave insensible from concussion of the brain, with my left arm and two ribs badly fractured. In the morning my note had been found, a search party of a dozen farmers assembled, and I had been tracked down and carried back to my bedroom, where I had lain in high delirium ever since. There was, it seems, no sign of the creature, and no bloodstain which would show that my bullet had found him as he passed. Save for my own plight and the marks upon the mud, there was nothing to prove that what I said was true.

Six weeks have now elapsed, and I am able to sit out once more in the sunshine. Just opposite me is the steep hillside, grey with shaly rock, and yonder on its flank is the dark cleft which marks the opening of the Blue John Gap. But it is no longer a source of terror. Never again through that ill-omened tunnel shall any strange shape flit out into the world of men. The educated and the scientific, the Dr. Johnsons and the like, may smile at my narrative, but the poorer folk of the countryside had never a doubt as to its truth. On the day after my recovering consciousness they assembled in their hundreds round the Blue John Gap. As the *Castleton Courier* said:

"It was useless for our correspondent, or for any of the adventurous gentlemen who had come from Matlock, Buxton, and other parts, to offer to descend, to explore the cave to the end, and to finally test the extraordinary narrative of Dr. James Hardcastle. The country people had taken the matter into their own hands, and from an early hour of the morning they had worked hard in stopping up the entrance of the tunnel. There is a sharp slope where the shaft begins, and great boulders, rolled along by many willing hands, were thrust down it until the Gap was absolutely sealed. So ends the episode which has caused such excitement throughout the country. Local opinion is fiercely divided upon the subject. On the one hand are those who point to Dr. Hardcastle's impaired health, and to the possibility of cerebral lesions of tubercular origin giving rise to strange hallucinations. Some *idee fixe*, according to these gentlemen, caused the doctor to wander down the tunnel, and a fall among the rocks was sufficient to account for his injuries. On the other hand, a legend of a strange creature in the Gap has existed for some months back, and the farmers look upon Dr. Hardcastle's narrative and his personal injuries as a final corroboration. So the matter stands, and so the matter will continue to stand, for no definite solution seems to us to be now possible. It transcends human wit to give any scientific explanation which could cover the alleged facts."

Perhaps before the *Courier* published these words they would have been wise to send their representative to me. I have thought the matter out, as no one else has occasion to do, and it is possible that I might have removed some of the more obvious difficulties of the narrative and brought it one degree nearer to scientific acceptance. Let me then write down the only explanation which seems to me to elucidate what I know to my cost to have been a series of facts. My theory may seem to be wildly improbable, but at least no one can venture to say that it is impossible.

My view is—and it was formed, as is shown by my diary, before my personal adventure—that in this part of England there is a vast subterranean lake or sea, which is fed by the great number of streams which pass down through the limestone. Where there is a large collection of water there must also be some evaporation, mists or rain, and a possibility of vegetation. This in turn suggests that there may be animal life, arising, as the vegetable life would also do, from those seeds and types which had been introduced at an early period of the world's history, when communication with the outer air was more easy. This place had then developed a fauna and flora of its own, including such monsters as the one which I had seen, which may well have been the old cave-bear, enormously enlarged and modified by its new environment. For countless aeons the internal and the external creation had kept apart, growing steadily away from each other. Then there had come some rift in the depths of the mountain which had enabled one creature to wander up and, by means of the Roman tunnel, to reach the open air. Like all subterranean life, it had lost the power of sight, but this had no doubt been compensated for by nature in other directions. Certainly it had some means of finding its way about, and of hunting down the sheep upon the hillside. As to its choice of dark nights, it is part of my theory that light was painful to those great white eyeballs, and that it was only a pitch-black world which it could tolerate. Perhaps, indeed, it was the glare of my lantern which saved my life at that awful moment when we were face to face. So I read the riddle. I leave these facts behind me, and if you can explain them, do so; or if you choose to doubt them, do so. Neither your belief nor your incredulity can alter them, nor affect one whose task is nearly over.

So ended the strange narrative of Dr. James Hardcastle.

Lightning Source UK Ltd.
Milton Keynes UK
UKOW06f0727190315

248094UK00001B/57/P